REFIRE

By E. J. Hopps

For David. Thank you for turning this enemy into a lover.

Prologue

She was late again. A habit she knew was wrong yet still managed to do with blatant disregard for basic social skills. It wasn't her fault. She was an escapist, a fantasy spinner— a woman who got lost in daydreams. Who bothered with timeliness when they could be dreaming up very big, intricate plans for themselves?

Evelyn finished painting rounded lips scarlet before pressing them together to blend with a pop. Standing out was imperative today and to do that, she needed to draw the eye. Being a touch late would lend itself to that objective, she thought.

When her car pulled up to the restaurant—all brick and windows and soft light—she barely held back a squeal of excitement. Working as a commis for the past three weeks had been a whirlwind of picking up literally any tasks that were available, working her ass off until she was bone tired, and *mostly* showing up on time. Falling in love with the restaurant had been the easy part. Now, all she needed to do was rise in the ranks, achieve her ultimate goal of chef de cuisine, and implant herself into the DNA of one of her favorite places on earth.

No problem.

The annual holiday party was a chance for Evelyn to meet every member of the staff in one place and she had big plans for this party. The fact that she was a woman working in fine dining was one that she loved, but also meant that she would have to work harder than everyone else in the usually male-dominated field. For Evelyn, this wasn't just a casual get-together where she could cut loose and shamelessly flirt with the front of house, this was an opportunity to control the "new girl" narrative. To showcase herself not only as a valuable member of the team, but someone to watch. Maybe it was a bit of a stretch to believe herself a threat to anyone standing in her way, but…

Evelyn Pimm was home. The feeling of rightness as she gazed at the restaurant's sign lightly swaying in the breeze coursed through her damn bones, through her entire being. There simply wasn't any other option besides fighting her way to the top.

A glance in the mirror one last time confirmed that her chocolate brown hair was staying in its intricate braid, light makeup in perfect contrast to the bold red of her lips. Lips that curled into a grin when she stepped out of the car and faced the front of the restaurant. Without any clue what the night would hold for her, she squared her shoulders and swung the double doors open with a flourish.

It was chaos. Music was blasting from speakers overhead; a drastic contrast to the muted levels they usually rested at during dinner service. A detail that Evelyn only knew from her own dining experience there, as she still worked mornings when the space was fairly empty. She sucked in an indulgent sniff, and the aroma of rich food and oak tables filled her nostrils, comforting her imme-diately. Smiling faces contended with dancing feet. Loud conversation faced off against clinking glasses. It was a proper party, and Evelyn had never felt more at home.

"Finally! Are you ever on time?" asked a teasing voice before she even had time to remove her coat.

She turned her brown eyes on the morning sous chef, Dorian. "Timeliness is boring," she threw back without much fanfare. Dorian was not her favorite person, but if she had to get in his good graces to move up…well maybe she would think about being on time more often.

"You rely on your charm to get you out of a lot, don't you?"

Then again, maybe not.

She met his flirty smile with as much politeness as she could muster. "Are you trying to tell me to work on my time management? Because I am happy to do that."

He waved her away, clearly not wanting to ruin whatever flirtatious fantasy was looming in his head.

"We are not working tonight. You interested in meeting the evening crew? I can get you a glass of Bordeaux. The minerality in this particular vintage pairs—"

"I am, but…" Evelyn trailed off as she spotted the owner of the restaurant across the dining room and, wanting to make a point to greet him first, slowly turned away from Dorian's lightly annoyed face. "I'm just going to take a quick circle around the room."

And with that, she left Dorian to his Bordeaux and headed straight for Harvey. Normally, she would have separated herself from a superior with a touch more grace, but Dorian's eyes tended to wander, and it was getting harder and harder to fake nice around him.

The moment he spotted her, Harvey's brown eyes crinkled at the corners, and he immediately reached behind himself for a bottle of champagne. His grey hair glinted in the dim light, sparkling red and green from the Christmas tree lights beside him.

"Aw Evie, join us," he trilled. His breezy voice lent additional lightness by, if she had to guess, several glasses of bubbly. "You can put your coat anywhere."

Oops, reminded of the thick coat still covering her frame, she began working the tie at her waist.

"I was just telling my son about you. I wish he had been able to try that dish you cooked up in your interview, it was truly a wonder."

Evie paused mid coat-shed, delighted by the massive compliment while also instantly feeling intimidated. Her gaze slid over to the man standing next to Harvey and was met with a hard jawline accompanied by painfully green eyes.

Eyes that were focused on her in a way that would make lesser folks squirm. She refused to squirm. Instead, she put on her best smile and held a hand out to introduce herself to Harvey's son and previous chef de cuisine of the restaurant.

Those green eyes glanced at her hand before darting back to her face. She watched in fascination as he slowly peeled himself off the wall and switched his champagne flute from one hand to another. Smile still planted on her face, confusion blossomed as he paused, and the corners of his mouth tipped down.

Before she could ask if he was alright, Dorian's voice broke through their conversation like the Kool-Aid Man. "You're still in your coat? Come on, Evelyn, stay a while," he said, before clambering over to her and reaching out to assist with a task that she absolutely didn't need assistance with. Not wanting to scowl at him and give the wrong impression, Evie began to shimmy out of her coat and give her attention back to the man who had held her dream position for years.

She barely registered Harvey's introduction as her jacket slid down her arms and was discarded, revealing one of her favorite dresses. Red, festive, and most definitely a statement. The man's eyes heated and darted down the length of her in a flash before his God-like features settled back into mild boredom.

Evie would have felt flattered if she were not trying to impress this man professionally, not physically dull his brain.

However, when his eyes met hers again, it was *her* brain that felt a little fried. She felt her cheeks flush under his steady gaze and wondered awkwardly how long was too long for her to hold out her hand.

"Where did you come from, Evelyn?" the man asked, his voice rolling over the music to hit her square in the forehead. *Max*, she drew up from the barely heard introduction.

Dorian scoffed beside her, answering the question before she could even open her mouth. *The prick.* "Evelyn was the pastry chef at Bloem before this. We're trying to give her a crash course in savory," he laughed.

Max did not. He simply handed her a glass of champagne to fill her still-extended hand, his eyes darting to Dorian for a brief second before landing back on her. If there had been fire in his gaze before, it was forgotten. Replaced by a smirk that Evelyn had seen about seven hundred times since becoming a chef.

These men.

It took massive amounts of practice for Evelyn to hold back an eye roll that was dying to fly from her face. Unfortunately, no amount of practice could save her from the strawberry wave of color that spread over her cheeks. The mortifying blush had plagued her since her teens, clearly attempting to convince her that embarrassment was the appropriate feeling for any situation.

Deciding that it was more important to maintain her relationship with Harvey rather than say something, though warranted, quite rude to his son, Evelyn squared her shoulders and schooled her lips into the softest smile she had.

She ignored Dorian altogether and sent a direct stare at Max's smirk.

"It's a shame that you won't be here to help Dorian with this *crash course*," she said, barely managing not to spit the last two words. "I've heard you and Harvey make quite the team."

"We did," Max said with a curt nod, and there was just something about it…

Evie didn't argue, she didn't push. She evaded confrontation with James Bond-like efficiency and was basically a special agent in people pleasing. But this was her restaurant—her mission. And this man was brushing her off like she was a Bond girl understudy.

That's why, instead of *nice to meet you*, or *cheers to your new job!* She said sweetly, "I hope to be able to fill a bit of the void you leave behind."

Evie caught a glimpse of a dark raised brow before turning all of her attention back to Harvey.

The night rolled on without issue. She chatted with Harvey, avoided Dorian with expert level ease and managed not to spill on her dress until the very end of the night. Still, after spending the evening getting more than a little tipsy with her new coworkers, Evie was more determined than ever. When the night ended, she held her goals in her brain until they filled her dreams. Her mission was clear: *be better than everyone, rise to the top, make yourself invaluable*.

A mission that would be all the easier since Maxwell Easton no longer wanted anything to do with the restaurant.

Chapter One

———

Six Years Later

Evelyn Pimm had a nasty habit of waking up at six in the morning, every day. It wasn't admirable. She wasn't waking up to do something ridiculous like go for a run or rising at dawn to perform sun salutations and journal her dreams.

No, Evie loved her mornings because they were the bringers of coffee.

Coffee that wafted into her nostrils and made her salivate in her sleep every morning—at six a.m.

It was a Wednesday. Which, for the normal people of the world, was just Wednesday. A day smack-dab in the middle of the workweek. Peak of the nine-to-five mountain.

Evelyn was not a normal gal in a cubicle, making cold calls and taking regular lunch breaks. She took one break a day, and the inside of a cubicle was what her nightmares were made of. She started her work week on so-called "hump day" and did not stop grinding until Sunday night, pushed forward every day by passion, determination, and a fair amount of adrenaline.

And coffee.

A sleepy glance out of her window revealed nothing beyond the fact that it was foggy yet again—a constant reminder that she lived in San Francisco. Her apartment was dark and eerily silent as she emerged from her room wrapped in a dark green comforter like a burrito; her head barely visible over the lush blanket as she trudged sluggishly in search of her heart's desire.

"Morning, my little angel!"

Evelyn let out a shriek of genuine terror at the sound of her roommate who was bent at the waist, hands flat on the floor in a stretch that shouldn't have even been considered until after nine a.m.

Shimmying the blanket down to her shoulders, she pointed a scowl at Shannon's overly peppy face while the insufferable woman transitioned to a quad stretch in the near-dark.

"Coffee," Evie growled, before wrapping the comforter even tighter around her shoulders.

"Don't I get a kiss first?"

"Shannon, I'll kiss you wherever you want if Mommy's medicine is ready."

"Baby, you know I have what you need," Shannon called after her, no doubt going back to her meticulous stretching.

Evie made her way to the kitchen, her blanket dragging behind her. The journey was not a far one, but with her inability to function enough to turn on the lights, she moved slowly and carefully through the apartment. Although she was not appreciating it at the moment, she loved her home. The landlord had decided that mustard yellow was an acceptable color for the walls, which her and her two roommates had made their mission to match with equally offensive shades. Rugs with fuchsia and baby blue accents rested underneath cream couches and natural wood. A ridiculous number of pillows and floor cushions splattered color around the room like a Jackson Pollock painting.

She stumbled into the tiny kitchen, its walls glowing a dull pink in the near-dark. The bulb on their fancy coffee maker burned bright red, a beacon of hope for her tired eyes before they landed on a full pot of steaming hot coffee. A whimper escaped her lips as she ditched the blanket in search of a much better comfort. One of the three cabinets held nothing but a collection of mugs which she blindly reached into, grabbing one at random. A mere vessel to bring liquid life force to her face.

Leaving the blanket behind, she sucked in the alluring scent of her coffee and shuffled back to the living room.

"I am reminded of my love for you every day," she whispered to Shannon while gazing longingly into her cup.

"Are you talking to me, or the beautiful display of eighties porn stars on your mug?" Laughing, Shannon pulled the tie out of her thick blonde hair and plopped next to Evelyn on the couch.

"You make me coffee every morning. You are the giver of life." Her voice was dreamy, the smell alone taking her to a better place.

"Aw, but it wasn't me this morning," she leaned in for a whisper. "Benjamin is awake."

Evelyn's gasp was not exaggerated in the least.

Shannon worked in a beautiful coffee shop in the Mission and was an all-around freak. She charged out of the apartment for a run every morning before making the non-functioning members of the household coffee, then bounced to work with such high functioning positivity, people were sure she was on heavy doses of medication.

Benjamin? He tended bar at The Church, a bougie rooftop spot in the middle of the constantly busy Castro.

He didn't have wet dreams any earlier than noon.

As if on cue, Benjamin came stomping into the room, his long red hair in a messy bun on his head, and a substance that looked alarmingly like mud plastered under his eyes and around his thick beard. A fluffy grey towel hung low on his hips exposing the mass amounts of tattoos that covered his arms and torso.

He flicked the lights on, the sudden illumination reflected off every colorful surface in the shared space and had Evie barely holding back a hiss.

"What does one wear to a breakfast date?" he growled, his deep voice contrasting his appearance in a way that was just so…Ben.

Evie's eyebrows shot up in interest. "What man has aroused your attention enough to get you out of bed this early? More importantly, what kind of nut job eats breakfast before nine?" They both ignored Shannon's hand as it shot into the air.

"The date isn't until nine, but I couldn't sleep. And because I couldn't sleep, my face started looking dry and puffy, so since I couldn't sleep and was getting puffy, I decided to exfoliate." He trailed off looking at his phone as if something super exciting was happening on the screen.

Looking back and forth from disheveled, half-naked Ben to Nike ad-perfect Shannon, she could not help but feel an immense amount of love for her friends. After years of knowing them, she still refused to believe how lucky she was. They met in their first year of college while working at a small Italian bistro, before ditching school and moving to the Bay with dreams of opening a restaurant together.

That dream had lasted for about two months before reality set in. Flash forward ten years and here they were. A barista, bartender, and chef, oh my!

Squinting, Evelyn focused on Ben. "Should I repeat my question?"

"Why? We both can agree that only Shannon eats breakfast this early." A bright blue pillow went sailing past Evie in a rush of color, hitting him in the crotch with amazing accuracy.

"Okay! I met him at the bar…"

Keeping the momentum going, Evie assured them that she was still listening as she ran to the kitchen for a refill. She heard Ben mention that his date worked in tech which immediately gave her the shivers. Office jobs were not her cup of life juice.

"…then he tells me his name is Jimmy."

Everyone froze.

Her roommates both glanced at her with sympathetic eyes as if Ben's declaration might cause her to fall to the floor and shatter.

Jimmy was not only the name of Benjamin's early riser. Sadly, it also belonged to Evie's ex-boyfriend. They had shared an apartment for two of the longest years of Evelyn's life, and the memory of the three of them moving all her shit from her old apartment in a frenzy still rested in her mind like an unwanted guest.

It had all been extremely dramatic. A break in her spirit, a truck rental within four hours of said break, and moving out every single thing that was hers while he was at work.

She hadn't seen him since.

Evie blinked out of her thoughts enough to respond. "Can you smudge a *person* with sage?"

Ben let out a deep belly laugh, "Maybe I can just dance around him with one of those Gwyneth Paltrow vagina candles."

And with that, the room erupted into laughter, the cloud that threatened to loom over her dissipated. Proof that Evie could, in fact, move on from the nightmare of her previous relationship.

"Alright," Shannon called, emerging from her room opposite Evie's. "I'm off to work, my little chickens."

Evie burst out of her own room wearing a plain white T-shirt, black pants, her signature bright-colored socks, and black kitchen clogs. Her rich brown hair was still air drying, making her shirt a little damp between the shoulder blades. "I'm coming with you. I need a decent cup of coffee for my commute."

"Oh! I almost forgot about your meeting with Harvey!" Shannon squealed before they both wished Ben good luck and made the trip down from their third-story apartment.

Her meeting with Harvey.

Evie worked at The Lennon; a two Michelin-starred restaurant tucked into a cozy neighborhood in the middle of the city. Originally hired as a commis, she rose in the ranks quickly and finally landed sous chef a little over two years ago. She loved the food there, and the atmosphere was amazing, but her real love of the restaurant came from the chef and owner, Harvey Easton. She was sure that Harvey wanted to promote her. He had to be nearing retirement, and as much as she hated to see it, she had noticed him slowing down a bit over the past couple of months.

After her fallout with Jimmy, she put everything she had into that restaurant. Her life revolved around the kitchen, all the cooks and servers, dishwashers, and hosts. It was her second home. It would be an honor to take on the role of chef de cuisine and run a kitchen that Harvey could be proud of.

The idea coursed through her on her commute. Her Lyft zipped past dumpling houses, florists, bars, and bookstores, giving her time to think about her meeting. She would accept the CDC position of course. Sous chef had taken her years to achieve and was incredibly fulfilling. It was the perfect position for her. Aside from the fact that her work ethic was similar to that of a treadmill in January, Evie loved to manage.

It was personal for her. There wasn't a single human in The Lennon that she didn't personally connect with on a daily basis. She knew that Cody's son won the spelling bee last month, and that Phil's level two wine course was giving him hives. If someone was struggling in the test kitchen or having a tough time with a new dish, she fixed it. She could be relied on—okay maybe not to be on time, but Evelyn Pimm was always there.

And now, she would be there for Harvey. He had been a bit distant all week, but that wasn't rare around this time of year. August was always a little rough for Harvey. Maybe he was worried that he would spill the beans about her promotion before their meeting. She smiled to herself at the thought.

When the car began to slow, Evie's small smile spread into a full grin, plumping her cheeks. The Lennon was one of her favorite places in the world and today, she was going to enter the kitchen as CDC.

"Cheers!" She called to the driver who graciously wore headphones the entire drive, leaving her to her daydreams.

The building was not large by any standards, but it stood out well enough. It was all brick, in a sea of stucco. Large floor-to-ceiling windows lined the top floor where the offices and prep kitchens were, and a small set of windows on the ground level showed off the main kitchen and dining room.

She smiled at the hanging sign above the rich, oak double doors which had a single, perfect strawberry carved into its dark wood.

Stepping through the inconspicuous kitchen door on the side of the building, she tried not to skip her way through the empty room. The sounds of The Lennon during dinner service were a joyous, bustling collection of laughter and sizzling dishes. Those sounds were a constant soundtrack in her life. But she loved being alone in the space. The quiet hum of equipment, the feel of clean stainless under her fingers. Evelyn navigated her way through the dark dining room with ease, familiar with every table placement, every chair.

Having seen his illuminated office from the street, she knew Harvey was already working. He had failed to turn on the remaining lights, however, leaving her to scale the stairs with coffees in hand in the early morning dark.

Feeling overly confident with her navigational skills, she rounded the corner into the familiar hallway just as the lights flicked on. Blinking at the sudden illumination burning her retinas, Evie slammed quite suddenly into a wall—spilling one of her coffees down her crisp white shirt and barely managing to stay on her feet.

"Oh, fuck me," she said gracefully.

"Charming," came a startled, dry retort. "Before or after I dress my second-degree burns?"

Evie froze the inspection of her ruined shirt, her head rising slowly as she realized the horrifying truth. She had run into a human. An annoyingly smug, pompous, wall of a human.

"Running late again, Evelyn?"

Chapter Two

"Maxwell," Evie replied stiffly. She could feel the warmth rising in her cheeks and was praying that her ears stayed blissfully dull colored.

Maxwell Easton. A man she loved to hate, which was incredibly inconvenient since she cared dearly for his father. Their shared blood, in Evelyn's opinion, was the single thing they had in common.

He was looking down at her with an annoyed expression, his full lips pulled into a tight line. If her eyes scanned over anybody else, she would have to admit that he was attractive. He had a sharp jawline that cut up to high cheekbones, while the contrast of his tan skin and evergreen eyes was just flat-out offensive. She always thought his thick black hair was begging to have fingers raked through it, muss up that too-perfect coif.

Warm.

That was her one idiotic thought as she realized they were still pressed together, one coffee smashed between them. Her brain groggily drummed up the fact that warm was actually hot, as in, scalding-coffee-running-down-your-cleavage hot, and she stepped away with a jolt. Aside from the extreme heat of coffee on her body, she had also had Maxwell Easton pressed against her skin. She and Maxwell did not touch.

"Oh my god." On second thought, she should not have stepped back; she should have remained blissfully unaware of the mutinous blob of near-black coffee that now ran down the length of his perfectly white chef coat. "I can buy you another one," she blurted in a panic. Normally, that sentence would be uttered after a heartfelt apology and potentially a pat on the shoulder for comfort. But not in this company. In this company, all of Evie's carefully practiced niceties splashed out of her body and onto the floor along with her coffee.

"Unfortunately for you, Evelyn, this is a Grayson," he said, equally as cold. She tried not to wince at the fact that she had just ruined a two-hundred-dollar coat and heated with annoyance instead.

It's a Grayson, Evelyn. What a prick!

"Oh," she mocked, a soft smile on her lips. "I meant the coffee. It's a natural Ethiopian, and I hate to see it go to waste on your shirt."

She shouldn't have said it, but this was Maxwell. They had been at each other's throats since her first Lennon Christmas party six years ago.

His narrowed eyes indicated he was about to spew his retort with as much stifled hatred as Evelyn had landed hers. Instead, his eyes cooled to a dark green and his stupid fucking mouth turned up at the corners. It could not have been a genuine smile; Maxwell and Evie did not smile at each other.

He took a slow step toward her, then another, forcing her to crane her neck to look him in the eye. She ignored her ridiculous urge to step back; years of working in kitchens with egotistical men had hardened her too much for that. She met his gaze head on, determined not to let him get to her.

16

He reached his hand up towards her and for a panicked, thick-headed moment, she thought he was reaching for her face. Her body stiffened and she sucked in a breath before he plucked the saved cup out of her hand and strode past her.

"Don't bother, I'll see you downstairs," he said as he descended.

"Pity, I thought you were leaving," she mumbled weakly after him.

Scowl still firmly in place, Evie quickly cleaned up her spilled coffee. The sight of it on the floor filled her body with sadness and she mopped up the last of the liquid with quick, angry swipes. Now she was going to be under-caffeinated and foggy for one of the most important meetings of her career.

Her meeting with Harvey should really be the only thing on her mind, yet she kept fuming over his devil incarnate son. She would never forget the smirk on his face when they met. She would never forget it because his previous look had nearly melted her down to a puddle, but that was beside the point. Had she imagined the heat in his eyes as they fell on her? Even if she hadn't, it was hard to imagine he had looked at her like that after getting to know his surly ass.

Maxwell was a bit of a poster boy for the San Francisco fine-dining scene. He had a reputation for earning restaurants additional Michelin stars and was responsible for the elevation of at least four well-known establishments in the Bay.

Yeah, you could find his irritatingly gorgeous face plastered on food magazines and restaurant websites across the city.

It wasn't her style. And thankfully, it wasn't Harvey's style either.

Her clogs smacked the tile as she charged away from the mess and through Harvey's office door without knocking. His kind face almost smothered her annoyance.

Almost.

A laugh burst out before he could help himself. "Run into Max, did you?"

"Literally. I think I ruined his Grayson." She smiled, feeling slightly victorious.

"Meh, he has fifteen more, I'm sure." Giving Evelyn a wink, he continued without a hitch. "Let's get right to it."

There was a sudden shift in the familiar office space. A thickening in the air at Harvey's serious tone. Usually carefree and rich, it went all cool and solemn in a blink. Zeroing in on him for an inspection, Evie noticed the dark circles under his kind brown eyes. His grey hair was full and swept back as if he had been running his hand through it. Harvey was like a father to her; she knew his face and all the emotions that it displayed.

Something was wrong.

"Hey," she pressed gently. "Everything okay?"

He glanced down at a small picture frame that rested next to a pile of business cards on his immaculate desk. The photo, she knew, was of a woman. Thick black hair, shockingly big, bright smile, and candy apple-green eyes. According to everyone that knew her, Lennon Easton had been a force of pure joy. Evie started shortly after Lennon passed away but whenever she looked at the photo, she was always blown away by how stunning she was—by how much Maxwell resembled her. If he ever genuinely smiled, he would have been a carbon copy of his mother.

"Evie, you've been with me for six years. You know this restaurant. You know the food, you know the staff, the guests. Hell," he let out a chuckle, "sometimes I think you know this restaurant better than I do."

His abruptness had her on edge and she fidgeted in her seat.

18

"I honestly don't believe The Lennon would be where it is today, without you." He smiled, the action not quite meeting his eyes.

"Thank you, Chef. You know that I would do anything for this place." She wanted to say *for you* but didn't want to sound desperate. His tone gave her a feeling of dread that she really didn't care for.

"I'm sorry, am I being fired?" she demanded. Her anger rising in the face of vulnerability. She didn't like solemn Harvey.

"No, Jesus Evie." He didn't smile. "But it might be worse."

In her panic, a thousand things burst into her mind at once.

Was he closing the restaurant? Selling to Apple? Oh, sweet Jesus was he opening a location in the airport?

"I'm handing The Lennon over to Max."

She blinked. A slow, dim sort of blink. One that you exhibit when someone has stated something so outrageous, it has no reasonable place in reality.

"Huh?" she managed pathetically.

He barreled ahead, clearly trying to take advantage of the stupor before the storm. "I have decided to take a step back, and to my surprise more than anyone Evie, I assure you, Max said he wanted to step in."

"No, please." Two more words down, she was improving.

"Look, I know you two don't exactly see eye-to-eye…"

"Don't see eye-to-eye?" she cut in, incredulous. "The man plates dishes with an eighty-dollar spoon and an ego that's one compliment away from imploding."

There was no fear of offending him when it came to his son. Harvey knew quite well that she and Maxwell were…well *enemies* wasn't too strong of a word in this case.

"He's going to tone it down. We have been discussing at length what I would like to see happen…"

"What?" She couldn't help the feeling of betrayal that bloomed through her body at his words. "How long have you been planning this?" Why had she been left out of these conversations? She had been a part of The Lennon far longer than Max and as the sous chef, these conversations should have been held with her. They should have considered her opinion.

Harvey flinched, his eyes falling to his hands in what, shame? Unable to get past her anger, she ignored the pang of sympathy before barreling on like an animal.

"He doesn't deserve this place, it's too wholesome. He's going to flip it into something pretentious and cold."

"He won't while you're around. I believe that this strange rivalry between the two of you will be squashed in no time. If you two work together, The Lennon can be something truly magical."

It already is she thought, a full pout filling her lips.

"Come on, Evie, the restaurant is named after his mother. It makes sense that he would want to inherit it."

She lost steam at that, finally taking a second to really look at her mentor.

He was sad. The mention of his late wife always made him a bit sad, but there was usually happiness tied in. As if just the thought of her face cut through his grief and reminded him of how lucky he was to have had her.

This was different.

Concern flooded every inch of her body as she reached a hand across the desk for his, words unnecessary for him to understand her gentle prompt.

"It's cancer," he sighed, the exhaustion finally leaking through his strong exterior. "Not as bad as Lennon's but, there it is." His voice didn't break, it didn't fold or expose his pain. His tone didn't waver or reveal that, although it may not be as bad as Lennon's, it had to be bad for him to break away from the restaurant.

Harvey's voice didn't crack one bit as he uttered words that nearly ripped her heart from her chest.

Evelyn's voice did in fact break, into a million uncontrollable sobs in a matter of seconds.

They rose from their chairs simultaneously, wrapping their arms around one another in an emotional, hang-on-for-dear-life kind of hug. Evie crying quietly into his shirt, ruining her second chef coat of the day while Harvey patted her head gently.

She blinked back tears as they pulled apart, needing to stay strong in the moment. Trying to be stoic, a support beam for her friend. Which was hilarious since she had already fallen apart.

"Treatment?" she inquired gently, searching his face.

"We'll discuss all of that later." Waving it away as if the new information wasn't lancing straight through her heart, he continued in his usual sing-song voice. "I will be announcing the transition at line-up today, I'd appreciate it if you would keep this to yourself. I don't want to worry the rest of the staff."

"Of course."

"Max will be trailing you all week." Her eyes flashed with annoyance as she was rocked back to face the Max problem against her will. "Don't look at me like that. He and I have an understanding that you both are going to run The Lennon cooperatively, while I referee from the sidelines." He grinned at her, a gleam in his eyes. "Congratulations, co-CDC. The job is yours if you want it."

She did. Her heart had skipped a beat when he mentioned the CDC position. Evelyn Pimm, second only to the owner of the restaurant. But her dream was dampened with that little "co" preceding her title.

Sharing the position with Max was an objectively bad idea. She could already hear his snarky voice questioning her every move.

For some reason she was blasted back to the first night they met. To Harvey looking at her like she was going to impress everyone and Max looking at her like she was going to crash and burn. Why would Max ever agree to this?

Harvey is sick, she reminded herself heatedly.

She agreed to everything he said without argument while holding back another bout of tears, and practically ran down the stairs and through the kitchen. She needed to go to her safe space.

Chapter Three

Max was fuming. He had thrown his ruined coat in the linen hamper and grabbed a generic one off the rack. His undershirt had been destroyed and chucked in the garbage, forcing him to wear only a thin, barely-there coat while he looked over the contents of the walk-in refrigerator.

He had walked by his dad's office just in time to hear Evelyn spouting about eighty-dollar spoons and egos.

Frustrated, he slammed a clear container of bright purple eggplants back in place and tried not to compare their color to her ridiculous socks. He would be lying to himself if he claimed he wasn't looking for something to pick apart. There was nothing.

It was a perfectly organized space. Green masking tape cut into perfect little squares adorned every container with meticulously written labels and dates.

He could not have been more irritated by the sight of it.

His thin chef coat was doing absolutely nothing against the cold of the refrigerator, but he was determined. He would find something to yell at Evelyn about.

"What a pain in the ass," he grumbled to himself.

It was nothing new, this feeling of extreme irritation towards her. She had been pushing his buttons since their very first encounter, when she showed up to the staff party in a ridiculously luscious dress. Red velvet, he recalled, making his stomach tighten like it did every time he thought of her.

Max's longing for Evelyn had burst through his body in an almost violent frenzy. Having neither the time nor mental capacity for a complicated relationship, he did what any intelligent man would do. He replaced his attraction with annoyance and avoided her like an ex in the supermarket.

The blame did not lie with Evelyn of course, Max knew this. He had relied on distance and her genuine dislike of him to help him through every single encounter. Every time he visited his dad or used the test kitchens; his survival had been so dependent on Evelyn hating him. Now he was voluntarily choosing to work beside her—a woman he had been borderline-obsessed with for years—sixteen hours a day, five days a week.

Attraction to Evie aside, Max had unfinished business with the restaurant and had to see it through.

The door of the walk-in suddenly whipped open, momentarily sucking out some of the chilled air and replacing it with Evelyn.

Oh shit.

The door closed gently behind her, and there they were. Alone, in a tiny icebox.

In a moment of hysteria, he ripped a label off the closest container and pulled it from the shelf before meeting her gaze.

She had been crying. Her caramel eyes were red-rimmed and puffy. Those ridiculously plump lips slightly more swollen and poutier, and her nose shone tomato red. Brown locks were pulled into a bun on top of her head, but she still wore her coffee-covered shirt. A very thin, very tight coffee-doused t-shirt.

Too close.

"What are you doing in here?" she asked suspiciously, crossing her arms at the chest.

Max put all his focus into the vegetables in his hands and miraculously managed to form a sentence.

"This container was mislabeled," he said casually, reverting to his classic defenses.

Not willing to wait for a reply, he strode towards the safety of the open kitchen.

To his horror, Evelyn unfolded her arms and reached for him before he could sneak past; revealing her cold chest, which he would absolutely *not* be glancing at because he wasn't a total pervert.

Christ, he had to get out of there.

Instead, his traitorous eyes met hers over the perfectly labeled container of cucumbers, prepared to see the usual look of barely suppressed hatred that lit up her eyes like fireworks. Nothing prepared him for the kind, soft look, and the tingle of her hand on his bare skin.

"I…ugh." She pulled her soft, warm hand away from him and raked it through her hair, realized it was in a bun, and gave up. "I'm sorry Maxwell. I understand that this is the second time you're going through this with a loved one, and I…well, I'm just so sorry."

Max stood still as stone. Unable to break eye contact, unable to process. He knew that he was pushing his feelings down—that he was using work to cope as he had done with his mother. As far as Max was concerned, when it came to channeling your emotions and grief into a creative outlet, he was a goddamn Olympian.

But standing in this compact space, receiving understanding and sympathy from Evie of all people…it was too much. She never apologized. Not after spilling coffee all over him, or that time she pulled his meringues out of the dehydrator too early, not even for her atrocious grasp of time management.

He felt his eyes begin to sting, his throat tighten. He couldn't stand to think about his dad being sick. Losing him would be...

Deciding he would rather walk into the ocean than break down in front of anyone, Max reverted to his old standby. Sarcasm.

"As much as I want to accept your sincerity, Evelyn, I can't take in any positive sentiments for fear of my *ego imploding*," he said, emphasizing her own words and using them against her like a weapon. His stomach knotted as he shuffled back into his usual mask.

Watching Evelyn's face transition from caring, to confused, to regret-induced unfiltered hatred was agonizing, and before he could shove his foot any further into his relentless mouth, he breezed past her, still clinging to the cucumbers like a lifeline.

Quick, angry footfalls sounded from behind as Evelyn immediately trailed him into the pristine kitchen. His anxiety was brimming. She was mad, determined, and awfully close. He was used to the first two, but the nearness of this fucking woman was making him feel too much. Like a lever had been pulled and Max's brain couldn't turn his defense mode back on.

"What is your problem, Maxwell? You know, you're going to have to kick this King of the Kitchen bullshit while you're working with me." Max had to blink back his shock. The evidence of her tears was completely wiped away, replaced with red-hot annoyance. The longest conversation they'd ever had was turning into a full-on brawl.

Because you're being a complete ass, he reminded himself before barreling on anyway.

"I know this is tough for you, having to work under me," *Why? Why are you still talking?* "But I'm taking over the restaurant, Evelyn. You can quit if you don't like it, but that's just the way it is."

He almost winced at his own arrogance. He was *really* laying it on thick today. But what else was he supposed to do? Max turned his back on her, afraid of what his features would give away, and began writing a new label.

"Under you? I'm not sure you comprehend the arrangement, *Chef*," she spat at him. The last word leaving her mouth as if it were poison. "Look, I understand that you care about this restaurant, but I am the one who has been running it alongside Harvey for the past six years." Evelyn grabbed his arm, whipping him around until their matching clogs were toe-to-toe. "I am not going anywhere."

Too close. The warning flashed in his mind again, but he did not step back. His brain burst full of conflicting thoughts and emotions: he was mad at her for calling him out on his absence from the restaurant, annoyed by his own big mouth for spouting a bunch of nonsense, and brutally aware of the proximity of her lips to his own.

Shoving all of it as far away as possible, he brought his face even closer because apparently, he liked to torture himself, his hands tensed at his sides in an attempt to keep them from doing something ridiculous like brushing the hair off her flushed cheek.

Evelyn's eyes widened in surprise, giving him a little jolt in his stomach. Guilt warred with interest. He wasn't trying to scare her for Christ's sake, he wasn't some bully who liked to intimidate women for fun. And yet this was the second time that morning that something achingly close to fear flashed across her features before she schooled them into a scowl.

Max knew all too well that he had been playing the part of the bully for quite some time, so why was her reaction making him feel like such a piece of shit? This is what he wanted. Evie's unbridled loathing was his first line of protection.

She licked her full, pouty lips, and his guilt turned to something else entirely in an instant.

"Want to make things interesting?" he asked before his brain could catch up to his mouth. "Let's work this out in the test kitchen."

***

Evelyn could feel her heart pounding through her ears.

Maxwell was just as self-important as ever and his arrogance always pushed her out of her shiny gilded mask to crash land into barely suppressed snarls and insults. Her inability to face confrontation completely dissipated when he was around. There was just something about this man that made Evie drop her Bob the Builder façade. Can she fix it? No—she absolutely couldn't fix any situation that involved this absolute devil of a chef.

She had never lingered this close to him before. Why did he smell like pine trees and soil in the middle of a city? Like Christmas. Like a fucking forest floor, on Christmas Day.

Convinced that she was losing her mind or needed more coffee, she pushed down the strange tingly sensation she felt with his intense eyes boring into hers and shoved on.

"Test kitchen?" Great, lovely. Nice follow-up, Evie.

"You still run the test kitchen every other Monday, right?"

They did. The restaurant was closed Monday and Tuesday, but the staff had complete access to the upstairs kitchen to test recipes. They would compile all their attempted dishes and present them to Harvey for his approval. If he liked the dish enough, it was added to the menu for the duration of that season—a way for his cooks to get creative and be fully represented.

Evelyn had almost thirty personal dishes featured on the menu, but who was counting?

"I don't see how that's relevant to our predicament." She stepped back; the reaction earned a slight frown from her nemesis.

She would love to wipe that smirk from his face.

"It's simple. The first person to get a dish approved, wins. They…"

"That's hardly fair, Maxwell."

"Why? I'll go easy on you."

She couldn't glare hard enough.

"It's unfair because I can't be beaten. I don't doubt that you can create a delicious dish with all sorts of luxury ingredients. Pretentious tweezer-work in abundance. But I know this restaurant and the food that works on this menu. I can't be beat." She watched as his lip twitched up at the corner, an almost smile working at his features.

"That's cute. But I'm not talking about fleeting seasonal dishes that will be gone in a week. No, to make things interesting, this has to be a staple," he said, a slow smile spreading across his face.

Again, it wasn't a smile, Maxwell *did not* smile at Evie. He looked absolutely mischievous.

A staple dish is exactly what it sounds like. Fine-dining restaurants usually have at least one. The components can change with the seasons, but the dish itself is too good to hold back—it must be offered year-round. A staple is a dish that has permanent ties to the restaurant. When someone mentions The Lennon, it was almost guaranteed that the conversation will turn to discussing their signature dishes.

No one aside from Harvey himself had ever created a staple Lennon dish.

"You're on, pretty boy." Pretty boy? Christ Evie... "I already know what I want when I win."

Max's non-smile fully filled his face at that, eliciting a blink from her at the unknown expression. Was he grinning?

"What are the terms then Miss Pimm? You want your old job back?"

A little shiver rolled across the back of Evie's neck. "Maxwell, I would rather stick my arm in a fryer than be your Sous Chef."

"As much as I would like to take a bite out of you, Evelyn, that doesn't scream winning dish to me." Max's jaw hardened as if he hadn't meant to say that out loud.

"Well, that's where you're wrong, I'm delicious," she teased, then snapped her mouth shut. She could feel the traitorous blush begin to fill her cheeks again as she tried to stifle her sudden feeling of…well she wasn't quite sure what she was feeling. "The fact remains that I absolutely will not step down. Pick something else."

"Fine…" Evie watched as the wheels turned. Max's dark brows furrowed as he thought of a better punishment for this ridiculous bet. Turning, he pulled a fine point sharpie out of a sleeve pocket and began writing a label for the cucumbers that Evie was certain had been labeled correctly. "I need someone to come with me to an event," he muttered, his back still turned toward her.

"What event?" she asked with raised brows. That was not the answer she had been expecting.

"Does it matter?" he threw back as he turned to face her, his features giving nothing away.

"No. I'm going to win anyway. I just want to make sure this *event* doesn't involve auctioning off my organs on the black market or something," she said while gazing at her nails in mock boredom.

He nodded. "And for you? What do you desire from me, Evelyn?"

"I—" Evelyn felt sweat bead between her shoulders as her cheeks flooded with warmth at his tone. It took her way too long to realize the change in him. He was laser focused on her, no scowl, no smirk—no completely unwarranted complaints about her socks. The way he was leaning against the counter screamed casual. But his shoulders were stiff, jaw slightly clenched. She was starting to wonder if he was a little nervous until he opened his stupid mouth.

"I understand it's hard to decide when you're scared of losing."

Evie watched the corner of his mouth twitch into one of those non-smiles again and scolded herself for letting her guard down. Of course this arrogant, robot of a human wasn't nervous around poor little Chef Evelyn.

"Respect," she blurted before she lost her nerve. "If I win, we work together Maxwell. You show me the respect I deserve for once instead of treating me like I barely know how to dress a salad."

She held her hand out to him to seal the deal and lifted her chin. She really hoped her expression was one of passionate determination, and not the nervous uncertainty that usually flooded her whenever she was met with conflict.

Green eyes narrowed as Max glanced down at her extended hand. He opened his mouth, then snapped it shut again as he unfolded his arms and reached out.

His gaze locked on hers and if she sensed a flicker of disappointment ripple through his face before taking her hand, she ignored it. She was going to do this, for Harvey and The Lennon, and her damn self.

She wouldn't run away from battle this time. The restaurant meant way too much to her—she had to fight for it. Max would destroy The Lennon. He would complicate the dishes, raise the prices and replace their cozy familial vibe with stuffiness.

She wasn't about to let that happen.

They shook hands and stared at one another for a second too long before the front door opened, and the first prep cooks began to arrive. Feeling relieved, Evelyn headed straight for the espresso machine. She needed to get her mind right before launching into the rest of her day, try to forget about the roller coaster of a man she was working with, and start dreaming up new dishes.

She had twelve days before the next test kitchen.

Chapter Four

Evelyn glanced at her phone as it lit up on her cluttered desk before answering immediately.

"Emily? God, I've been calling you for a week!"

"I've been busy," her sister replied in her classic dry tone.

She ignored her and launched into an animated rundown of her conversation with Harvey, her voice rising when she told her about Max and their deal.

Emily made sounds of outrage and cursed at all the right moments. There was never a time where she would challenge Evie with ridiculous questions of right or wrong. She could have just told her sister that she murdered Max in cold blood and Emily would immediately start looking into the best routes to flee the country.

They could not be more different, but they always had each other's backs. That is why, when she finished her story, she received this response:

"Fuck that. You don't need to share the top spot with anyone."

"Right?" That felt better. "And he's an impossible person! The other day, I caught him yelling at our dishwasher, Cody, about plate breakage like a lunatic."

Evie could hear frantic typing on the line indicating that her sister was expertly multitasking during her little rant. She looked down at her own hands, still as stone on top of her forgotten recipe.

"You named your dishwasher?"

A bubble of laughter filled her throat at her sweet sister. She was incredibly successful, knew exactly what she wanted in life right after high school, and didn't stop working toward it until she had a six-figure salary and a white picket fence.

Hospitality work still puzzled her.

"Cody is a person, not an actual dishwashing machine." Emily's burst of laughter rang through the phone, forcing her smile to widen.

"Whatever. I'm going to recap, Max sounds like a dick. End of recap." There was a brief pause in typing before Emily asked, "Have you bought Dad a birthday gift yet?"

Tense, sore shoulders always followed that particular line of questioning.

She had a complicated relationship with her dad. He wasn't a bad guy, but he certainly hadn't been a decent father either—not that he would remember any of it. Her childhood had mostly consisted of failed attempts to seem more important than whatever substance was coursing through his bloodstream.

She had just accepted that.

The thing about Evie was, she was a runner. The idea of a genuine, head-to-head argument gave her the nervous sweats, and her fight or flight response was one-hundred percent fly bitch, fly!

The last time she spoke to her dad had been a nightmare. She had broken down and told him about how hard it had been to coddle his addiction and toxic behavior. After her relationship with Jimmy shit the bed, she couldn't help but notice the similarities between him and the man who barely raised her. The fact that Evelyn had put herself in that position still grated on her while, shocking no one, her dad had forgotten their conversation by the end of the week.

"I don't know. I don't really know what to get for him." She heard a heavy sigh from the speaker.

"Fair enough. Maybe I'll take him out to dinner, and you can just pay for half."

Emily prattled on about her life, while Evelyn attempted to shake her guilty conscience. Letting people down was devastating to a professional people pleaser, and Evie was nothing but professional.

She promised Emily she would say hello to the roommates for her before hanging up and resting her chin in her hands.

Evelyn considered herself a very lucky person. She had amazing friends, a mother who not only raised her alone, but raised her to be strong and independent. She loved her sister and knew that these amazing people would be there for her whenever she needed them.

But Harvey had filled a void in her life that her father had been unable to. He had helped her through the insecurities of the past years with such softness and caring, she wasn't sure how it all would have panned out without him.

If Evie was honest with herself, she would admit that the competition with Max was a distraction from Harvey's illness. Barely able to stand Harvey's voice without her eyes burning with hot tears, she would practically jog to the walk-in to regain her composure before breaking in front of the staff. The last thing they all needed was for her to fall apart.

And she would rather consume an entire bus tire than give Max the satisfaction.

Harvey had told the staff about the dreaded takeover like one would rip a bandage off an arm. The suddenness of it all had the staff bombarding Evie with questions when they weren't hitting her with sympathetic looks. Clearly, they were concerned about her mental stability now that she was sharing a workload with her mortal enemy.

Not wanting to make it all about her and Max, Evelyn turned up the charm and played nice whenever Harvey was around. He didn't need her stress on top of his own, and she would make it so.

Unfortunately, Max made it Frodo-and-the-ring level impossible to be nice to him.

He trailed her all week, his closeness grating on her every nerve, and Evelyn almost turned her knife on him after he suggested for the fifth time that they change their kitchen towel policy.

"Giving everyone four towels in one day is too many, Evelyn. You're not teaching the staff restraint or encouraging them to work cleaner."

"That's because my staff is respectful. And if they aren't working clean, I have a conversation with them." She turned her bright, narrowed eyes on him, sarcasm dripping from her tongue like honey. "A conversation is a series of words strung together to communicate a thought or idea. It can be very useful when managing employees. Some might say *more* effective than taking away two of their towels."

Ridiculous conversations like this bounced between them all week. Mostly in hushed tones during dinner service and always with forced smiles for Harvey. Evelyn would grit her teeth through introductions with food purveyors who already knew of Max and his reputation for achieving three stars. She could practically see the dollar signs in their eyes as they shook his hand and immediately started gabbing about luxury ingredients.

The number of eye rolls she had forced back was starting to give her a migraine. The staff that had grown so used to 'Evie the fix-all' was instead seeing a bickering, stubborn, ice-cold Chef Evelyn. She wasn't about to unpack which version was the genuine one.

Sitting back from her desk she looked past her bright office space to the open door across the hallway. Max's office sat empty and silent and would have been identical to hers if it didn't look like it was prepped for a surgical procedure. The space was organized so perfectly that it took all of her willpower not to rearrange some books just to see if he'd notice.

It was Sunday, which meant they had made it to Harvey's official last day in the kitchen. A thought that she abruptly sailed over before her emotional dam burst from the pressure.

Instead, she took a breath, finished her coffee, and tried to collect her thoughts.

Thoughts that unwillingly kept circling back to Max.

The more Evelyn worked with him the less she felt she knew the man. Max was more confusing than a David Lynch film.

Towel arguments and rude comments about her socks aside, he actually had a way of surprising her with kindness. She had to admit, over the past week she had seen more Harvey-like qualities in him than she ever thought possible. He had a way of talking to the staff that was stern, yet respectful. The way he asked her opinion on literally everything delighted and confused her. Delighted, because he clearly valued her opinion, and confused because he *should*, so why was she even delighted by that fact?

Conflicting feelings and thoughts began bouncing around in her body whenever she thought about his stare holding hers for a beat too long.

In fact, there was truly only one thing that was crystal clear to her after spending the week with him: Max absolutely adored his father.

She would catch him doing odd jobs for Harvey around the kitchen so he wouldn't strain himself. Max's booming laugh came much more frequently when they were together, and Evie almost completely softened when he dished up family meal for Harvey every day to make sure he ate.

If that didn't soften her, the man kept bringing her coffee for their morning meetings.

As if alerted the minute her cup was empty, Max waltzed in with two steaming mugs.

"You beauty," she said lovingly.

"Me, or the coffee?"

She let out an elegant snort before accepting the offered mug. "Is that really a question you need answered?"

"Not if it's the final straw for my massive ego," he tossed back, taking the chair across from her comfortably.

She finally let an eye roll fly, relieving the muscles in her strained face.

Relaxing a little, Evie immediately brought the fresh coffee to her lips, sucking in its alluring aroma before allowing her eyes to close. Medium roast, notes of blueberry and milk chocolate *heaven*.

A moan of pleasure escaped her lips after taking a sip. Velvety crema rolled over her tongue in a wave of caffeine that practically begged her to take an indulgent moment to savor it. She licked her lips to spread the slight bitterness as far as possible.

On a sigh, her eyes fluttered open to find Max staring at her—laser-focused on her lips. His eyes looked heavy and mossy green, his own lips slightly parted and wet. Had he just licked them?

And why was she thinking about his tongue?

Before she could come up with something ridiculous to say, a small blush ran up his neck and he flicked his eyes from her face to her desk, suddenly fascinated by multiple inanimate objects.

In a moment of blatant poor judgment, she wondered if that was lust she had seen on his face.

Stop thinking.

"You go to The Valencia Gym in the Mission?" he asked suddenly, his blush fading.

"Huh?" Trying to keep up, she followed his decidedly non-lusty gaze to her keys, a little gym tag hanging off of the ring. "Oh yeah, but I only go once a week."

He raised an eyebrow at that, making her fidget. She didn't need to let her eyes wander to know he had muscles that could make grown women weep, certain that he wore his chef coat a size too small just to prove that point.

"That might explain why I've never seen you there."

"Oh, I don't linger in your section," she said. "I've never been one for grunting and mirror selfies."

His smile was quick and natural, and Evie really needed to get a handle on herself. It was ridiculous that she felt so much satisfaction from a mere lip twitch. He was smiling at her, not licking her neck.

Stop thinking about his tongue!

"What does one do with a *single* day at the gym?" he asked, leaning back comfortably in his chair.

"One has a personal training session on Tuesday mornings. They're at seven, which is more likely why you haven't seen me."

"In the morning? Are you lacing your protein shakes with espresso?"

Her lip quirked in response, a smile teasing her lips as she realized that not only was she enjoying a conversation about exercise, but she was enjoying him. Maxwell *Yes Chef, Pompous Boy* Easton.

"Of course I do, I'm not a robot. So, do you want to go over the dishes that are transitioning tonight? We can have our outline ready before Harvey gets here."

"What kind of personal training?" he asked, ignoring her question. "Are you weightlifting?"

That image made Evelyn laugh from her belly, a full, genuine smile plumping her mouth. She was not a fan of exercise.

"Oh yeah. I'm coming along too," she said, humor lighting her tone. "I can now squat with the weight bar. I think that's like, five whole pounds."

"Wow, are you training for the Olympics?"

"Working with you sure feels like an Olympic sport. Can someone win a gold medal in patience?"

Max sipped from his coffee, a laugh brimming in his eyes over his cup. She tried not to feel disappointed by his lack of smile. The brightness in his eyes should have been more than enough encouragement to keep bantering on, yet there was something about this man that presented a challenge. She was dying to wrench a smile out of his stoic features.

Plus, the banter…wasn't horribly unpleasant.

As if he could hear her thoughts—as if he could just sense her dwindling hatred towards him, Max's brows drew together as he broke eye contact to scowl down at her desk.

"How can you work so clean in the kitchen, but live in complete squalor in this office?"

She blinked at his sudden change in demeanor. What just happened? If Evie didn't know any better, she would say that Max had been enjoying their conversation—that he had been enjoying her as much as she, admittedly, had been enjoying him.

But she did—know better, that is.

"I'd be happy to meet in your office, but I'm afraid you'll short-circuit if I move one of your pens out of place." She caught a little flash of something pass over his face and his lips twitched again with that almost-smile that was starting to drive her insane. She wasn't sure and certainly had too little time to figure it out before he glanced down at his phone and unfolded out of his chair.

"Dad's going to be late, we should just meet up when he gets here. I also want to discuss changing the music today. It's a little too casual for my taste."

She stared at his back until the office door shut behind him, breaking her gaze. His staccato voice bouncing around her head as if it was still trying to catch up.

David. Lynch. She thought as she suppressed the urge to go after him and demand an explanation for the sudden change. The nerve of the man. Confusing her with easy— dare she say, flirty—conversation before slipping back into his usual state of smugness.

Evie wasn't quite sure what was making her so upset. It wasn't like Max owed her anything. She supposed it was the subtle shifts that were throwing her off balance. Max had always been so cold to her, so distant. But now he was dealing in friendly banter and coffee deliveries on the table. Personal questions and get-to-know-you type conversation that was so surprising, she felt compelled to answer. He had to have an angle. But why be hot and cold all of a sudden when cold suited him just fine before?

She let out a huff, realizing that, instead of working on her pathetic excuse for a test recipe, she had occupied her thoughts with Max for an alarming amount of time. And he had managed to roll through her morning like the twenty-four-hour flu, leaving Evie like he always did, feeling confused, distracted, and annoyed.

His cold demeanor continued through their meeting with Harvey and straight on to family meal. It was pasta day which was Evie's absolute favorite. How could anyone be sad about carbs and gelato-laced espresso? Family meal was her one break during the day. A chance for the staff to make a simple meal and sit down with each other to shoot the shit.

Lunch was followed by line-up, where she and Harvey would go through every single guest that was dining that night and discuss allergies or preferences. Well, now it was her and Maxwell. Harvey decided to make himself sparse on his last day in the hopes that it would help transition the staff effortlessly. So, Evie ran line-up instead, her head filled with mild self-doubt but her voice strong and confident.

As she was talking about the special dishes they had prepared for a couple that was dining with them for the third time that month, an affogato was placed in front of her. The smell of vanilla and espresso mixing with…something else.

The smile froze on her face when she turned to see Maxwell behind her standing awfully close, his arm still outstretched from setting down the cup.

She hadn't been expecting him. Why did they keep ending up so close to each other and why the fuck was he bringing her coffee again?

Their eyes met and she quickly looked away, a flush threatening her skin as the realization that she had cut off mid-sentence punched her in the head. The staff watched patiently as she struggled to pick up where she left off.

A couple of knowing glances were exchanged amongst the cooks which made her want to throw herself into the oven.

As soon as line-up ended, she downed her affogato and strode to the kitchen to set up.

"How was the beverage?" Max had shuffled in across from her to set his own station straight. His face was unreadable, but she was sure he was making fun of her somehow.

"Palatable," she said dryly without looking up from her work.

"Yeah, I used your gelato. You don't add enough stabilizer and it develops a grainy texture."

She snapped her eyes to his, a retort hot on her tongue.

Max had a smirk on his face the likes of which she had never seen before, a bowl of gelato in his hands to accompany it. He brought a spoonful to his mouth while his eyes lit with amusement. She willed herself not to stare as the rich cream glossed over his lips.

"You seem to be enjoying it just fine," she huffed.

Max lifted a shoulder in response before setting aside the bowl and giving her his full attention. "Should we talk about the music now?" he asked, all business in an instant.

"Maxwell," she gave in and massaged the bridge of her nose. "The music is staying as is. It's representative of Lennon, and since she is the soul of this restaurant, I don't think Harvey…" Evelyn snapped her mouth shut when she zeroed in on Max again.

He stood tall and rigid as if frozen halfway through a movement. A pained expression drenched his features making Evie's chest crack wide open.

"I…I didn't mean to offend." It was weak, but she couldn't think of anything else to say. This stream of conversation was not an enjoyable one with a great friend— let alone someone you are desperately trying to just coexist with.

He pulled out of it enough to silently guard his features and get back to work, and Evelyn felt a thousand different forms of guilt. Obviously, she knew he cared for Lennon, but they had never talked about the pain he must have felt when her brightness wasn't lighting up his life anymore.

Of course they hadn't talked about it—it was none of her business and they weren't remotely close to being friends. Truth was, Max didn't owe her anything just like she didn't owe him. Her tough-love answer was that Harvey evolved The Lennon after her death. The restaurant was his way of keeping her spirit alive, and Maxwell simply hadn't been around enough to understand that.

But Max certainly wouldn't want to hear that, and she wasn't about to be the one to say it.

During dinner service, she glanced in his direction about a hundred times. Waiting for his mood to shift, waiting for his humor to kick in again. Instead, she got short orders and minimal communication all night.

The second seating of guests were being led to tables when she decided to squash it. Max was a grown man after all, if he wanted to brood over the fact that she was right, he could brood until Christmas for all she cared. Instead, she turned her attention to the guests that were slowly shuffling into the warmly lit dining room. A smile tugged at the corners of her mouth as she watched a set of regulars snuggle into their usual seats.

Sparkling wine to start, she thought to herself right before the server came back with glasses of crisp bubbly. She returned their enthusiastic waves as they caught her watching and smiled fully. Evie loved seeing guests return; loved seeing their excitement and happy anticipation of a meal that *she* prepared.

"Chef Evelyn, the customers at table four wanted to say hi personally." This from a new front of house employee with soft eyes.

"Guests," Evie corrected gently.

"They're not buying chicken fingers and fries or perusing the cheeses at their favorite grocery store. These people are coming into our home and sitting down to a carefully curated experience. They're not our customers, they're our guests," Maxwell added.

Aside from barked directions to the servers, it was the first she had heard him speak all night.

"Yes, chef," the girl squeaked.

"Will you let them know that I'll run their first course, Amanda?"

She nodded in acknowledgment and quite literally ran away.

The sweet thing.

Six plates were placed between her and Max, capturing her attention once more as they quickly got to work. The plates were what dreams were made of, charcoal-colored disks made by her favorite ceramicist. She spooned rich, creamy sauce onto the plate while Max delicately laid fresh flowers and herbs on top.

His hands were large and steady. They dwarfed the shiny tweezers, making the act of plating look silly. Still, he gracefully plopped tiny herbs and petals onto the dishes. Their bright colors contrasting with the grey ceramics beautifully. Evelyn was so caught up in the sight of it that she failed to notice Max pause, his hand coming out of nowhere to grasp her wrist.

She went still immediately, her hands steadying before spilling sauce all over the perfect dishes and forcing them to refire the entire thing.

Evelyn's gaze swirled up to meet his, which was most definitely a mistake. They hadn't looked at each other since she had mentioned his mother, or more accurately, he'd been avoiding her as if she were a food blogger.

A hard jaw and drawn brows met her, his eyes forest green and bright. Passionate creativity lit up his features giving him an almost otherworldly glow, and he was close enough for her to see little flecks of amber in those forest eyes.

Oh boy.

His fingers tightened around her wrist, the pressure of it had her sucking in a breath. Heat shot up her arm and tingled in her chest, and for God's sake, her nipples hardened immediately. Max's expression shifted slightly at her reaction. He raised a dark brow before sliding his thumb over her wrist, the gentle caress doing zero in terms of helping her control her nipples.

She had no idea what was happening. Her mind felt like mush, her skin was alive with sensation and flushed with heat.

What the actual fuck?

She jerked her hand away, breaking the moment and cursing her absurd loins.

"That plate is for seat two. They need the—"

"Gluten-free sauce, got it," she threw out before sputtering about and finding the right pot.

"Hands," she and Max called in unison as soon as the plates were finished. A few servers rushed up to run the food as Evie herself grabbed two plates and immediately walked towards table four.

"Offline," she called over her shoulder as she removed herself from the kitchen line. The cooks called back a unified *yes, chef* in acknowledgment, allowing her to fly through the dining room to deliver the plates.

The weekend could *not* come soon enough. After years of actively avoiding Maxwell, she was clearly having some sort of allergic reaction to his touch. Evie would have to be completely oblivious not to notice how attractive the man was, she wasn't a doorknob. But having such a strong reaction to physical contact like that had never happened to her.

Plastering a smile on her face as she neared the table, Evie shut off the thoughts of her co-CDC, knowing damn well that she would be thinking about him all night anyway.

Chapter Five

Max tried for the hundredth time not to react to Evie's movements from across the hall. They had made it through week two and his nerves were completely shot. Staring hard at his agenda for the test kitchen, he was about to give up and just get started when Evelyn rose from her desk and stretched her arms over her head.

Don't look. Don't look. Don't look.

He looked. His eyes roamed over the curve of her ass as she arched her back, pale skin exposed as her white shirt lifted above worn jeans. It tightened around the full curve of her breasts which were settling as she lowered her arms and—his eyes snapped to her face, and he froze. Evelyn's narrowed gaze was locked on him for a split second before they both looked away and Max was certain he was going to die. She had just caught him staring at her stretch like a pervert, a brute. A perverted brute.

Hearing her approach his office, he stared hard at his computer in complete terror.

"Hey," she said from the doorway. She didn't sound mad, but he barely glanced up this time in the hopes that it would make up for the ogling. "I'm going to get started. I can brew a full pot of coffee if you're planning on coming soon?"

Planning on coming…Max blinked hard at the screen.

"Coffee would be great; I'll be there shortly." Jesus, he sounded like a character from Madmen after ordering a martini from his secretary. "Thanks," he added weakly.

She paused for a beat before spinning on her heel and heading for the kitchen.

Max leaned back in his chair and closed his tired eyes. This had been a terrible idea. From the moment he was put within yelling distance of Evelyn he had been a complete disaster. There were moments where he would let his guard down and things felt so naturally good between them, he thought he could do it. He could just let go and see what happened. Then, his anxiety would kick in and the cold demeanor that he used against her cloaked him in a matter of seconds.

His event was next week. A detail that he had failed to tell Evelyn when they had set the terms of their bet but one that kept pushing at his temples nonetheless. He had been completely selfish when he picked it as his win, but the truth was, he desperately needed someone to go with him. Evelyn's pick, well—it had nearly destroyed him.

Respect.

The regret he felt in that moment made him want to tell Evelyn everything.

He didn't have friends. He didn't date. Max didn't surround himself with people he would grow to care for, because inevitably, they would end up leaving. Learning that the hard way, he developed a system that would keep him from that kind of heartache again.

But the thing was, Evelyn deserved so much more than respect. She had risen in the ranks quicker than anyone Max had seen at The Lennon. Her determination to be a solid part of the restaurant was maddening mostly because she was so effortlessly good at it. She darted around that kitchen fixing every little problem for a team that so clearly admired her, and she was just so fucking good at cooking.

Max didn't just respect Evelyn, he worshipped her. Which was clearly not doing him any good since she couldn't even stretch in her own office without him fantasizing about running his hands over that sliver of pale skin. She asked him for respect, and instead, he stared at her exposed midriff like a complete dick. And, staying on brand, he had not only decided to work with her for the foreseeable future, but he had intertwined their lives with his ridiculous bet.

His brand was being a dick in case that wasn't clear.

A text from his dad brought him out of his self-loathing, prompting a rise from the comfort of his meticulously organized desk.

Morning! I'll be in for tasters around noon. Evie says that works for her if it works for you

Of course it worked for her. Evelyn had already been cooking for forty minutes while Max sat on his ass brooding over her. He rattled off a quick confirmation to Harvey before launching toward the test kitchen.

The first thing he noticed when he walked through the door was the smell. It smelled like honey, like caramelized honey. Something toasty, nutty and spicy—a hint of cinnamon. It smelled like the best granola in the world which was not nearly a good enough description for it.

He tried to be subtle as he zeroed in on Evelyn at one of the stovetops that lined the perimeter of the kitchen, and that's when he noticed the second thing. She was singing. She was singing *really* well.

It being a test kitchen day, there were other chef de partie and commis at their own stations testing recipes for Harvey's approval. Max greeted them absently as he moved closer to where Evelyn was working. He vaguely noticed the music coming out of a small speaker somewhere in the large space, all his attention on his co-CDC's swinging hips as she went into a high note. Someone whooped as another let out a piercing whistle when she nailed it, earning a carefree, slightly embarrassed laugh from Evelyn.

Maybe it was the laughter that did it. Maybe it was the way that, even through a performance like that, she wasn't missing a step as she cooked over an open flame. He didn't register the cause and barely registered the result, which was Max, mouth slack, staring at Evelyn's back in shock.

She swung around, smile still lighting her face and froze halfway through bringing a steaming pot to her pristine station. Max had enough discipline to snap his mouth shut, but barely managed not to grasp his chest at the heart.

"Maxwell," she gasped. Her cheeks became a violent red as she averted her eyes and began pouring whatever delicious substance she had been cooking into a food processor. "Don't tell me there's a no singing policy," she mumbled.

He continued to stare; his eyes drawn to the blush of her cheeks.

"I think you've stunned him Chef," called Phil, one of their cold-line cooks from Evie's left.

Max shook his head to try and clear his shock. This was too perfect…

"You can sing," he said, the words sounding more like an accusation than a statement.

Her brows drew together in a skeptical gaze.

"Yes, I can carry a tune. I can also line dance and whistle so if those aren't allowed in the restaurant you better let me know now," she said coldly, blush still clinging to her cheeks.

Max barely heard Phil beg her to go to karaoke and sing A Whole New World with him as he fled Evelyn's side of the kitchen without another word. The suddenness seemed to put everyone on edge, for the music was turned down and he could have sworn someone muffled a cough. He didn't care.

Max wasn't exactly one for signs, but this new development made his heart race as he thought about the following week. A couple of nervous eyes darted in his direction as he set up, but he focused his mind on his station. Hands rapidly began working on his dish with a determination that was a bit manic. It could have been three minutes, or three hours, but his nerves settled into a small knot at the base of his neck when finishing touches were being made and he heard a familiar greeting as his dad entered the room.

***

David. Lynch. Evie thought for the hundredth time in the past two weeks.

She watched Maxwell out of the corner of her eye as he cooked like his life depended on it. He was mad at her again, that she was certain of. She just couldn't figure out what set him off. Did he hate singing, or was it just other people's happiness that gave him a bitter taste in his mouth? She wouldn't be surprised if kittens and doughnuts were on his short list of least favorite things as well.

A couple of hours ago, she could have sworn Evie's innocent stretching had been on his list of *favorite* things. The thought brought heat to her neck as she remembered catching him staring at her, his eyes taking in the length of her body.

Ridiculous.

Evie almost laughed out loud at herself. The man was obviously picking her apart. He had probably been inspecting her outfit and logging away all of the new uniform policies he was going to make. In fact, she wouldn't be surprised if he had a running list of things to change about Evie, starting with her colorful socks.

Max brought a tasting spoon to his lips, slammed the spoon back into his utensil crock and cursed under his breath. The commis nearest to him cleaned his station and left so fast, she was sure he had just shoved his dirty things in his knife roll and would clean them all when he got as far away from Max as possible.

Phil leaned in towards Evie from the station next to hers. His thick brown hair was swept back from his face, but he ran a hand through it in an attempt to subtly cover his mouth from view.

"Do you think he hates rainbows as much as he hates your singing?" he asked in a low whisper. "Puppies? Cupcakes?"

Evie snorted out a laugh, delighted that they were on the same page. She was about to suggest that maybe it was just her that he hated when Harvey burst through the swinging doors.

"Tasters up everyone, Daddy's hungry," he yelled, causing a few people to jump.

"Ew Chef, please do not refer to yourself as 'Daddy'. I have to remind you of that way too often," Evie said with a grin. Harvey's wide smile shot at her in return, then dimmed a bit when his gaze found Max, slumped over his dish, eyes blazing with determination. He didn't jump, flinch, or bother to even look up from his plating.

Unnerved by his behavior, Evie looked down at her dessert feeling slightly less confident. It was beautiful, but hardly perfect. She had been looking forward to Harvey's feedback on this iteration of the dish until the truth of her situation went right for the jugular. This wasn't a winning dish, and Max had been cooking across the room with…persistence.

She craned her neck to try and get a better look at his plate-up, but he was too damn far away.

Competition had always been Evie's preferred method of battle. Winning fair and square was the perfect way to come out on top with minimal argument. She liked to win. Thrived off of it. Evelyn knew what she needed to do to succeed in this male dominated industry, and that was—quite simply— to be better than everyone else. There was a constant, silent war waging in her head every day while on the surface, she oozed quiet confidence. It was an art form.

An art form that she clearly couldn't master while Max was around.

Panic struck her as Harvey began tasting two stations away, offering feedback that wasn't exactly gentle, but wouldn't send you home crying into your cold brew either. The tone of his voice as he matter-of-factly told Phil that the cracker he had spent two hours on tasted like bland birdseed made her palms sweat.

Evelyn had thick skin and could take feedback for what it was. A necessary step in her training for the battlefield. No dish was perfect on the first try…

Her eyes rose of their own accord from her less-than-perfect dessert to find a green gaze locked on her. Max's lips were curved up, his cheeks plumped in a way that she had never before seen, teeth white and gleaming. She blinked at him, shocked to see the smile on his face. Blinked, as comprehension dawned that Max didn't smile at her.

A smile from Max could only mean one thing—he thought he had a winning dish.

"Okay Chef Evie," Harvey chimed, jolting her out of her staring contest with his devil-child. "What have you made today?"

She cleared her throat which had grown tight with nerves. Fuck fuck *fuck.*

"Here we have caramelized white chocolate mousse, a spiced oat crumble, and crystallized blueberries."

"Mmmmm." Harvey closed his eyes and rested with the bite he had taken. The hum that rumbled his chest gave absolutely nothing away before he said, "Tell me about the blueberries."

"Yes, Chef. I tossed the berries in an egg white mixture, then dusted them with a generous portion of sugar. They went into the dehydrator overnight until the egg whites and sugar formed a crystallized skin over each whole berry. I was hoping it would be a crunchy, sweet crust while—"

"While maintaining the integrity of the fruit," Harvey finished for her. "It's a triumph Evie," he finally said, and her shoulders relaxed a bit.

"But..."

"But?" she asked, her shoulders tightening again.

"The dish is unbalanced. When you get everything together in one bite, it's too much. You lose the magic of the berries, which should be the focal point of the entire plate. Simplify," he said easily. Completely unaware of the bet, her poor choices, and her miserable life if she lost and had to actually spend time with Max.

He looked up and seemed almost startled by the expression on her face. She must have been radiating cold fury.

"Uh, do you want to meet next week to chat about it? I know it's your day off, but I could make some time on Tuesday to discuss ideas," he said a little too casually.

Evie schooled her features immediately. She knew why this week wouldn't work, and her heart cracked open at the thought of him leaving the oncologist to discuss her unimportant dessert. She gave him a smile, ready to refuse when an irritatingly familiar scent of cypress tingled her nose and Max sidled up next to her.

His arm brushed against hers, and it took all of her energy not to shove him as far away as possible as he set his own dish next to hers on the stainless. Then he spoke, and she reconsidered that shove.

"Evie's going to be busy helping me with a project next Tuesday I'm afraid, but I'd be happy to discuss some ideas with you," he said with a grin in her direction.

She held back a protest as he snagged a tasting spoon from her utensil crock, scooped himself a hefty portion of her dessert, and devoured a bite for himself.

The glare she sent in his direction didn't quite hit as she laughed at the sheer boldness of the move. "I haven't agreed to help you with that project yet, *Chef*," she said the title as if it were somehow an insult. "And it's not your turn, so you can bring your dish back to your station."

He winked, *winked* at her. Then proceeded to ignore the order of things and looked at his father with nothing but confidence.

"Sorry Chef, but my dish is a little time sensitive." He looked to the commis next in line. "Is that okay Conor?"

Conor, who was borderline obsessed with Max, and he obviously knew it, barely managed not to bat his eyelashes before nodding affirmation.

Traitor.

"Okay then," Harvey glanced nervously between her and Max before snagging a new tasting spoon. "What do we have Max?"

"Actually, this is a spin on one of your classics, Chef," he replied. Evelyn almost didn't recognize his voice as he spoke. He had softened, almost sounded kind. "We have a chickpea panisse topped with tomato-braised abalone and anchovies. The anchovies are there for salt and umami, and I thought the tomato could be replaced with either preserves, or maybe even an acidic broth when tomatoes are out of season."

Jesus, the man was already talking components going out of season as if the dish had already won. Reluctantly, Evie conceded to the fact that it was beautiful. A small disc of chickpea cake had been pan-fried to utter perfection. Layers of thinly sliced abalone, garlic, and anchovies rested on top in a bright red sauce. She watched as Harvey scooped a spoonful, the layers coming apart beautifully.

Feeling bold herself, she snagged the same spoon Max had used to try her dessert and swooped up a bite.

Fuck.

Fuck fuck *fuck*.

It was heaven. The tenderness of the abalone was so perfect, it made her toes curl in her clogs. Briny, acidic, salty, sweet. She glanced up at Max who was laser-focused on Harvey, who was laser-focused on the dish. His face gave nothing away.

"Let's see if the farm has any chervil ready. Add a little greenery to the dish. Can you get abalone delivered this week Evie?"

"Yes, Chef," Evelyn said, peeling her eyes away from Max's profile. "Are we putting this on the menu this week?"

Harvey smiled. A big smile that beamed with happiness, and pride, and a whole lot of trouble for her. "I think this should replace the abalone dish permanently," he stated as if it didn't doom Evelyn to a life of misery. No, he had no idea how utterly fucked she was as he simply shook Max's hand and moved on to Conor's station.

Evie had gone still as stone, her limbs unmoving and straight. She had lost.

Just like that.

In her head, she had been convinced that it wouldn't happen that fast. That she had months before she would have to worry about Max coming up with a winning dish.

Thoughts whirred around as she recalled his stare that morning, gaping at her singing, his constant abuse of her undeserving socks.

Evelyn managed to move, one hand in front of the other as she dumped the rest of her dessert into the trash and began cleaning.

"So," Max began. And although there was no identifiable smugness in his tone, she gritted her teeth in preparation of his next words. "My event is next Tuesday." Someone laughed as Harvey finished his tasters for the day, and she couldn't have been more annoyed with the sound. "I can give you the details now, or…"

"You are unbelievable," Evie whispered, without turning to face him. Hot anger filled her throat, dying to escape her mouth. Cleaning her knives with a hostility they didn't deserve, she halfheartedly tried to maintain her composure. "Last week, you huffed into this kitchen, grumbled at your cutting board for an hour, and left before Harvey even got here." Her movements were downright abrasive at this point as she sheathed her knives and placed them in her knife roll, each one sliding into place with cold efficiency.

Max huffed out a breath next to her, barely moving. "Are you a sore loser Miss Pimm?"

"You cheated," she whispered, heat tingling her ears. "You just morphed a dish that was already a staple."

"The old dish, and this new iteration have nothing in common save for the abalone. It was time for a change, and Chef agreed."

"You mean *Dad* agreed," she threw back, the words searing her tongue on their way out. She knew she was stooping low. She knew that Harvey would never take sides or show favoritism like that. She also knew that Max's dish had been fucking perfect. But those were all realities that she wanted to stay blissfully ignorant of at the moment.

Max stepped toward her, eyes narrowing in frustration. He lowered his voice even further, face close enough that his whisper vibrated through her chest.

"I have been dreaming up that dish for a long ass time Evelyn. I had a plan to surprise him with it, to…" he trailed off before finishing the thought. "This dish is next to perfect, and I used it to win, end of story."

Ignoring her guilty conscious, Evie turned to face Max fully. A mistake, since he had been brutally close to her. She locked her gaze to his, ignoring his tight jaw and stiff shoulders. The kitchen was almost empty at this point, with more than a couple of nervous eyes avoiding their whispered brawl.

"Why?" she asked, surprising herself with the question.

He blinked. "Why what?"

"Why waste a perfect dish reveal on me?" she muttered. *Is the idea of showing me the respect I deserve so repulsive to you?*

She couldn't say it. Wouldn't. But she knew without a doubt what had gotten into him today. It had taken two weeks to break him. Two weeks, and Max's hatred toward her filled to overflowing. Towel policies, colorful socks, messy buns, and coffee addictions had sent him into this kitchen with a fire under his ass to fix his Evie sized problem. He pulled a legacy dish out of his back pocket so that he would never have to be level with her. Maxwell Easton would *never* share the top spot with Evelyn Pimm.

His eyes shuttered, confirming the truth to her—his face a mask of utter coldness, revealing nothing and everything at the same time.

"Guys!" Harvey's voice careened through their bubble, popping it instantly and bringing Evelyn back to the kitchen. They were standing toe-to-toe, arms crossed, faces inches apart in a whisper battle that must have sounded like a symphony of hissing. She snapped her eyes to Harvey, his face wary as he took in the sight of them.

"What the hell is going on?" His voice came out thin and tired, and she couldn't stand the sound of it. Her actions had been the cause of that voice. The cause of that utter exhaustion.

She stepped back so suddenly; her ass bumped the garbage can causing it to wobble in place before she slapped her steadying hands upon it.

The silence in the kitchen was edible. Bitter, and chewy.

Max picked up his forgotten plate and smiled at his dad. "I was just offering my feedback on Evelyn's dish," he lied.

"Although," she cut in. Shame filled her gut with something sour, and before she could change her mind she said, "I told him to save it for Tuesday when I help him with that project." And then, because she couldn't help it, "But, your stubborn ass son couldn't keep his mouth shut."

Despite the insult, or maybe because of its familiarity, Harvey's face softened with relief. His brown eyes gleamed with amusement before he told her that Max's stubbornness came from Lennon, said his goodbyes, and left.

Bitter. Chewy. Silence.

Feeling Max's eyes on her, she gathered her things and headed for the door.

"Evelyn," he said from behind her.

"I *am* a sore loser," she called over her shoulder. The only form of apology she could offer him. "E-mail me the details of your event."

And with that, she fled the kitchen with pride in how she managed not to run out of the restaurant and away from Max's overwhelming presence.

Chapter Six

This is complete and utter bullshit, Evelyn thought as she held back yet another eye roll. At the rate she was going, she was going to have to stretch the muscles of her face every morning from the strain of holding them back.

The guest gazed up at her expectantly, his chin jutting out at an angle that made him look extremely self-important. Which, to be fair, he was.

"I understand your frustration Mr. Walker, but this is our policy. Given the highly specialized nature of our food, menu substitutions are unfortunately not available." God, she sounded like a robot programmed to self-destruct before upsetting anyone in the slightest. If this were an email, it would be filled with apologies and exclamation points. Maybe an emoji or two.

The guest ran a hand through his thick, blond hair and rolled his eyes at his date. He was well within his rights to do so, but apparently that sort of behavior was unacceptable for Evelyn. She turned her gaze to the woman next to him with a kind smile.

"My apologies, but we truly can't accommodate a vegan menu," she said as softly as possible. It really wasn't his date's fault. Mr. Walker and his pointy chin and cheesy blazers was one of their regular guests. He had a different date every time, which, good for him—but he really should have known better than to pull Evie off the line for this.

Her mind was already circling back to the kitchen where she belonged when Pointy Chin asked what was quickly becoming one of her least favorite questions of all time.

"Can I speak to the chef?" he inquired, voice rising a full octave. "I mean, I know you have the ingredients to pull this off back there. I come here all the time, you should be able to just," he waved his hand in front of him in a circular gesture. "Make it happen."

The increase in volume from Dick Chin startled her into a blink. Look, she was used to entitled guests. In fact, she loved an entitled guest. The Lennon was a two-star that probably should have been a no-star because Harvey firmly believed that, yes—they're in hospitality. But the guest was most certainly *not* always right. In fact, they were usually dead wrong.

Like at this moment.

Evie watched as Mr. Walker's date squirmed in her seat at the shear condescension in his words. *Just make it happen.* The demand grated on Evelyn even more than the request for the chef. That one line represented what was so inherently wrong with the majority of Yelp reviewers and self-proclaimed foodies. They simply didn't take restaurant work seriously. Dick Chin wholeheartedly believed that what Evie did every day wasn't difficult. He believed, like so many others, that it was an easy thing to just go to the walk-in, pull out all of the veggies they had, and make an eight-course, vegan meal worthy of two stars without any testing or tasting.

But it was even more than that. Because what really got to Evelyn was how ignorant he was about it all. How offensive it actually was to hear someone say, "Can you just make me a grilled cheese?" when you have tirelessly used your skills, and knowledge, and years of training to develop a carefully curated dining experience. How was Dick Chin going to tell her how to do the job that she had been studying for almost fifteen years? She didn't go to his office and tell him how to swindle people out of money or whatever horrendous thing this guy obviously did for a living.

Why was it always okay for people to tell restaurant and hospitality workers how to do a job that they knew nothing about? It didn't matter. What mattered was the fact that Evie loved entitled people because she didn't have to appease them. At the end of the day, this vision was Harvey's. Nobody else's.

Not to mention the fact that it actually was impossible to create a vegan menu with five minutes notice.

Sadly, that inner dialogue didn't stop Evie from sweating as she geared up to hand her guests a final refusal. Even through all his condescension, she hated disappointing guests and feared the conflict that would inevitably follow. No amount of inner pep talk would make it easier, so, she softened her gaze and prepared to drive the final nail into the vegan coffin.

Before she could begin, Mr. Walker sat up a little straighter and lowered his voice. "Perfect. The actual chef is here."

She turned to find Max with a strange, sugar-coated smile on his face and just managed to smother a groan. Max's event was in two days, and she had been doing a very thorough job of avoiding him until Mr. Walker decided to ruin her night. He had probably stopped while running food because this moron had kept her from her job for far too long.

Maxwell's eyes shone bright and fiery as they left her face to find his target. Because that's exactly what it looked like he was doing, lining up a target. His candy smile was still locked in place as he stepped forward and spoke directly to Mr. Walker's chin.

"Pardon the interruption Chef Evelyn, but you are needed back in the kitchen," he said, without looking her way.

Relief loosened her stiff shoulders even as her stomach tightened. What was he about to do? Step in as The Chef and save the day? They were fully booked, and there was absolutely no way they could pull off this request, but Evelyn simply accepted defeat with a nod and fled back to the safety of the kitchen.

Stepping back into the chaotic fray of a busy night was heaven and Evie immediately hopped into motion. Her movements natural and efficient. She was just finishing a plate-up when Maxwell returned to the pass. A quick glance revealed Mr. Walker, following his date out of the restaurant with a flush that could battle hers any day.

"Yikes, he doesn't look happy," she mumbled to Maxwell.

"Oh, he's not," Max said in a cheerful tone.

Evie nodded, seeing his false joy as a sign of annoyance. "I'm sorry you had to take over for me. He was being relentless, and I just—"

"You don't have to apologize to me Evelyn," he cut in, annoyance definitely shining through. "You're my co-CDC, people don't get to talk to you that way. To any of the staff that way," he added quickly as his hands moved over dark blue plates. "I simply told him to give us a week's notice and come back another time. I needed you here."

Evie's hands shook with a small tremor, her tweezers vibrating slightly as she strategically draped bright orange calendula petals over crisp greens. She would tell herself for the next hour that the encounter with Mr. Walker had set her on edge. It had absolutely nothing to do with the deepening of Max's voice, intense and focused and oh so close, saying *I needed you.*

"You okay?" he asked impatiently.

Evelyn raised a brow and barely gave his too-close face a glance. "I'm fine Maxwell. I assure you I can handle a rude guest without falling to pieces."

"Then," he said before catching her wrist in his and stilling her slight tremor. "Why are you shaking?"

Goosebumps popped up slowly on Evelyn's arm as he pulled away, fingers raking over her skin. Recognition that he had called hands and stepped back, allowing the servers to rush in and walk the perfect plates to their tables, didn't hit as quickly as it should have.

Jesus, how was she supposed to spend a night with this man? She could barely make it through a shift without her mind turning to a place that she never thought possible with Maxwell. He was confusing and rude. Pompous. A thousand different unsavory adjectives.

And she'd felt a thousand different versions of embarrassment since he showed up in those tight chef coats.

Evelyn glared at the next round of plates as if they personally offended her with their presence. This was all her fault. Apparently, throwing yourself from a toxic relationship straight into a world of work-induced celibacy wasn't great for the nervous system. She was convinced that even the tiny hairs on her arms leaned in Maxwells direction, begging for more skin-on-skin action. It was an insane thought, and one that she vehemently rejected as Phil sidled up next to her.

"That was awesome," he said with a little jab of his elbow. Evie refused to acknowledge how her skin stayed goosebump-less at Phil's touch.

"What was awesome? My perfect distribution of calendula?" she asked as her now-stable hands plucked petals and placed them once again on the next round of salads.

Max was across the kitchen, face in profile as he spoke to another cook, features serious and slightly terrifying. His jaw was just fine, she told herself as a muscle flexed in his neck. It definitely wasn't chiseled to perfection as if carved out of stone by practiced hands.

For fuck's sake…

"No. Well, yes, but no," Phil went on. "The way Chef Max told off that douche with the floral blazer."

"Dick Chin," she clarified with an indulgent grin. "And telling him to give us notice next time was pretty standard Phil. The man doesn't deserve a James Beard Award for that." Annoyance lit her tone, and she scolded herself for it. She didn't need her strained relationship with Maxwell hovering over the rest of the staff.

"Chef, he said a lot more than that," Phil prattled on. He plucked two plates from the pass to run them to a table himself and paused to tell her, "His face, when Max called him out?" Evie looked up at him in surprise, but Phil's face was delighted as he fled to deliver the plates. "It was priceless," he threw over his shoulder before navigating to the appropriate table.

"What was priceless?"

Evelyn nearly jumped at Maxwell's voice. She had been staring at Phil's back, shock stilling her body.

She whirled to find him already plating the next course. His abalone dish, she noted with dislike coating her throat. The sight of it reminded her that she lost which was enough to launch her into a state of complete defense.

"What did you say to Mr. Walker?" she demanded. Her fingers moved swiftly over the dishes, adjusting the beautiful piles of abalone until they were perfect.

Max didn't so much as blink as he continued to plate.

"I told him to give us notice next time," he hedged.

"And?" she pushed, matching his pace, head down.

"And," he said sheepishly. "I told him that if he wanted to continue to bring his dates here, it would be smart for him to show the chef the respect she deserves."

Evie blinked up at him, aware of the fact that her mouth was gaping and doing nothing to snap it shut again.

"Then," he continued.

"Then?" Evelyn shrieked, unsure of whether she wanted the answer or not.

"I reminded him that last week's date had been gluten free, and we received notice. And the week before that, one date had a shellfish allergy, and the next day he came in with that girl that didn't like music with lyrics in it. Remember her? We ended up seating them in a quiet corner..." he trailed off to call hands and finally met her eyes.

Evie's mouth still hung open, her eyes felt wide and round in her head. No wonder Mr. Walker practically ran out the door.

"Maxwell..."

"It's like I said," he cut in casually while plucking two plates from the pass and turning towards the dining room. "People don't get to talk to you that way."

Chapter Seven

Max ran a hand through his perfectly smoothed hair for, he promised himself, the last time. He always had to work hard to mold the dark locks into submission and this particular nervous habit wasn't doing him any favors.

The air was cool as the last beams of sunlight showered rooftops around him in burnt oranges and yellows. A honk and incoherent yell sounded from somewhere in the distance, barely heard over a man in overalls playing an accordion on the corner.

Overall's hair was smooth and perfect, he noted before catching himself in a nervous gesture and shoving his hand back into the pockets of his suit pants.

He had gone with the dark green suit today. Something that he only pulled out when he wanted to impress, but not go overboard. A ridiculous goal seeing as he was about to step into an event where Overboard was basically the theme of the night. But the suit fit him like a glove and the olive, floral tie was about as flashy as he was willing to get.

He hadn't told Evelyn much about the event, worried that she would fake an illness before voluntarily walking into the chaos. It was a requirement that everyone dress to impress though, which he made sure she understood before leaving the restaurant on Sunday. She had simply told him that she wouldn't show up in leggings and a crop top if he stopped commenting on her socks, flashed him a fake smile and darted out of his general area. Unfortunately, Evie's curvy body in leggings and a crop top refused to leave his traitorous brain since the words were released into the universe.

Oh, and his fantasies didn't stop there. Max crossed his arms, legs stiff as he fought the urge to pace along the sidewalk, waiting for her to arrive. The minutes ticked on as his imagination flew to Evie exiting a Lyft in front of him. Strappy heels hugging her ankles, a red velvet dress clinging to wide hips. Lips pouty and murderously red…

This woman was going to ruin him.

If he had been smart, he would have never returned to The Lennon. There were other ways he could support his father…ways that didn't involve torturing himself with an infuriatingly temping brunette. But that thought brought him up short and gave him a sour taste in his mouth. Taking the pressure of work off Harvey's shoulders was the least he could do. It was important for his dad to know that Max was there, that he could rely on him not only at work, but in every facet of this terrible, unfair journey he was on. He wouldn't fuck everything up this time.

"There's a small kind of comfort in knowing you scowl at things that aren't me."

Max fell out of his thoughts with a thud. His eyes adjusted to the now-dim light of the street, and he zeroed in on the woman walking towards him.

Words escaped him. Maybe even oxygen escaped him, he couldn't tell. His chest was moving up and down, but he certainly didn't feel like he was breathing. Evelyn sauntered up to him, heels clicking on the cement. She stopped a good two feet away and swirled herself around to show off her outfit. Not even a hint of a smile painted her features.

"Am I impressive?" she asked sarcastically.

"You…" he tried. But nope. It was confirmed; he wasn't breathing.

She wore a dark blue jumpsuit that was tied around the perfect spot at her waist, sash dangling to her knee and whirling slightly in the breeze. One sleeve curved over her shoulder while the other was left bare, the neckline swooping across her chest as if someone ripped the other half away. Tiny stars curled along the length of it all, catching the streetlight and twinkling as if she was draped in the night sky.

She had clearly taken some time to apply makeup, for her whisky eyes were somehow even more piercing, lined in coal and glaring at him with distaste. Chocolate hair was knotted at one side with a few sweet locks framing her stupid fucking face.

Lips.

Dark red, and killing him slowly.

Those lethal lips quirked up at his stumbling. She crossed her arms, pulling his gaze to her bare shoulder. He wanted to chew on it. Start at the pulse in her wrist and lazily travel up to that shoulder, nipping and licking his way along to the next pulse point below her ear…

"Where's your jacket?" he rasped. God, he sounded like he had been thinking about exactly what he had been thinking about.

Evie blinked. Her almost smile curving into a full-on scowl.

Without a word, she lifted her bag and gestured to it as if it was obvious and he was one-hundred percent stupid.

"I also have stretchy pants for after I make you buy me a full dinner and maybe an entire bottle of wine," she said with false enthusiasm.

If her current outfit; the one that clung to every curve and fit her like a second skin, wasn't considered stretchy pants, he didn't want to see it. Didn't need another image of Evie to actively suppress.

"Well, all the food is included, and I'll buy you whatever drinks you want. You might need some liquid courage," he mumbled under his breath.

Max nodded to the building they were loitering in front of. "Ready?"

They both turned their attention to their destination. There was nothing showy about the front door. In fact, if there hadn't been an intricately designed iron bench resting next to the entrance, you wouldn't know anything was there at all. The building was old and kind of scary looking. It was a miracle there were no gargoyles accompanying the wrought iron gates and stained brick. A single round sign with the letter F hung just to the left indicating absolutely nothing.

"Undecided," she said at last.

He considered her for a moment. She definitely looked apprehensive standing in front of what appeared to be an abandoned building, dressed like she was going to a gala and probably wondering what the hell she was doing here with him. Honestly, that question was also soaring through him as well. Their rivalry had been years in the building, yet here she was. Just because of some idiotic bet that he had truthfully had no intention of holding her to.

"Smart, it's good to keep your guard up in this place," he said without any additional explanation as he swung the door open and waited for her to pass through.

They ended up in a gallery. Art in various forms hung from the walls and adorned high, pedestal-like tables. It was simple, nothing flashy to take away from the pieces on display.

"Welcome to Frankie's…oh, hi Maxie!"

He turned to the familiar man sitting at an ornate mahogany desk at the back of the gallery. Noting the glass of wine he was drinking, he raised an eyebrow at Colin.

"Does that mean you'll be joining us a little later?"

"Pfff," he huffed while running a hand through his long smooth hair. "As if I need a reason to enjoy the simple things in life. Who's the midnight sky?" he asked, gaze sliding to Evelyn. He tried not to pout at the full, genuine smile she gave Colin.

Max introduced the two, all while watching her reactions out of the corner of his eye. He was dying to know what was running through that brain of hers. Her eyes bounced casually around the empty space while listening to Colin ramble on about the benefits of drinking on the job. A full laugh erupted from her painted lips, hitting him right between the eyes.

"Wait, who is Frankie?" Evelyn asked as she looked over a business card.

"Oh, Frankie is the reason The Show even exists, Starshine," Colin answered. She beamed at the nickname like he had told her she was the most beautiful woman on the planet. The prick. "Well, him and Lennon of course."

Colin patted Max on the shoulder as he said this. An attempt to ease the pain that cracked his chest in two anytime his mom was brought up in conversation.

"So, what's your talent this year?" Colin asked casually.

Max gently pressed Evelyn toward the door to Colin's right and failed miserably in his attempt not to focus on how thin the fabric of her outfit was.

"Starshine," he replied simply, before leading them through the door and into utter chaos.

***

A neon pink, six-inch heel went soaring past as the crowd erupted into cheers and applause. Music flowed through the room, bouncing off the padding on the walls and high ceilings like bumper cars. An entire wall was lined with food. Charcuterie and cheeses, savory pastries and salads with bright vegetables. Was that a whole pig…

A bell was rung at the bar and the room broke out in applause once more, checking the levels of the contents in their glasses. Some rose to fill their drinks, some remained seated, chatting animatedly. There were feathers, leathers, mesh and patterns. So. Many. Patterns. Someone was in the corner next to a good-sized stage, hula hooping while casually sipping from what appeared to be a large tiki drink with a swirly straw. Swaying over the stage was an oddly patterned banner that read *Welcome to the 8th Annual Show*, a phrase that made absolutely no sense.

Evie didn't know where to look, how to feel, or how to continue on with her life knowing that this magical place existed.

"What the shit?" she asked no one in particular. When Maxwell had led her through the back door and down a very poorly lit staircase, she was certain he was taking her to some kind of underground murder cave. Colin had just been a decoy, sweetening her up for the slaughter.

Instead, they were met with a large metal door where they apparently tumbled through the looking glass into Alice's dizziest daydream.

"What am I looking at?" she tried again, just as the music quieted a bit causing several heads to turn in her direction. Her confusion didn't lessen one bit as almost eighty people yelled *Maxie* then continued to bombard the man with laughed greetings and hugs—as if he wasn't Satan's spawn.

"You need a drink," *Maxie* stated after making it out of the throng of silk-draped bodies, his lips pressed together in a suppressed laugh. How could he look so comfortable in this setting?

"Yes. And potentially a CT scan, MRI—let's just schedule a full range of brain scans when this episode is over shall we?"

"You bet," he called over his shoulder, greeting more people on his way to the bar.

Trailing behind him, mouth shut, but hanging open in shock in her mind, she had to give it to him. Her determination to thoroughly hate this evening was bulldozed the minute they walked through the doors. Maybe even the minute they walked into the gallery. She had not been expecting it. Some might say that blindly going out with a man you have practiced hating with the determination of a professional athlete, was not a great idea. Evie had been telling herself that she relented just to have the opportunity to make his life a living hell for a full evening, but she knew—could feel the truth of it between her shoulder blades—that she truly just wanted to see behind the curtain.

Lights bounced chaotically off Max's dark hair, glinting from the grays starting to peek through. She let her eyes wander down the length of him. An indulgence she carelessly accepted yet would never admit to.

That suit had no right to fit him like that. It was tailored to perfection around his middle, accentuating his broad shoulders and long legs simultaneously. The fact that he was painfully gorgeous made her furious. He was doing it on purpose, she was sure of it.

"That, is a man who knows how to wear a suit."

Evelyn continued to stare at Max as he ordered drinks, reluctant appreciation hanging heavy in her gut.

"He does it to piss me off," she replied without looking at the source of the rich, honey-dripped voice.

Her companion chuckled into his drink. "Oh, so you know him well then. It's not like him to date, so I just assumed you were a cousin or something. Well, until you started looking at him like he was another offering on the buffet table.”

Mortified, Evie jolted herself into movement, removing her gaze from a luscious, green-shrouded frame to her new companion. And it is truly a marvel that she was able to fully suppress the squeal that flew up her throat when she came face-to-face with Beyoncé.

The man was in full drag and looked so much like the queen herself, Evie wasn’t fully convinced it wasn’t her. Suddenly, she felt like her star covered jumpsuit was akin to a burlap sack.

“I’m sorry, I’m not sure why I was looking anywhere but in your direction. Look at you!” She exclaimed, forgetting about Maxwell’s existence in an instant. “You’re absolutely stunning.”

The man fanned himself before flipping long caramel locks over one shoulder.

“Yes, thank you,” he sang. “I am finally gifting the world with my Single Ladies performance tonight. I’m Frances by the way.”

“Evelyn,” she responded with a smile. “Wait, do you own this place?”

“Guilty,” he replied without sounding guilty at all.

A drink appeared in front of Evie, and she grabbed it without asking questions. Max handed a drink to Frances as well causing him to fan himself and throw a wink her way.

Scowl still in place, Max gave the man a nod. “Toned it down from last year I see,” he grumbled.

“Ha! You’ll be whistling a different tune when I take that trophy home again.”

“Your confidence has always been admirable Frankie, but I have a secret weapon this year…” Max trailed off, eyes finding hers.

His usual scowl was still there, but softer. An easy camaraderie settled over the two men as they discussed their issues last year, and how Grace never deserved to win.

She was having a really hard time keeping up and finally decided to just ask what the hell was going on.

"I'm sorry, where am I right now?"

Frances fanned his arm out in a Vanna White style wave. "You're in Frankie's Speakeasy, honey. This has been a safe space for folks to relax, raise money, and have a damn good time for nearly fifteen years."

"And what is this particular event?" she asked, completely enthralled with Frankie and his bouffant.

"What?" He looked at Max with one elegantly raised brow. "You didn't tell your girlfriend where you were bringing her, and she still managed to dress like an intergalactic daydream?"

Max's scowl deepened. "Evelyn is my coworker," he clarified, draining the rest of his drink in one go.

"Yeah, we actually hate each other with a white-hot intensity," she said, grinning at them. "I lost a bet," she added.

"Huh." Frankie was looking at her now, focused and a little too smug for her liking. "Well, I'll let Maxie explain The Show to you, it's going to start in thirty minutes, and I need to get limber."

Evie watched in wonder as Frances kissed Maxwell's cheek, whispered something in his ear that had his neck flushing red, and sauntered off. All swishing hips and swaying hair.

"I think I'm in love," Evelyn said as she watched him go.

"You'll have to get in line. Come on," Max nodded to the wall of food. "Let's get something to eat."

"And then you'll tell me what I'm doing here?" It came out harsher than she had intended. Usually, when she was attempting to be blunt and unapologetic, she had to work for it. It was strange how a weight was lifted in the presence of this impossible man. Funny that she worked so hard to please everyone else, then felt comforted by that relaxed pressure around him—The Devil himself.

He nodded. "Yeah, but I want to make sure you are buttered up with a full buffet offering first," he said, voice teasing, scowl still firmly in place.

"Very smart," she said as they began to navigate the crowd.

***

"At its core, The Show is a fundraiser," Max said before shoving a bite of leafy greens in his mouth. "We sell tickets, which include food and mass amounts of entertainment, and all proceeds are donated to Frances' non-profit. They spread the funds between cancer research, assistance for people going through chemo…stuff like that."

Evelyn listened while stuffing salty pork into a roll. She had taken a closer look at the banner after finally being let in on the secret of this magical event. The pattern that at first had been confusing, revealed itself to be *fuck cancer* repeated thousands of times in hundreds of different fonts.

"And my love for Frankie grows." Batting her eyelashes at Maxwell felt wrong, but she couldn't help settling into a comfortable form of herself. Maybe she was comforted by the fact that nothing made sense around her.

"It will grow even bigger as time goes on, I assure you of that."

Huh. Well shit. Evelyn's middle performed a hesitant flip at the soft affection in his voice. It was abundantly clear that he cared dearly for Frankie, and probably a fair number of people in this room.

A bell sounded from the bar again causing everyone to inspect the levels of their drinks and either take a large pull or get up for another. It was strangely robotic.

Max chuckled at her confused expression. "That sound is to remind people to keep drinking," he clarified. "All beverage sales are donated."

She looked down at her drink, almost empty and practically glaring at her. Evelyn wasn't the biggest drinker. That is, she loved a good drink, but hated getting drunk. She had seen too many people lose themselves in the substance to enjoy anything past a good buzz. Nevertheless, she began to rise to buy another. It was a good cause after all.

"You don't have to drink Evie," Max spit out before she could leave. "Besides, I'm buying everything tonight, remember?"

"Oh right, so you can get all of the donation glory?"

He laughed a full laugh and she sat with a thump. The sound was so foreign, so unexpected. It was certainly never performed in front of her. She got a strange sense of accomplishment from pulling that laugh out of him.

"Only you would turn a charity fundraiser into a competition."

"Untrue," she stated before turning back to her plate of food. "Some of those marathon runners are intense with their fundraising efforts. So, what *is* The Show then?"

"It's an adult talent contest," he stated simply.

"Be serious. I'm starting to regret not drilling you for more information. If I had known ahead of time that Beyoncé was an outfit option, I would have shown up in something flashier. Now, spill the tea."

"First of all, you look perfect," he said, distracted by the stage lights as they started to dim and still. "And second, I'm one-hundred percent serious. This is a talent show, where grown ass adults get to live out whatever twisted fantasy they have while they pretend to work all day."

"My god..." At that moment, Evie had zeroed in on someone dressed up like a cat, whiskers and all, as they set up a mini trampoline on stage. "How did this all start?" Where was she? What was the meaning of life? All of these questions were flying through her head as she tried to navigate this dreamscape. But there was one question that trumped all the rest.

Why am I here with you?

He hesitated for a brief second, eyes darting everywhere for a moment before landing on hers.

"Frankie and my mom met during chemo treatments." The words were said in a rush. As if he had rehearsed the lines but struggled with the delivery. "They obviously became fast friends. Planned the entire thing from a hospital. They decided to host the first annual Show after they both finished treatments."

She didn't need him to go on to know the end of this particular story. Lennon hadn't made it to the first fundraiser. Occasionally, Harvey would open up about his late wife, about how he thought he had more time until—he didn't. And something that was so constant was suddenly gone. He told her it was like losing a limb. An extremely important, extremely solid part of your very being, was just gone.

She couldn't begin to imagine it. And as she looked at Max, uncomfortable as hell in a full suit, attending a fuck cancer fundraiser with the fear of losing another parent to the disease resting on his back. It made her angry that the universe could be so cruel.

A need to express that clunked in her belly. In that moment, this overwhelming desire to comfort and console her mortal enemy was so strong, she gripped the sides of her chair to keep them from doing something ridiculous. She didn't touch Maxwell Easton and all that. But she couldn't help the impulse. Seeing that far-off, sad look in his features—knowing that rehashing the story had brought him pain—it made her itch to fix everything.

Max cleared his throat and ran a hand through his hair. Slicking it back from his forehead while somehow mussing the locks simultaneously. "Anyway, that's how this all started. Frankie made it through, started his nonprofit, and immediately started planning the fundraiser." A lightness returned to his tone and Evie almost didn't recognize him without the scowl. Then his features turned a bit mischievous.

She was more than happy to move on from somber.

"Now, over the years, this has turned into a fiery hot battle. You see that trophy over there?" Evelyn turned her gaze to a raised pedestal next to the stage. A tall, bright green trophy with, you guessed it, mass amounts of different patterns, sequins, glitter, and what appeared to be a Barbie that had seen better days on top, stood in all its glory.

"I can't unsee it," she replied before turning back to him. She was fully enthralled by this whole thing. Could feel it in the way she leaned toward him, hanging on to his next words.

"Every year there's a panel of random judges. If they pick you as the champion of The Show, you get to take the trophy home until the next fundraiser."

"You get to have that eye-melting, plastic tower of whimsy in your house? For a full year?"

"Uh, huh," he confirmed, a whisper of a grin on his face. "And all the bragging rights that come with it. My dad and I haven't won for six years, but this year…"

"Wait, *you* actually participate?" Evie had to lift her chin off the damn floor.

"Oh, absolutely," he said without missing a beat.

"And what do you do?" she asked in utter delight.

"Well, the last year Dad and I won, we acted out an 80's montage. My Flashdance clip was pretty good, but Dad sealed the deal with his Top Gun volleyball scene."

Evelyn choked on her drink; the sweet, tangy liquid came horrifyingly close to spraying out of her nose.

"Was he," she cut off on a cough. "Shirtless?"

Max patted her back, a full grin splitting his features. "Cut. Off. Shorts."

Evelyn closed her eyes. She pressed her lips together to try and suppress the full laugh that was dying to escape.

"My god," she said again. "And *I'm* the one turning a charity event into a competition?"

"Uh huh, you fit right in," he said simply. "But none of that matters today. What matters is what *you're* doing. Now, there's a full karaoke setup, so…"

"Wait," Evie stammered, holding a hand up to stop him. "What do you mean me? I'm not getting up there," she squeaked.

Max turned to her and scooted his chair closer. His eyes were a little crazed and focused directly on her face. The lights at the stage began to shift as the music faded and a microphone let out a screech. Frankie sauntered on stage, hair swaying in a move that was clearly practiced to perfection. Max leaned in, whispering over Frankie's introduction.

"Look, I know this is the craziest thing to just walk into, and I know I didn't give you any information beforehand, but honestly," he paused to nervously run his hand through his hair again. "I never thought you'd actually come. I didn't even know what I was planning to do. Usually Dad and I…" Max trailed off, looking vulnerable and sad, and cracking her chest wide open.

She felt bad for him. Rivalry floated around them like it was the scent they put on every morning and yet, she could feel for him in this moment. Feel for Harvey.

Maybe it was her deep-rooted need to make people happy that lowered her walls a bit and made her woefully unprepared when he grabbed the edge of her chair and pulled her closer to him as if she were light as a feather.

In the blink of an eye, she had ended up between Max's legs, cheek to cheek. He still smelled like pine and nutmeg, and fucking Christmas.

"Okay, I admit that I really needed someone to come with me this year. That's why I picked this as my win. But then, I heard you singing the other day," he moved away slightly, his eyes burning into hers. "And I just thought—"

"Okay," Evelyn said in a whisper. She didn't dare breathe, didn't dare move. Any kind of shift would bring her skin to his, and she was just too uncertain of what that would do to her.

This whole thing was insane.

"Okay?" he asked, sitting back and allowing her to release her breath.

"Okay," she said nodding. "But you're coming with me" she stated before standing to get another drink.

"What?"

She heard Max rise from the table and scramble after her.

"I saw a box of props and costumes next to the stage, are those available for everyone?" she asked, all business as she tried to catch the eye of the bartender.

The room erupted into applause as Frankie finished his speech and flipped his hair. He introduced the cat-trampoline lady and Evie took that as a sign that The Eighth Annual Show had officially begun. She ordered another round for her and her frenemy for the night before meeting his eye.

"Yes, but Evelyn, I'm not getting up there with you. It usually takes Dad and I months to prepare for this. I don't have your," he gestured to her entire body, his hand pointing from her head to toes and back again. "Natural talent."

She smiled. Couldn't help herself. The image of Maxwell and Harvey practicing their performance for an adult talent show was officially too much for her overstimulated brain.

"Listen to me Maxwell." Evie threw caution to the wind, ignored her no touching rule and grabbed him by the chin. She held his gaze and annoyingly had to keep her eyes from drifting to his lips. "This changes nothing between us. You and me? We still dislike each other with a white-hot intensity." Max's scowl returned in a blink, but she rallied on. "But we both care for Harvey, and this may come as a surprise to you, but I am REALLY competitive."

Max's lips turned up in a lopsided grin at that, which gave her the enthusiasm to continue.

"We are getting on that stage, giving these people the performance of a lifetime, and taking that horrendous trophy home to Harvey."

She released his chin, but he didn't step back. Their faces were as close as they had been back at the test kitchen, but this was different. They weren't tearing into each other.

They were teaming up.

He smiled. A big, bright, genuine smile.

"Let's keep with the 80's theme. Tell me, how familiar are you with Dirty Dancing?" she asked before pounding her drink.

Chapter Eight

The regret he felt was vast, to put it mildly.

Max looked at himself in the dim bathroom light, his reflection showing him a side of himself that he never thought he'd see. *Definitely* never thought Evelyn would see.

And yet here he was, a grown ass man in a white, sleeveless undershirt sporting a very pink, very puffy skirt.

It wasn't necessarily a tutu but…

He could hear that Frankie's performance was not only amazing, but coming to an abrupt close and a cold sweat began spreading along his forehead at the thought of getting on that stage with Evelyn.

This entire event was so out of character for him, he was actively considering climbing through the air ducts to escape acting out her plan. A plan she had animatedly explained to him before shoving the skirt in his hands, telling him she'd see him on the other side, and heading into the restroom to change herself.

Applause broke out as Frankie finished up his performance. Max's eyes widened, bolting to the air duct again to gauge the distance. A knock broke through his escape plans, and he literally started shaking. Why? Why did he torture himself like this? Yes, he knew most of the people out there, but his anxiety was taking the reins on this one.

"Baby?" Evelyn called from the other side of the door. And damned if that one word didn't bring him out of his panic in a blink. The way she used baby in reference to him would be burned in his brain for the remainder of his existence. "I hope you're ready 'cause I'm coming in," she announced.

His wide eyes locked on hers immediately as she poked her head into the small room, a plain, black tank top and yoga pants visible from behind the door. Of course she had actually brought them.

Her whisky gaze ran down the length of him once, twice…

"This is the best day of my life," she managed before collapsing into a fit of giggles.

"I can't do this," he stated. He made to slam the door in her face, but she pushed her way through.

"Oh, come on! I was joking Max, really," she laughed out. "I'm telling you; this is a winning performance. I won't waste a classic 'nobody puts Baby in the corner' reference on this, because Harvey is about to have a full year of sleepless nights knowing that monstrosity of a trophy is somewhere in his house."

"I can't get up there." He could hear the nerves in his voice. Felt no shame about it. Although he had managed to make quite a name for himself over the years, a reputation that had him attending dining awards and photo shoots, the spotlight was a terrifying, miserable place. Being the center of attention was meant for people like Evelyn, people who didn't scowl at rainbows for not being pronounced enough.

The background, or more accurately the kitchen, was the only place he felt truly comfortable. But as Evie rolled her eyes and tugged his arm, dragging him to the stage with a literal spotlight, he followed. Hearing her sing had given him a determination to win. To bring some joy to Harvey's life. Seeing his dad's face fall into a genuine, toddler-like pout when he realized he wouldn't be able to make The Show this year had been heartbreaking. It felt silly, especially in a fucking pink skirt and dress shoes, but he really wanted to bring a win home for him.

He told himself that was why Evie was there. Why he trailed after her with very little resistance and amped himself up for this ridiculous performance. She could help him do something meaningful for Harvey.

It had nothing to do with getting closer to her. Feeling her hand wrapped around his arm as she tugged him to the stage. Nothing to do with the view of her round ass in those yoga pants…

They reached the bottom of the stage steps and Evie turned so suddenly; Max ran into her chest. Her soft breasts pressed against him sliding up his body as she rose to her tippy toes and whispered in his ear. "Go get 'em, Baby." Her hot breath danced along his ear and goosebumps spread along the sensitive skin just below. He should have felt nothing but shock at her closeness, the press of her breasts and the lustiness in her voice, but his body moved of its own accord. As if reaching for her, embracing her, holding her against him like she was meant to be there was the most natural thing in the world.

But before any of that could happen, she bounced out of his reach and headed straight for the karaoke table. Hips swaying as she navigated the path.

This is when the shock set in. Shock, and the realization that he was horrifyingly close to having a full hard-on in a skirt. His mind raced through what had just happened as Frankie prattled out a small intro for them.

A round of cheering went up and before his mind could properly catch up— before he could fully process the feel of Evelyn pressed against him, her lips grazing his ear—

Frankie slipped by on the steps. A look of sheer delight covered his gorgeously contoured face as he saw Max's new outfit.

Still in an Evie induced stupor, he passed Frankie in silence, taking his spot in the middle of the stage. He couldn't see her yet. He truly couldn't see much of anything as the lights blinded him, but he ached to get his eyes on her. It was hot on the stage and sweat began building, his mind racing as he tried to remember what he was supposed to do. He grabbed the mic and his sweaty palms almost let it slip through to the floor.

A chime of a laugh sounded from the other side of the stage and his eyes connected with Evie. She was smiling at him, mic held comfortably in her no doubt dry hand. He barely registered the crowd chanting *Maxie, Maxie, Maxie* when the lights glinted off her rosy cheeks and she beamed at him like that.

He was a goner.

Music began playing but he didn't break her gaze. Her caramel eyes widened as he held the mic to his mouth and actually did what he was supposed to do, he sang the opening lines to "The Time of My Life" as she sauntered on stage lip syncing his part. His voice was awful. He couldn't carry a tune in a cooler, and when he told her he knew the song, it was a bit of an embellishment. She had played the last dance scene from *Dirty Dancing* for him twice before they went to change, so that brought his total of actually listening to the musical number up to an impressive four.

He turned to face her as she paused inches away from him, bringing her mic to her own lips. Her voice was amazing. Rich and smooth and caressing the air around him in comfort. Well, as much comfort as he could muster while lip syncing along to her voice. He looked like a complete moron, but he didn't care while Evie was holding his gaze and singing. Then, they were holding each other. His hand came around her waist, the other holding the mic in a death grip as he took over and Evie began lip syncing his part. They were dancing. Dirty dancing to the delight of the crowd watching the entire thing unfold. His face split into a grin which was starting to become painful. He had smiled more in this one night with Evie than he had in the past year.

They sang together, Evie sounding angelic, him sounding like Skuttle from *The Little Mermaid*, all while dancing painfully close. She kept spinning him in these ridiculous lopsided twirls. He had a good foot on her, forcing her to her tiptoes whenever she attempted the move. Their performance was clumsy at best, but he supposed that dancing with one another wouldn't necessarily come naturally after years of hatred.

Before he could grab her, stop her, do anything to keep her from leaving his space, she twirled and leapt off the stage. The crowd roared in delight as Evelyn landed on her feet and lifted her arms in triumph, all while still maintaining the sway of her hips and rhythmic bounce of her feet to the music. He watched in complete awe as she shook her ass towards Frankie who didn't hesitate one bit and took the mic she offered to continue singing the song.

He knew what was supposed to come next, but he flat out refused to jump off the stage in a skirt. A detail, he realized with a start, he had completely forgotten most likely due to Evelyn's enthusiasm.

He used the dancing crowd as a distraction and bolted down the stairs and to the front center of the stage. On cue, Evelyn whipped around to face him, gave him a questioning look to which he responded with a nod. A nod that he was certain was him just agreeing to a painful, embarrassing death. The crowd parted to make way as he kicked into a jog and charged toward his nemesis.

He had tried with all of his might to talk her out of doing The Move. There was absolutely no good reason for him to expose himself in this skirt, not even for the trophy. But aside from that, he was one thousand percent certain that Evelyn wouldn't be able to lift him.

Max remembered in this moment how she had goaded him into it.

"What, you don't think I'm strong enough?" she had asked his smirk after the first rundown of her plan.

"Evelyn, I'm like two hundred pounds. You told me you could barely lift the weight bar the other day, remember?"

"That was obviously a joke. I am strong," she said while flexing muscles that clearly didn't exist. "It takes loads of strength to deal with you on a daily basis." And then, she smiled. Hit him with a grin he had seen a million times yet never, ever tired of. It was a smile that said, *come back at me. I dare you.*

Yeah, it was that smile that flashed in his mind as he ran through the parted crowd towards Evelyn. She was already laughing, eyes wide before he even reached her. He felt her hands curl around his upper abs, crushing his ribs in a death grip as he launched all of his weight at her with far too much confidence.

For a second, as "The Time of My Life" rang out from Frankie's lips and the crowd lost it with applause and cheers, he was elevated.

It was a very brief second.

Their fall was not a graceful one. Evelyn lost her grip and decided to wrap her arms around him in a bear hug instead, both of them crashing towards the floor, limbs entangling. He barely had the presence of mind to flip Evie around, so he crumbled to the floor first. She landed with a thud on top of him, his skirt hiked up to his boxers and Evelyn's legs tangled in his own.

God, it hurt. He was a large man, and he did *not* fall softly. But damned if he would take it back. His mind was on another plane before he realized he held Evie in his arms.

She was smiling so warmly down at him, a silent laugh in her eyes, he wanted it to last forever. To have Evie pressed against him, his arms trailing up her body. He watched, almost from outside of himself as his hand came up to cup her face.

The flush in her cheeks intensified as her smile wavered a bit.

"Are you alright?" he asked in a rough voice. He wasn't. He knew the scowl that he usually had stamped on his face was long gone. Would she know where his thoughts were right now? How the crowd simply disappeared as he looked into her doe eyes and felt hot lust tighten his stomach?

Her wide eyes flashed to his lips then back up as he rubbed his thumb along her jaw. They were close. He just needed to raise his head a couple of inches and finally catch her full lips in his. Finally taste her.

He felt her tug away and immediately drew his brows together in confusion. Why would Evelyn's body be anywhere but on top of his? Then he realized that multiple people were helping her to her feet, something that he should have been doing instead of fantasizing about her fucking mouth.

Multiple people were helping her to her feet...right, because they were in a room with over fifty witnesses.

Max bolted upright; his own flush heated his neck bringing a stream of sweat right between his shoulder blades.

Jesus *fucking* Christ. He avoided Evie's gaze as people surrounded him, clapping him on the back or sending big hugs and laughs his way. Apparently, they had really enjoyed their little performance. He glanced up once to find her eyes on him, watching him warily as folks gave her praise as well.

His eyes darted away. He didn't care if it made him a coward. An imagined kiss. One that he tried (and failed) not to daydream about or wish for, had come brutally close to coming to fruition. Max officially had too hard of a time keeping his walls up around Evelyn Pimm. Right then and there, as the crowd began to move back to their seats and his scowl was set firmly in place again, he called himself out.

It doesn't fucking matter if you're working together, yelling at each other or close to killing each other, you will always want this woman. You adore her. You...

Max beelined for the bathroom to change out of his stupid outfit. He had never yearned to put a suit back on in his life but tonight, it seemed, was a night of firsts. His gaze drifted back to the full room just before he reached the bathroom and found Evelyn thankfully not giving him the time of day. He changed, brooded, and cursed himself for being such an idiot. A sick voice in his head told him that he had wanted this all along. That he wanted to trap himself in her presence so they would be closer. Become closer.

That simply couldn't happen, and he knew it.

He strode back out of the bathroom just as the next act was going on.

"How dare you?"

Max stiffened immediately before his intelligence caught up with him and registered Frankie's voice, not Evie's.

"How dare I look that good in a skirt?" he tried.

"How dare you," Frankie said again, flipping his hair for the millionth time that night. "Keep that woman away from us for so long. She is brilliant for you."

"Calm down Frances, we are simply coworkers."

Beyoncé lifted a hip and crossed his arms. "I hope you are able to lie to yourself better than you are lying to me right now. I see the way you look at her. It's like you've been waiting for her your whole life."

Max felt the panic rise in his throat. If Frankie picked up on it, Evelyn had to see it too. A thought rose up from a dark place, bringing with it a knot in his chest. What if she knew, and wanted it too? She was here wasn't she...

90

Nope. No.

He couldn't get close to Evelyn, and he needed everyone to know it.

"You've always been a romantic Frankie but trust me when I say that Evelyn is here for one reason. Because my dad likes her. If she can help me make him happy, help me achieve my goals for the restaurant? She gets to stay. But the minute that stops being the case, you'll see that the look I've been giving her is more from shock that she's still around after all these years."

Max rubbed at his chest where the knot intensified and tried to ignore the look of disappointment in his friends' eyes. A lecture was brewing behind his disappointed stare, and he knew that Frankie had seen right through the façade. He was one of the only people in his life who knew him that well. But before the lecture came, Max was faced with a far worse confrontation as Evie cleared her throat from behind him.

***

She felt a cold rage coursing through her blood and hoped anyone she cared for was as far away from the explosion as possible. Max's little proclamation had dissuaded *any* thoughts she had held previously. Thoughts of his lust-filled eyes on her tits, his hands stroking up her body and his fucking lips almost brushing against her own. No, those thoughts were long gone as she watched Frankie's eyes go wide before, at a swift pace, he sashayed away.

To his credit, Max's gaze stayed locked on hers. His face was making a strange back and forth between his usual scowl and an attempted word. It was reminiscent of a fish out of water which oddly made her want to laugh through her anger.

A thousand strong words pressed on her brain in an attempt to be expressed. Words that would effectively formulate the utter betrayal she felt in her gut. How she could have ever let her guard down around Max was a complete mystery. She was kicking herself over the knowledge that she had felt sorry for him mere moments before, bringing her own weaknesses into stark focus.

Heat rushed to her face as her actions in the last hour came flooding back to her. Seeing Max nervous and vulnerable for the first time in her life must have caused an essential wire in her system to simply snap, and fizzle. She had rubbed herself against him like a cat in heat, whispered in his ear. Called him *Baby* in the sultriest voice she knew how to use, all to distract him out of his fear. The worst part of it all, is that she had felt accomplished when it had worked. Watching Max's features go from terrified to horny in a matter of seconds had filled her with smug, unashamed pride. Like she had the power to move someone as unmovable as Chef Easton. Well, she had certainly read that scene wrong. She hadn't distracted Max out of his panic; she had played into his hands. She had recklessly used whatever twisted heat she thought she felt between them, ultimately making her look unprofessional and foolish.

Ultimately, turning her into the vulnerable one.

But no, she thought as her embarrassment continued to push on her cheeks, the worst part was that *she* had liked it. The feel of Max's skin on hers, his hands trailing up her body and the pressure of his hard chest against her...

"I hope this helped," she said before he could get a word in. The statement sounded hollow, even to her. It didn't even begin to compare to the multiple expletives she would have preferred to spit at him, but Evelyn had realized something at that moment. Things with him had always been heated. So much so, that Evie barely recognized herself around him. She had decided years ago to ditch her people pleasing ways around him, and this is where it got her. Right where she ended up with everyone else. Used, walked all over then discarded like a well-utilized door mat.

He cocked his head in confusion as she went on. Settling herself into a familiar mask usually reserved for people like Dick Chin. "That is, I hope Harvey has to find a way to live with that Barbie hellscape on his mantle," she said with her best smile.

He blinked at her, a look of alarm flashing on his face.

"Evelyn," he began.

"Oh, no need to thank me," she cut in. Expertly steering the conversation away from confrontational and directly to light. "I reenact eighties movies to help win adult talent contests, all the time. It's actually becoming a bit tedious if I'm being honest."

She tried her smile again but Max didn't return it. Instead, his brows knit together giving off a look of annoyance that grated on her patience.

Just take the out Easton, she thought even as she fought the urge to tell him how she actually felt about his little outburst.

"Don't do that," he said quietly.

Her smile faltered a bit. "Do what?" she asked between her teeth.

"Don't," he waved a hand between them as he took a step closer. "Evade. I know you heard what I just said, don't pretend you're not mad to spare me Evelyn."

Lights flashed as another act began on stage, but all of Evie's focus was on the man in front of her. She took a step forward herself, ready to take his advice and release all of the hurt and anger she felt but stopped herself before the words could tumble out. The truth was, she wasn't doing it to spare Max, she was softening the situation solely for her own comfort. If he was going to use her like everyone else

did, then she was going to do what she did best and save
them both from an uncomfortable conversation.

She shoved everything back, went inward and radiated
calm. But she couldn't help a last-minute lifeline before
running for her life.

"I did hear something," she confirmed. "Frankie saying
something about the way you look at me..." she said
ruthlessly and knew the minute her stunt worked. Red crept
from his crisp collar up his neck and his whole body
stiffened. He had gone right back to the fish out of water look
he had at the beginning of the conversation and that's when
she made her escape.

The laugh she pushed out was false and completely
foreign to her own ears as she slung her bag across her body
and began turning towards the exit.

"Clearly, we were better at acting than we thought. Tell
Frankie I said thanks, and let Harvey know that he can thank
me for taking home the win," she threw at him as she all but
ran from the room.

He didn't follow her, which she thanked every star that
glistened on her jumpsuit for. Distance from the man was the
only thing she needed. A sigh of relief softened her shoulders
when she found the gallery empty and moved towards the
exit.

She needed tomorrow. She would finally have time to tell
Shannon and Ben all about her time with Max. They were
going to skin her alive when they found out she did this, but
she couldn't help that now. All she knew was that things had
changed. She had been closer to Maxwell than she had ever
come, seen a personal side of him that she was certain not
many others had seen. And yet, she felt her walls go up,
stronger and higher than before and knew, deep in her bones,
that her and her co-CDC had just crossed some kind of line.

Chapter Nine

He had no idea what he was doing.

Max glared at his miserable reflection as it bobbed up and down in the dark gym window. He was running, a form of cardio that he literally never chose for himself, at seven-thirty in the morning on one of his only days off.

His reason for being there was so painfully obvious, he almost ran back out the door two minutes after walking in.

Avoiding Evelyn had been a skill of his for the past six years. He had managed to meet her perfect face with cold indifference and a strength-of-will that could bend a spoon. After his mother passed, he put up so many walls around himself it was like a fucking paintball course. One that he was happy to hide in for the rest of his life.

Three weeks with Evie had it all crashing down around his ears.

He had most likely imagined her reaction to his touch, and yet the image of her red cheeks and parted lips refused to leave his mind. It was much better to focus on that look than it was to stress about her indifference.

He knew the minute she decided not to argue. Painfully watched as she shrouded herself in a mask usually reserved for everyone else. Having that mask pointed at him was new and unwelcome. It made him realize just how special it was to have Evelyn snapping and glaring at him rather than placating him. Made him realize how much more genuine that reaction had been. He needed to talk to her. Get her to glare, and yell, and call him Chef in that way that drove him crazy. Which was how he ended up sweating his balls off, watching the window's reflection like an absolute stalker.

Yeah, maybe it was time for him to go.

Fumbling with the controls on the treadmill, he muffled a curse as it began to incline rather than slow down. He slammed the bright red stop button before he could trip over his own feet and embarrass himself further.

"Not much of a runner, huh?"

A set of icy blue eyes greeted him when he glanced at the machine to his left.

"What gave me away?" he panted, smiling sheepishly.

"Oh nothing, you were an absolute gazelle." The girl hit her own red button before taking a chug of water.

"Honestly, I do enough running in my line of work. I usually stick to the water when I'm here." Which is exactly where he was headed now, he decided. A lap around the pool would help clear his mind of Evie…hopefully.

"Are you a doctor?" she asked, flipping her blonde ponytail over one shoulder.

He held back a sigh and faced the woman again. It was nothing personal, Max just despised small talk. Meeting new people, trying to relate to complete strangers—it made his palms sweat and his left eye twitch.

Still, he put on a nice face and answered. He may have anxiety about meeting new people, but he wasn't an asshole. "No, I'm a chef."

"Oh! So is my roommate!"

He would have winced at her peppiness at that hour if her words hadn't splashed over him like ice water.

96

"Oh yeah?" *Doesn't matter. Don't ask.* "It's not Evelyn, is it?" *Why are you asking? Go, run, save yourself.*

Her big eyes grew even bigger, giving him his answer before she opened her mouth. "Yes!" She clapped her hands together in pure joy. "How do you know Evie? She's here by the way," she went on before he could answer. "She's trying not to get her ass kicked in the aerobics room."

Max attempted to keep up as the complete stranger grabbed his hand and led him towards the back of the gym. They made their way past workout equipment that he had no idea how to use, past the weights and mirrors.

He fought back a laugh when he caught sight of a man with obscene biceps, grunting at his own reflection. The scene reminded him of Evie's easy teasing in their shared moments before he ruined everything. *Those* moments were only reserved for a less-guarded Max. One who was brave enough to let his walls down for a brief moment—a fleeting instant of allotted happiness.

God, he was a miserable sap. He dreamt of having genuine conversation with Evie throughout the day yet fought the urge to lower his walls in five-minute intervals. Where were his walls now, as he was being led to the only woman who could knock them down?

Whipping his eyes away from the mystery equipment and bland grey tile, he focused instead on two figures sparring in a dimly lit room.

He had no idea what he had been expecting. He just knew that Evelyn sending a roundhouse kick, chin high to a two-hundred-pound man, was not it.

Her hair was in its usual state, piled messy and high on her head. Gone was the boxy cut of her chef coat which had been replaced with a skin-tight outfit of emerald green spandex. Her hands were wrapped in tape and held in tight fists in front of her jaw.

Max sucked in a breath as she dodged punches from a man two sizes bigger than her, then another as he watched her bounce back and forth in a boxer shuffle, her curvy body doing absolutely everything to him.

"I'm Shannon, by the way." He vaguely registered the bright voice next to him, transfixed by Evelyn's every move.

"Max," he hissed as the giant man blocked an uppercut from Evie.

"Aha," she drawled, drawing a glance from him before he looked eagerly back to Evelyn. He was about to tell her that her "aha" sounded extremely loaded when the giant man kicked Evelyn's legs out from under her. She hit the mat flat on her back with a smack that echoed through the entire gym.

"Hey!" Hot, anger-filled recklessness hit Max so quickly, he barely had time to think before barreling into the room and to Evie's side in two steps. She sucked in a breath, her eyes widening at the sight of him. "Evie, are you alright?"

Rather than answer, she sucked in another wide-eyed breath and attempted to roll away from him. He grabbed her waist and lifted her to her feet, gently running his hands over her and ignoring his own rules about touching. Her breaths were coming in gasps now, the sound of it tearing at something deep in his gut, then twisting when he noticed the tears in her whisky eyes.

He took a quick moment to check for any other signs of injury before turning his fiery gaze towards her sparring partner.

The man was smiling at him, and he had never wanted to wipe a grin off someone's face more. "What the fuck was that?" he demanded, placing himself between them with his hand lightly resting on her hip.

"Max," she sucked in a breath, "It's fine."

"You knocked the wind out of her," he accused, outrage lacing his tone.

"Yes, she asked me to. Besides, if she had been more focused, Evie could have dodged it." His smug smile was starting to piss Max off.

He looked back at Evie who had managed to collect herself enough to let out a nervous laugh. She threw a stream of curses towards the large man before turning an awkward smile on Max.

"Michael's my trainer, he's just showing me…"

"How to get her ass kicked." Shannon supplied from behind her.

Their eyes met, his full of worried rage, hers full of embarrassed amusement.

He must have been losing his goddamn mind, but he couldn't help it. A slow grin spread across his face as he realized how utterly ridiculous he was. Laughter bubbled up and out, his anger turning to amusement in a strange shift. Embarrassment should have been the victor in this emotional warfare and yet, he felt something natural settle over him. As if his desire to protect the woman next to him was exactly what he should be feeling.

Evie started to laugh with him. "Oh good, I thought you were going to be worried about me. Laughing at my injuries is way more appropriate."

"All right, Evie?" the instructor asked her, amusement lighting his own face.

"It's okay," Shannon called from the doorway. "This is completely normal behavior for chefs before their coffee."

***

Evelyn was mortified and delighted as she left the aerobics room with Max by her side. Two conflicting emotions seemed to be her trending mental state when he was around.

She had quickly gotten over her initial shock of seeing him at all and went straight to horrified at seeing him in that very moment—sweaty and gasping for breath. Her turn to look like a fish out of water.

Her mortification was swiftly drowned by delight at his concern for her, at his anger at Michael for potentially— definitely—hurting her. At his hands floating across her body, reminding her of the previous night before it had all gone to shit.

She tried and failed not to think about that last bit when they met up with Shannon, her anger flaring against her will.

"So Max," Shannon trilled, "what are you doing today?" Evie's anger redirected itself in an instant.

They had a ritual. Every Tuesday, they went to the gym, swung by the store for provisions and a gallon of caffeine, then met up with Ben at Dolores Park.

It was their only day off together, and they made the most of it. All the week's stories, complaints, and confessions were thrown at each other in rapid succession. They went into Tuesdays in the park with an understanding that they would either end up in tears or be slightly hungover on Wednesday.

It was her church. Her holiest of days.

To be fair, she had been complaining about Max for almost a full month through texts and passing moments, but still—she had big plans for this particular park session.

"Well since my workout was such a success, I was planning on doing absolutely nothing for the rest of the day." Max threw a smile at Shannon that had Evie's guts twisting. He was different in this setting. A little more casual and a little less Hell's Kitchen. A knot of frustration formed in her shoulder when she realized his casualness was mostly directed at her roommate, however.

Ignoring it, she turned her scowl on Shannon. "Very important plans. We should get out of his hair."

"Or," Shannon chimed, ignoring Evie's face entirely. "You could come to the park with us. Eat, drink, tell us your secrets. Oh, and you can meet Ben!"

Max's face fell slightly before his stony exterior returned, facing her. "Ben? Is that your…" he cut off looking highly uncomfortable.

"Roommate." Evie clarified, unsure of why she was talking so loudly and clarifying with such force. "My other roommate," she finished dully.

"And second favorite," Shannon said with a wink in his direction.

Max's shoulders relaxed a bit, and he turned his easy smile on her, interrupting her mental list of the many ways she was going to murder Shannon. He raised a brow, his smile wavering as if the look on her face was convincing him not to come. Was he considering spending an afternoon with her? Willfully? After their almost argument last night, she was completely dumbfounded by the idea.

She had no idea what was happening, but she was certain he had multiple personalities. Max had hated her from day one, treated her with nothing but fiery sarcasm since then, and verbally confirmed that she was only around to help him with Harvey, like, eight hours ago. But maybe her plan had worked a little too well, and now Max was attempting to keep the peace as well. His dad was sick, and their constant drama might just be the perfect distraction. Their teasing, arguing, and occasional camaraderie was just chaotic enough to take his mind off Harvey. Always the empathetic one, Shannon must have zeroed in on it before she had.

Because I'm clearly a selfish asshole, she thought. Evie had been so focused on pretending to keep the peace with

Max, that she didn't register that maybe he needed the diversion.

"You should come. Tell us your secrets and all that," she said in an almost convincing tease.

"Aw yeah, the secrets of a man who lives alone, and works sixty hours a week."

"So, it's decided!" They both jumped when Shannon clapped, then spun on her heel towards the exit. "You and Evie are on drink detail; I'll grab some snacks and see you in the usual spot."

Silence hung between them as they watched her traitorous friend go. *What the hell just happened?*

"What the hell just happened?" Max asked out loud, mirroring her thoughts.

Evie's guilt crept in and smacked her in the back of the head; a warring emotion to the flat distaste she felt about spending more time than necessary with Maxwell. Still, how could she not have seen this before? He was hurting and vulnerable, which Evie had to save space for.

She had two seconds to decide what to do and went with her instincts. Looks like they were calling a truce for the day.

"Didn't you hear our orders, Chef? We're on 'drink detail,'" she teased as she began walking, pausing only to look back when he didn't follow. "Oh, do you need to shower or something?" she asked, a little less sure of herself.

Okay—she definitely shouldn't have put Max and showers together in her relentless brain.

He gave her a strange half-smile, his eyes shining with amusement. "So, we're going to the park," he stated, the meaning behind his words hitting without the details.

Were they about to spend an afternoon with each other? It wasn't like either of them had lost a bet this time. If he came with her to the park, he was voluntarily spending time in her presence.

"Well, first we have to fulfill our duties," she said as casually as possible as she strode to the exit, Max in tow.

Leaving the gym together felt like a much bigger deal than it looked, yet they fell into step next to one another at a comfortable pace. The streets were just starting to fill with activity while they headed for her usual grocery store. Cars whipped past, and joggers panted while skirting past them on the sidewalk.

She glanced at Max under her lashes, his silence giving her a minute to think. It wasn't a coincidence that he showed up for her *one hour* at the gym after their conversation. He had to have known he would run into her; she just failed to work out why. She had given the man an out—a lifeline. He could have just left it alone and gone right back to talking shit about her favorite socks.

Could it be that Max was a little lonely? She wasn't sure why that tugged at her heart so much, especially after meeting Frankie and having witnessed an entire party of people who knew and clearly cared for him. But the chance of Max not having friends like Shannon and Ben to lean on made her ache for him a little.

Okay, maybe she was starting to ache for him a lot.

This whole thing was ridiculous to her. She didn't love confrontation and wasn't loving the idea of revisiting their conversation from last night, but she hated her insecurity just as much. The right move was to be straightforward and simply ask him why he was stalking her.

"So, kickboxing huh?" Max asked, cutting off her inner pep-talk. Although she had been dreading the question, it caught her off guard. There was no easy way to explain her obsession with self-defense.

She looked down at her hands coming together to fidget with nervous energy. They were still slightly pink where she had peeled off the tape.

"Yeah well, I need quick reflexes for when you start throwing plates at the restaurant."

"Ha! Tell that to my coffee-stained Grayson," Max shot back.

"Oh, I bet you *do* talk to them, don't you? Whisper sweet nothings as you gently iron them every night." She bumped her shoulder against his, her teasing mood getting away from her a bit. The feel of their bodies connecting made her light and bubbly, and she really needed to remind herself that she disliked the man next to her.

"Only to complain about you," he said, his hand reaching up suddenly as if he was moving before his brain caught up to his arm.

He tugged on a strand of hair that had escaped her messy bun—and she flinched. The tenderness of the move was thoroughly crushed at her intake of breath and sudden jolt of fear.

Max yanked his hand back, eyes searching her face. "Wow," he whispered, "are you always that jumpy or are you genuinely scared of me?" His face registered a mixture of shock and mild hurt, as if he found the idea of her being afraid of him appalling.

"Not you," she said without thinking. Oh, how Evie wished Michael was around to kick her feet out from under her and whisk the air from her lungs at that very moment. Unsure of why she was telling him anything about herself, she changed the subject. "So, what brought you into the gym so early?"

There, that wasn't so hard.

Although now that she had blurted out the question Evelyn wasn't sure she wanted the answer.

A blush, one she was dangerously close to getting used to, came creeping up his neck again. "Oh no, don't change the subject. Is there someone you're scared of?" he pressed, concern creeping through his stony exterior.

104

"Nope," she said with a pop as irritation built. Harvey, Ben, Shannon—all of them jump to protect her the minute she stubs her damn toe. Evie didn't need to be protected; she could do that all on her own. Yes, she was afraid of someone, but that had been her own fault. Now she needed to face her fears in her own way.

More and more people began filling the sidewalk as they went. Café doors were propped open, the smell of coffee and fresh pastries wafting into the air. Car horns honked in the distance, but Evie's one-track mind was already focused on her next caffeine fix.

"Weren't you living with some guy?" Max asked suddenly.

She whipped her eyes to his, shocked. How had he known that?

"Uhm..."

"I remember him. You brought him to one of The Lennon's staff parties..." The memory made her flinch before her face turned tomato red. Oblivious to her mortification, Max sailed on, brows drawn as he tried to recall her ex. "I remember now, not Ben...Jake? Jim?"

Jimmy had been a nightmare at that party. He had gotten rip-roaring drunk, used her cardigan as a napkin, then proceeded to pick a fight with any man that talked to her. Evelyn had made a million excuses for his behavior before they left early to save her from her embarrassment.

Which of course, was flowing right back into her body.

"That's over."

Crystal clear relief coated his expression, but she wouldn't be reacting to that. If she did, she might just warm up to the man completely. Which was ridiculous of course. Anyone with a pinky-sized amount of sense could have told her that Jimmy was a bad choice.

"But not really," he guessed, pinning her immediately.

She shrugged. Evie didn't want to admit that she had put herself in a fragile situation and certainly didn't want to discuss it with Maxwell Easton.

Still, when he softly asked, "He was violent?" Her carefully curated indifference dissipated until her heart beat too loudly in her hollow chest.

Evie realized too late that they had eased to a stop in front of a busy playground. Kids hopped around and yelped in a heated game of tag as they talked about a past she would rather forget. She should just ignore the question and walk on; Evie didn't want sympathy from him. From anyone. But the anger that burned through her veins at the memory of that party smothered her embarrassment and burst out of her like a volcano.

"Violent," she mumbled, turning the word over in her mouth. "Amongst other things. It was mostly the walls that took the brunt of the damage." Evelyn had two seconds of shock before accepting the fact that she was speaking out loud and barreling on. As if her words were finally active after lying dormant for months. "Jimmy liked to throw things, but luckily for me, his aim was terrible after a few drinks. Except for the insults. They hit the bullseye *every* time. I was uptight, boring, getting fat…" She trailed off, memories swarming her like a gang of murder hornets.

"He used to blame *me* for our lackluster sex life when in reality, he just couldn't stay awake with the amount of alcohol he had coursing through his veins."

It felt good…sort of freeing to tell someone about it. The wounds were fresh, and the kickboxing could only help her so much. But it felt powerful to say the words out loud and know that she didn't have to feel the way she had. Evie wasn't letting Jimmy's words get to her anymore. She wasn't uptight or boring.

She wouldn't look at Max's reaction, so maybe she was a bit of a coward.

106

Baby steps.

"I guess my final straw came when he was particularly mad one night. I had caught him stashing beers in the tank of the toilet when he was supposed to be attempting to quit." A sad laugh tumbled out at the memory. Evie's gaze darted from kid to kid, actively watching the game of tag and avoiding Max's gaze. "He had me pressed against a wall, yelling at me for being so rigid."

She felt Max stiffen beside her. Most likely shocked by her complete lack of judgement and naivety. What he didn't know was how disappointed she already felt in herself.

Evie squared her shoulders, but still avoided his eyes. She watched as the kids ran in circles, completely care-free and spirited.

"Anyway, he finally scared me enough to make me abandon ship. He punched the wall so close to my face, I had to pick paint and drywall out of my hair for hours. Ben and Shannon helped me move out while he was gone the next day, and that's that."

Evie couldn't stand the look of pity that was guaranteed to be painted on his face. Moving on from Jimmy might have left a few scars, but it had been an easy decision nonetheless. She didn't need anyone's pity.

Evelyn wasn't helpless.

She didn't flinch when his hand rose to her face. Instead, a warm comfort radiated from his fingers as he gently lifted her chin to look at him—his soft touch a complete contrast to the molten rage illuminating his eyes.

There was no pity in his expression.

Her breath caught in her throat at the fire in his features, barely suppressed anger bubbled under the surface, but she was absolutely not scared. A strong desire to take a step closer to him stung her temples and escalated quickly when he ran his thumb gently over her chin.

"I'm fine," she said mostly to herself.

"I know," he responded, his voice thick with emotion. "But Jimmy might not be if I ever run into him on the street." The smile he gave her didn't calm the heat in his eyes in the slightest.

"You'd have to line up behind Shannon and Ben. And Harvey for that matter," she said before reluctantly stepping back from his comfort.

He tugged on her hair again, this time earning a signature eye roll before they fell back into a lazy walk toward the store. His arm casually kept sweeping into hers as if they walked this close all the time and God, she really liked it. Maybe she didn't need to be saved, but the idea that Max cared about her enough to barge into the gym and casually threaten her abusive ex had her feeling…feels.

Affection for him spilled over and she had to admit, it felt lovely. Uncomfortably lovely. Like soft serve dripping over your waffle cone and making your fingers sticky.

Getting involved with Max wasn't realistic in any realm of possibility but still—she kind of leaned into this little tug of attraction to him instead of pushing at him like usual.

"So, why were you at the gym at such an ungodly hour, Chef?" she asked playfully.

"I think you know why, Evie," he said without looking at her, and her playfulness caught in her throat.

She could feel her heartbeat through her fingers, her mind racing as they made their way through the doors of her favorite corner store.

Did she know why? She had a guess, but it didn't make a lick of sense because Maxwell Easton HATED HER. There was no sensible reason for her to feel as if he liked her—like he wanted her. There was no reasonable explanation for the way she felt around him either. As if…

Nope. That wasn't going to happen.

"Were you plotting to get me on the weight bench? Give me a spot and then let the bar crush me to death?"

It was an out. She was giving him *another* out. Evelyn was running because a smart woman knew how to take the route of self-preservation.

Max cocked his head at her, his eyes narrowing. "I just wanted to try one of those espresso laced protein shakes you were telling me about," he murmured. His deep voice still held heat in it which did *not* lighten the mood.

As they walked down separate aisles, Evie reminded herself that he was just using her as a much-needed distraction before she started blushing, yet again. She needed to have a severe pep talk with her skin before it turned red permanently.

"Where's the champagne in this place?" Max asked, his head and shoulders the only things visible over a short rack filled with various hot sauces.

Get a grip, Evelyn.

She held up a twelve-pack of Tecate. "It's not that kind of party. You oversee the limes; I'm going to grab the mezcal."

***

So, it was *this* kind of party, Max thought as he sucked down a sip of smoky mezcal at eleven a.m. Shannon had arrived before them and set up what he personally thought of as an absurd number of various blankets. She had piled chips, cookies, movie theater-style candy, and an array of artisan chocolates in the middle of their camp.

They had started with coffee, then cracked into the booze as soon as a lanky kid jumped from his slackline to serenade the park with Sublime.

He was having fun. He realized it sometime between the potato chip breakfast and the first sip of beer. Shannon was a bright, bubble of enthusiasm, and it made him realize that he missed having a solid group of friends. People he could depend on and…well, tell his secrets to.

The proximity of Evie's body to his own was concerning but hell, he had been reckless all morning and to his surprise—Evie had been too.

He was stretched comfortably next to her, both of them listening as Shannon animatedly recounted every minute of her week. The current subject was someone she referred to as Shoulders, who slipped her his number with the cash he had used to pay for his coffee.

"Just call him," Evie demanded before taking a sip from her mezcal soda. He was close enough to smell the tangy citrus of the lime in her cup. "If not for the conversation, then for the shoulders."

Shannon wrinkled her nose. "He added soy milk to his pour-over."

They all groaned in complete understanding.

"Some people's children." Evelyn shook her head looking crushed.

A deep accusatory voice broke through their Shoulders conversation. "You started without me," he said.

"Yes, but I remembered that it was your week, and got mezcal," Evie told the man that walked up. His blue eyes brightened at the mention of the spirit. He looked to be a little shorter than Max, with a nice face and bright red hair tied in a bun at the nape of his neck.

"Who's the new guy?" he asked with a wicked grin.

"This is Evie's Max," Shannon threw out without any consideration for Max's insides.

Ben's eyebrows flew up in surprise before he plopped down next to Shannon and launched into his own week.

He forced himself to calm down, working on each muscle group one at a time.

Evie's Max.

How could a phrase like that be thrown around so casually?

It was a busy day in the park. The fog had burned off and he was starting to sweat a little under the glare of the afternoon sun. The group next to them was playing giant Jenga, their screams echoing through the park whenever the blocks came tumbling down. He snuck a glance at Evie who sat cross-legged next to him, clearly unaffected by the comment that was making his stomach dance. Swept up in his own stress, he jerked away with a start when her knee brushed the side of his thigh. A blush covered her cheeks as she muffled an apology and scooted a full foot away from him.

Jesus.

"Here you go," Shannon chimed, breaking him out of his self-deprecating thoughts. She held out a phone with a hot pink case covered in pineapples. "You have B."

"Huh?" he asked intelligently. Had he missed something?

Evie saved him with a bright smile that made him want to sit on his hands. If she kept smiling at him like that, he was at serious risk of going way beyond playful hair tugs.

"Pick a song," she said easily. "The artist has to start with a B. Pass it to me and I'll pick a C artist."

"D goes to me," Ben added, then covered Shannon's mouth when she tried to make a dick joke.

The small speaker next to them was playing some Anderson .Paak song as he silently ran through all of the ways that he could mess this up.

Max suffered from anxiety and generally hated being put on the spot. Things that had an influence greater than his own small bubble tended to send him into a state of barely suppressed panic. Which was the reason why something as simple as choosing a song to play had him sweating through his t-shirt.

You literally danced in a bright pink skirt in front of fifty plus people, he told himself. Sadly, logic helped as much as it did every time. It didn't.

He went with the first thing that popped into his head which of course, was The Beatles. Hopefully, that counted…

"Dear Prudence." Evie beamed at him, sending a chill of pleasure up his spine. "This is one of my favorite songs."

"Mine too." He beamed back and breathed a sigh of relief. Grabbing a box of Butterfingers, he popped one in his mouth before handing one to Evie.

"You play a lot of The Beatles at the restaurant too," Ben said as he tossed a Milk Dud in the air and tried to catch it in his mouth.

"Yeah, my dad is a big softy. Loves listening to anything that reminds him of Mom. She had been in love with the band from the time she was eight and fully understood the inspiration for her name." He chuckled a little. "I was uncomfortably close to being named Jude."

Blank stares met him in return.

"You should have played Maxwell's Silver Hammer," Evie whispered to him knowingly.

"Okay Evie, your turn to dish on the week," Ben said while slicing lime wedges for their beers on a fancy cutting board.

Evelyn squirmed a little, her knee brushing against him again. He didn't jolt away this time. In fact, he had no idea how they closed the gap between their bodies again, but he was a smart man and didn't argue with fate. Max watched her brows draw together and her full lips, *Christ those lips*, pop out in a pout.

His thumb itched to caress that pout.

Deciding that was one hundred percent not what she wanted, he filled one hand with his cup and shoved the other into a pocket.

"My week wasn't very eventful."

She wasn't very good at lying.

Max knew he shouldn't poke the bear, but he simply could not help himself. In fact, there were a lot of things that he shouldn't be doing that he was flat out ignoring at the moment. "Downplaying our win, Miss Pimm? I heard you sang a duet with a very impressive chef."

He had never seen an eye roll so large.

"It's impressive how his giant head stays balanced on his neck," she shot back. He caught Shannon and Ben's glance at one another, but his focus stayed solely on her. All so he could watch the moment she fully understood what he said.

Her eyes became big, rounded orbs in her face, shock taking over her features before she grinned fully, directly at him. This time he couldn't help it, he gripped his chest at the heart. God, she was insanely beautiful.

"We won?" she squeaked. Disbelief and awe lighting up her features. He just nodded, removing his hand from his chest and shoving it right back into his pocket so he didn't pull her in for a celebratory kiss. It would feel so natural. Instead, they grinned at each other like a couple of lunatics, and he truly couldn't believe he had managed to stay away from her for so long.

A voice cleared, and Evie nearly jumped out of her skin. "So Max," Shannon began for the second time that day. "If Evelyn is skipping her turn, tell us about yourself, and then you can explain this duet."

He tried to smooth his features and not spook at her question. This is a perfectly normal conversation. "What would you like to know?"

"How did you meet our Evie?"

"At a Christmas party," he stated honestly as Evie blurted out, *we work together*.

Oops.

Shannon pounced immediately. "Ooohhh I love a good Christmas party. Ugly sweater?"

Max fought back a snort as he remembered the day. "Not if you're Evelyn," he replied before his brain could catch up with his mouth. "I wasn't even wearing a tie, and she walked in wearing this dark red dress that made every person in the room sweat into their champagne." He cut himself off suddenly, mortified.

Was he drunk?

He had gotten way too comfortable, his guard lowered way too much. He was rambling on about a dress he saw her in six years ago like a complete psychopath.

Looking around at the group in silence Max took in their surprised expressions before glancing into his cup.

"What's in this thing?"

He could feel Evie's eyes on him when the other two burst out in joyful laughter. Reluctantly, he met her surprised expression and tried to calm his nerves. He needed to get a hold of himself.

"Well," he said hesitantly, unsure of what he was about to do. "It was a nice dress," he mumbled like a complete dumb ass.

"What the fuck Max?" she whispered back, eyes wide. "When I think about that night, I remember you telling me that the kitchen was going to quote 'chew me up and spit me into a nine-to-five.'" He winced at the memory and his careless defense techniques finally coming back to bite him in the ass cheek, then focused on his appalling behavior rather than how Evelyn moved her body closer to him. She stared straight into his eyes with intensity. "Do you know how much tension and loathing could have been avoided if you had just said *nice dress* instead?"

Max dragged a hand through his dark hair, thankful that the other two members of the group were in their own intense conversation.

This is where you run, bud. The thought burst into his brain and pressed on his temples like a migraine. He needed to turn his sarcasm on, say something offensive, and jet out of that park, taking out the Sublime singer as he fled.

But, he realized with a start; he didn't want to. And the yearning to give in to Evie was becoming more and more difficult to fight.

Ben's deep voice cut through his musing like a sword.

"Hey, there's Jimmy. Everyone act crazy so I look like the normal one." Ben bounced up, and Max snapped his gaze away from Evie's red-cheeked face.

Fire burned in his belly, the heat rising until it met his neck and began the slow climb to his face. The knowledge that Ben hated Evie's ex just as much as him didn't register. His anger snapped at the thought of the man being in the same space as him at that very moment.

He felt Evelyn's hand on his arm before he could stand up, cooling the instant bout of rage coursing through his body.

"Not that Jimmy," she affirmed desperately, her grip tightening around his arm.

Shannon's brows shot in the air at Evelyn's words and her lips parted in surprise as she assessed him. Max must have looked exactly how he felt—a hop-skip away from murder.

"Yeah, don't worry," Ben threw over his shoulder, completely oblivious to the tension behind him. "I already smudged him with Gwyneth's vagina."

Max faltered at that and shook his head as if that would help him understand in any way. *Gwyneth's...*

Deciding that he didn't need to know, Max ignored everyone including his own blazing emotions, and turned back to face the woman he had dreamed of for years. Maybe the alcohol had made him a little carefree, maybe his father's illness had given him strength and loosened his tongue. Or maybe he was just tired of smothering his attraction to Evelyn Pimm.

"It was a *really* nice dress," he said lamely. *And can you hold my beer? I need to walk into traffic now.*

Chapter Ten

She was an absolute coward, and you know what? That didn't bother her one bit. After their shared day at the park, going back to the restaurant with indifference towards Max was harder than ignoring the samples at Costco.

Aside from her dehydration, Wednesday went off without a hitch. By the time Max had made it in, looking a little rough around the edges, she had created a prep list the size of a CVS receipt.

Filling her day with busy work had been easy enough. Avoiding Max was proving to be a bit more difficult. Her body was doing incredibly funny things to her, reacting every time their eyes met and embarrassing her with waves of lust that she couldn't even begin to explain. Her best option—her ONLY option—was to keep the man at arm's length.

Things got a little harder for her when he began bringing her coffee again. What she didn't need, was to be confined to a small space with Maxwell Easton, breathing in his Christmas sweat while sipping her love juice.

Evie made herself so busy, her staff began every interaction with an exasperated *there you are!* And by the time Saturday rolled around, Shannon and Ben had resorted to cornering her in their living room.

"Tell us about your week dammit," Shannon had demanded, while Ben opted for a more direct approach.

"Did he look at you with those bedroom eyes again? You should wear the red dress to work tomorrow!" he had called after her as she covered her ears like a child and ran from the apartment.

Coward.

She couldn't help it. The realization of how much she was enjoying Max's company was alarming.

"Stockholm syndrome," she grumbled to herself at her desk. An unfinished recipe for the new dessert she was testing sat untouched in front of her.

Tomorrow was Monday and the next test Kitchen shared with Max. Losing the bet didn't change a thing as far as she was concerned. Max still threatened the integrity of The Lennon. She had to prove that not only could she get a staple dish onto the menu, but she could do it while maintaining the style and practices that made her restaurant so special. Because it was her restaurant, she had to bring the heat.

No more park hangs and thumb caresses.

Thumb caresses, thumb caresses.

"Ugh." Evelyn shoved away from her desk and began pacing. He was making her crazy with his stupid green eyes and soft touches. She was so turned on she couldn't focus on her job, and that was a problem. She had already turned to her vibrator more times than she cared to admit, but nothing stifled her lust for Max. Evelyn was officially pining over her sworn enemy.

"Masochist," she grumbled as a knock sounded at her office door. She would not call herself a coward again, every inanimate object in the room knew exactly why she had closed it in the first place.

Straightening her hair, she jumped back to her desk and tried to look calm before calling out a welcome.

Harvey peaked his head in the door cautiously with a baffled expression. "You must be hard at work in here if the door is closed."

Her sigh of relief was quickly cut off when Max trailed in behind him, three lattes balanced in his hands.

Red dress, thumb caresses, coffee, vibrator. Fuck fuck fuck.

"Mmm." She nodded smoothly.

"I just wanted to meet up with you two and talk about tomorrow's test kitchen," he said happily, taking the only other chair in the room. He looked good. Having had only one round of radiation, Harvey looked like a slightly tired version of his usual self. But she selfishly feared that it would show. That she would have to watch as her friend's health deteriorated. "You still working on that dessert?"

Evie's unfinished recipe shamelessly rested on her desk for all to see. "Yes, it's coming along nicely."

"Nice enough to be a staple recipe?" Max asked as he leaned over her shoulder to deliver her coffee. Evelyn moved the mug right over the page to block his view and glared up at him. The man wasn't helping her mental stability at all. He was still as self-important as ever, but something had shifted after their day at the park.

Evie was sure that she would mistake it for flirting if she allowed herself to be around him long enough.

"Well, the first iteration of it came damn close," Harvey contributed, oblivious to the tension between them. Or more likely chalking it off to their usual dislike of one another.

Max's grin wavered; brows furrowed as he looked up at his dad in surprise. "Really?"

"Shocking right? No caviar or gold leaf in sight," Evelyn said, pulling a heavy sigh from Harvey.

"Okay before you two start taking bites out of one another," *shove that thought away, immediately.* "Let's talk about what's coming into season..."

Harvey went on and on about seasonal fruits and veggies while Evelyn desperately tried to pay attention. Maxwell had terrible instincts and stood next to her over the desk, the muscles in his arm flexing as he leaned over a pad of paper. His hip kept bumping into the side of her chair, making her fingers itch to stop the movement. To touch him. The disloyalty of her body continued as her gaze mercilessly flicked over to thick biceps again and again as he took notes. Treachery strengthened, forcing her to suck in a deep breath when he sipped his coffee, the smell wafting into her nostrils to mix with his pine needle scent.

Harvey is talking to you.

"Evie?"

She tore her eyes away from Max's biceps and laser-focused her attention on Harvey.

"Hmmm?"

"I was asking if blackberries would be okay for your dessert? We just got a flat from the farm," he repeated.

"You're distracted this morning," Max added sounding positively smitten with the idea.

"Yes, yup. That will be perfect," Evelyn squeaked. She stood and ushered them to the door with a fervor that could only be described as desperate.

The power dynamics between her and Max were miserably one-sided. She needed him, and his god-like features to be out of her line of sight.

"You need me to bring you a couple more coffees before service starts? You seem a bit unfocused."

Gritting her teeth, she shoved him out of the door and patted Harvey on the back as he passed. The poor man looked back at her with an odd look, his warm eyes questioning.

If she had any kind of explanation for the way she was feeling, she would have given it to him. As it was, she had no fucking clue what was happening to her.

The minute they left, Evie flopped back in relief, her muscles finally relaxing. It was ridiculous, the way she felt around Max. He had this strange power over her that she couldn't manage to shake. Suddenly the pompous Michelin-obsessed man she had known, was likable and setting her insides on fire—after one month and a single bout of day drinking.

Her week had been filled with avoidance and, well—fear. She didn't want to like Max. For the longest time, he had been the only person she hadn't felt the overwhelming need to please. Like they were already enemies so why work harder than she needed to? It was a welcome relief after having to mold herself into the perfect female chef. Hard-working and stern, but likable and kind. There was no space for her to be one hundred percent herself in this industry.

She instantly felt guilty for having the thought because of course she was herself around Harvey. But this whole situation with his son had her diving into emotional places that she didn't want to go.

Evie sat up straight as an idea bloomed in her mind.

What if he knew exactly what he was doing to her? Her stomach dropped at the thought, and she picked up her sad test recipe. He was trying to stir her up so he could win. Distract and confuse her enough to let her guard down so he could fully take over the restaurant.

You'll see that the look I've been giving her is more from shock that she's still around after all these years.

She knew two things about Max at this point: he loved his dad, and he hated her. A day of exercise, and one afternoon filled with conversations that didn't include death threats hadn't changed that in the slightest.

Evie's fluttering disposition all week was beautifully convenient for him, wasn't it? All the while, he was probably ordering white truffles behind her back and changing the sock policy.

A pulsing ache pushed insistently at her chest as her breathing became labored. Ridiculous. She was getting upset by the betrayal of her longest foe. She truly was a full-blown enabler if she allowed *him* to pull one over on her. The man had played nice, squeezed information out of her, and now intended to use it to his advantage.

It was a really nice dress.

Well, she could certainly fight fire with fire.

Evelyn got to work on her recipe, with a new determination—writing out every step and flavor combination that she was going to attempt the following day.

With a bounce in her step, she launched into the walk-in and gathered her ingredients, setting them aside on a tray labeled *Evie, test kitchen*.

She received passing greetings from busy cooks as they worked, then surprised smiles when she actually stopped and talked to them about service. Their reactions just reinforced her theory that Max was trying to distract her—and was clearly doing the job well.

Tonight, she was going to balance the scales.

Smile in place, she bounded into lineup a little late to find that Max had started without her—which really burned her ass, but she would allow it. He needed a head start on the evening.

"Alright, the first turn of the night is as follows: Mark and Sue Gladstone will be at table one. Remember, Mark is left-handed everyone. When you place his silverware, make sure you do it correctly. Next, we have..."

He droned on in his professional voice, which was *not* sexy, and she had the satisfaction of hearing him falter

122

whenever their eyes met. Following the sixth table, he actively stopped looking in her direction. After a good week of avoiding eye contact as if she were working next to Medusa, her sudden interest in his face had the desired effect.

Confidence soared through her muscles after line-up, leading her straight to the kitchen to set up right next to her target.

"Maybe we should try working on the same side of the pass tonight," she said easily.

The pass was a table at the end of The Lennon's beautiful open kitchen. All of the plated courses were placed there to receive final inspection and garnishes from either her or Max before they went to the appropriate table.

He gave her an odd look, clearly thrown off by her sudden closeness. Recovering quickly, he muttered, "Okay, sure." And scooted over to make space for her.

They were painfully close. She may have been torturing herself more than him, but she committed.

The Ballroom Blitz came streaming out of the speakers, sending everyone into a quick frenzy as they picked up the pace. The song was their indicator that service was about to begin and if you weren't ready, well you better get ready.

Evelyn sang along to the tune, swinging her hips as she tied a grey apron tight at the waist.

"You seem…different," Max said, brows drawing together as he watched her.

"I'm just testing something out." She flashed her best smile, spirits rising when he blinked at her in surprise. She didn't elaborate, however, causing him to fidget a little before he started to turn back to his board.

"Wait, your collar is all messed up."

She placed her hands on Max's broad shoulders and angled him to face her. His small intake of breath sent her stomach fluttering, her knuckles grazed the side of his neck as she fussed with his perfectly crisp collar.

Even though she had to curse herself for the little flip in her own belly, she continued to hold his gaze with soft eyes. Well, tried to hold his gaze. His seemed to be dancing everywhere other than her face.

When she released him, his chest heaved out as he let out a breath, before muffling a thanks and flipping back to his board in two seconds.

Perfect.

Service flew by with Evie taking every opportunity she had to brush a knuckle over his skin or place her hand on his back when she walked past. A pesky little voice in her head told her she was being unprofessional, and she shoved it away like a plate of bad oysters.

Her resolve stumbled a bit when Max began leaning into her flirtation.

Goosebumps bloomed over her neck when he whispered in her ear between seatings. Although his mouth remained a good three inches away from her face, the feel of his breath on her sensitive skin had her feeling quite hot.

"What are you doing Miss Pimm?"

A server silently dropped off her usual mid-service espresso before turning on one heel and speeding off. Hopefully, he mistook their narrowed eyes and flushed cheeks for anger.

"I told you; I'm testing something out." *How to make Max blush in 100 different ways.*

After a long pause, he shrugged, and she tried not to feel disappointed. The recklessness in her wanted to banter with sexual undertones until Max looked like a tomato.

Okay, she needed to ease up a bit. Her own body was having too strong of a positive reaction to the man that she had dimly set well within her personal bubble.

As the second wave of guests were seated, Evie tried to reign in her dirty thoughts and focus on service.

That lasted all of ten minutes before Max decided it was a great idea to feed her.

Their eyes met over the tasting spoon he held up, his narrowing when she let him raise it to her lips, a small moan escaping in approval.

"That is a really nice dress…ing," she murmured. Then she slowly ran her tongue over her lips because she was fully out of control. Or, judging by the way Max's jaw set, and his muscles tightened as if holding himself back from her—maybe she had *all* the control.

"Hands," he murmured to no one. It was barely more than a whisper, and Evelyn was the only one close enough to hear. *Hands*. One simple word said with so much stifled heat it had her entire body breaking out in goosebumps. She felt warmth rising in her cheeks, his tortured eyes still pinned on her. "Hands," he repeated with more force.

Three eager servers walked up to the pass; hands held out to receive plates. He peeled his eyes away from her face and told them where to run the food before actively avoiding eye contact.

Well shit. She was aggressively turned on, and the idea that this little game could backfire came creeping up on her from a dark place. It wasn't her imagination—couldn't be, right? Maybe she was a fool after all because she was quite certain that the heat radiating off of the person next to her was real. Even more alarming was the fact that she felt searingly close to Max and all of this lust flying between them. As if they were meant to be inappropriately flirting at work.

The end of the night arrived in a confusing wave of disappointment.

Shameless woman.

Thoroughly enjoying yourself while batting your eyes at an impossible man, not to mention coworker, was not her usual pastime. How had she gotten to this point again? Oh right, she didn't trust him as far as she could throw him and spoiler alert, that wasn't very far. Balancing the scales and all that.

Her plan wasn't finished just yet.

Every Sunday, the staff would hang back and drink the opened bottles of wine that wouldn't remain sound over the weekend. It was a chance for everyone to cut loose after the stress of the week. If any of the staff had noticed the electricity between them during service, they didn't show it. Everyone forgot about the pressure of the kitchen for an hour, relaxing enough to just enjoy each other's company.

Music blasted out of a portable speaker as they filled various mugs and deli cups with wine they would normally never be able to afford. Evie indulged in a beautiful Alsatian Riesling and leaned back against her freshly scrubbed counter. She smiled over at Max who was stuck in a deep conversation about *that couple* at table five with Karla, their Sommelier.

The cooks launched animatedly into the challenges they had faced during service and how if they had still been at *that* restaurant the chef would have thrown a wine glass at their head. Chatter about the nights highs and lows circulated over the constant hum of refrigeration fans.

"Good night?" Evie softened instantly at the familiar voice. Cody was The Lennon's most senior employee, even longer than her. He was soft in every way: soft blond hair, soft peachy skin—soft around the middle. He always had a kind word or encouraged her through a bad day.

Gentle demeanor aside, Cody could have a dish-pit cleaned and shining, every single glass polished, with the same speed and determination of a NASCAR pit crew.

"It was good, yeah," she mumbled, distracted by her mission.

"You seemed a little…preoccupied," he said with a little nudge on her shoulder.

Evelyn's heart started racing. Cody, a man who spends almost the entirety of service in the confines of the dish-pit, had noticed her highly inappropriate behavior. If he was on to her…

When a server announced that they were taking the party to a bar around the corner, it gave Evelyn the out she needed.

Relief flooded her as Cody immediately turned away, no doubt planning to Irish goodbye and avoid the drunken mess of a kitchen crew going out on their Friday night. She turned her attention casually to Karla as she tried to convince Max to join them, then jumped into the conversation herself. "Come on Maxwell, it's our Friday night," she said with a little push on his arm.

He looked down at her hand where she touched him then hesitated. "I really should close up."

"You closed last week," she said quickly. "Besides, it'll take me five minutes to close up and I'll join all of you," she said, raising her voice a bit towards the end.

It had the desired effect. Everyone around her whooped, excited about her *finally* ditching her managerial duties and coming out with them. She had no intention of doing that, but they wouldn't care after a couple of drinks.

After everyone was ushered out the door, she bounced through the restaurant for her final inspection of the kitchen.

Hopefully, she had managed to make Max curious enough to be deliciously miserable when she didn't show up to the bar. Not only would he be ghosted, but there was a good chance he'd be hungover tomorrow for their cook-off. The idea had her practically skipping as she circled the dining room turning lights off as she went.

The Lennon was a beautiful restaurant. The tables were small and intimate and spaced far enough apart that you could be ticking off House of Dragons spoilers to the ignorance of the surrounding guests.

Small antique shelves were placed strategically around the room draped in dried flowers, books, and vintage Hobart scales. It looked like a cabin that your artsy aunt Rose spent two weeks out of the year in.

Although she usually preferred to linger a little in the dark, empty restaurant, time was of the essence. The last remaining lights still beamed down in the kitchen shrouding her in shadow as she made her way through the dining room.

Before she could make it through the tables, the kitchen door flew open, making her pause just outside of the pool of light. She squinted at the interruption, then froze as Max's bulky frame pushed into the restaurant, pulling the door shut behind him.

Shit.

"Forget something?" she asked casually from the dark.

His eyes followed her voice and pinned her with an achingly serious gaze, mouth turned up slightly at the corners.

Nothing, she told herself even as her body reacted, dancing bolts of electric sex zipping down her stomach and straight between her thighs.

"Yeah," he said simply before walking toward her in what seemed like three strides. Ever the coward, Evie took a tentative step back and was met with a very ill-placed pillar.

"What are you doing?" she whispered as he placed his hands flat against the wood on either side of her head.

"I'm testing something out," he murmured, using her own casual answer from earlier in a way that wasn't casual at all.

Evie sucked in a breath as Max's gaze lowered to her lips and, unable to help herself, she licked them in response, her hands held in fists by her sides. If there was a single coherent thought in her head, she was not capable of finding it.

"What were you testing tonight, Evelyn?" His voice was all gravel and smoke, and she felt her body respond against her will.

"I was…" What? Nothing mattered when he brought his lips closer, a whisper away from her own. She raised her hands to his chest, intending to push him away and allow herself to suck in some air. Instead, she was met with hard muscles that flexed at her touch and had her sucking in air *without* pushing him away, hands clenched into fists against his hard body.

He didn't touch her, didn't kiss her, didn't lift her onto table three and rub his hands all over her hot, hungry body. He didn't even do that thumb caress thing she couldn't stop thinking about. But the look on his face said that he wanted to.

And the feeling was painfully mutual.

She wasn't afraid. It was a dull thought compared to all of the whirling emotions that curled through her limbs, but one that stuck in her brain, nonetheless. He had stormed in here with an intensity that could slice through stone, yet the fear never came. No flinching or evading. She wasn't shying away from Max.

"Fuck it," she panted out before unclenching her fists and curling them into his silken hair. She caught a flicker of surprise wave over his features causing a brief feeling of uncertainty before, ditching her cowardice, she dragged his lips down to meet her own.

His surprise didn't last long. Max let out a groan, a deep ragged thing that made his chest rumble. Frantic in his movements, he immediately brought strong hands to her face, circling one around her neck and burying it into her hair.

Which was encouragement enough for her.

Evie shot her tongue out, sighing when he let her separate his lips and taste him. He tasted sweet and sharp at the same time. Like the Riesling she couldn't afford. She sucked it up like it was the last glass she'd ever have.

Max's hand left her cheek and got to work skimming down her side, caressing her curves and managing to make her crazy with desire.

A shiver sailed through her body before she bit down softly on his lower lip, smiling as another low groan escaped. Pulling her body against his was a feeling she could get used to. Hard muscles rippled against her, setting her blood on fire.

He muttered a curse in response, his breath coming out in gasps to match her own when he broke their kiss and rested his forehead against hers.

A protest was hot on her tongue just as he began to move again. As if mind-reading was a particularly special skill of his, he gripped her waist and lifted her off her feet, stealing the breath from her lungs. Her legs curled around his waist automatically as Max carefully circled her around, kicking a chair out of the way before setting her on table three after all.

She was losing whatever game they were playing, but she didn't care. All she knew was that she wanted Max and would suffer the consequences later.

Evelyn enjoyed sex. Loved the feeling of sinking into intimacy and exploring. The idea of it was thrilling, and she tried not to ruin the moment by focusing on how it had mostly been an idea for her rather than reality. Unfortunately, after the toxicity of her last relationship, she had dedicated all of herself to the restaurant and depended on her vibrator and broad imagination.

Her imagination, as it turned out, hadn't dredged up anything close to the actual feel of Max between her legs.

She pressed her feet into him, bringing his body into hers and nearly losing it when his erection pressed hard between her thighs. She moaned against his lips at the glorious pressure. It felt good to give in. It felt so good to be wanted.

"Fuck," he gasped out. She understood, the sexual energy between them was a force she hadn't been expecting, and now that she was experiencing it, she couldn't pull away.

Before she could get to work on the buttons of his shirt, he did what she couldn't. Max pulled away from her hands, his warmth leaving her as her legs unwrapped themselves, the low light from the kitchen glinting off the untamed desire in his eyes.

Chapter Eleven

He held her at arm's length, too afraid to reconnect their bodies but aggressively unwilling to let go. Panting, they stared at each other. Her whiskey eyes were heavy with lust, her lips swollen. She looked so fucking delicious he almost forgot his own name.

He wished he could forget why he stopped.

"Are you worried I'll ruin another chef coat?" Her voice was husky and dripping in sex, eliciting an immediate reaction from his dick.

"Christ." He closed his eyes hoping that would help. It didn't. He was certain that he would see Evelyn everywhere from this moment on. "I need a minute," he said before reluctantly removing his hands from her soft skin.

"Oh," she replied, her smile wavering.

"Hey," watching her face fall was like a knife to the gut. "Don't do that. I need a minute Evie, before I quite literally explode."

"Oh," she repeated, color returning rapidly to her cheeks.

His skin still tingled where she had touched, he still tasted her on his tongue, his mind was completely jumbled with thoughts of the woman in front of him. He had gone too far and had no intention of going back. Not in a million years had he expected that mind erasing reaction from her. Not after she had avoided him all week, no doubt remembering all that she had heard at the fundraiser. A reminder that they were supposed to hate each other.

But then tonight rolled around and he didn't stand a fucking chance. Every atom he possessed told him to get close to her, push the boundaries. After all the ups and downs of the past month, Evie had decided to test something out, and he didn't care if he lost, won, broke even or crash landed. He wanted her, and all he wanted to do was ignore the feeling in his gut that told him to go slow, but his brain relentlessly reminded him to be gentle. Even after she had opened up about her ex, he still stormed in and practically dry-humped her against the wall. It was a small miracle she hadn't punched him in the face.

Still panting, they stared at one another for way too long. Max knew that he should say something, literally anything to try and keep her from running, but he couldn't seem to be able to form the words.

Watching Evie's features light with desire had been a beautiful torture, and maybe he liked to be tortured. He was actively running out of reasons not to reconnect their mouths so yeah; he definitely liked it.

A small click sounded, breaking the silence and freezing Max to the spot. The kitchen door swept open, and he realized that there were much worse forms of torture. He snapped his gaze over to the unwelcome interruption to find Karla, squinting at the empty kitchen from the doorway.

"Chef?" she called, unable to see them just outside of the kitchen's light.

Max looked back to Evie in a panic. He needed to hide his arousal before he embarrassed them all. Barely having any time to register the change in her face, his stomach sank at the mask Evie slid on without issue. Longing for the fire in her eyes and the pout that had filled her lips seconds before gripped him immediately.

Evie expertly shifted herself in front of Max and stepped into the dim light of the kitchen.

"Yes Karla?" She sounded calm and collected and not at all how he felt.

"Oh, I was just coming to grab you…two," she added the last word reluctantly. Her disappointment at finding Evie instead of Max was written all over her face, making him fidget in discomfort. "Phil just bought a round for everyone."

"Excellent. Max and I got into an intense conversation about closing procedures, but we're about to lock up and head over." She stepped into the kitchen as she spoke, and though he couldn't see her, he knew the light would be shining onto her bright, forced smile.

Max managed to take one step then thought better of it. His head was still reeling from his kiss with Evie, and she was doing a much better job of handling the situation than he would be. He really wasn't sure why that gave him an empty feeling in his stomach.

Karla flashed a matching false smile and reluctantly left them in silence.

He could feel the change in the air. The magic of the moment had completely drained, leaving him feeling unsure and admittedly, a little worried. *That's just your anxiety messing with you. You shouldn't be worried about losing someone that was never yours.*

Unfortunately, that inner pep talk made his chest ache. Quite the opposite of helpful.

Evelyn slowly turned around and Max's stomach twisted into a million little knots at her expression. He fought back the need to close the sudden space between them with impressive determination.

"You better get back to the bar." Her voice was so painfully distant, Max's walls began shifting around him for better protection.

"I'm not leaving like that." He took a tentative step toward her and stopped abruptly when she quickly moved back. "We should talk about what just happened."

"What just happened is, I let you seduce me into thinking this was anything more than a twisted attempt to distract me. Karla nearly catching us in the act would have been a laugh for you, but you certainly know that as a woman, I would not get off that easy."

Max felt a flush creep up his neck. Did she honestly think so little of him? That he would use her like that? The thought left him idiotically speechless as she continued in a nervous prattle.

"I can't believe I let this happen. You know that I've been *so* distracted with thoughts of you all week? I am letting you interfere with my work—but of course, you know that. Me being preoccupied with thumb caresses is extremely convenient for your takeover, isn't it?"

"Evie," he cut in, barely managing to shake his head clear. What did she mean by 'thumb caresses?' His delight at hearing that she had been thinking about him all week was embarrassing and ill-timed at best. It was also being smothered by the sheer panic that her words were eliciting. Memories of the week, of him teasing her for being distracted, flooded his mind. "This is not some elaborate plan to sabotage you. That's not what I was doing."

Arms crossed tightly across her chest; she let out a nervous laugh.

"Then how do you explain this, Max? Showing up at the gym, that fucking story about how we met. Talk me through us going from mortal enemies to…" she unfolded her arms only to wave them back and forth between them. "Whatever that just was."

He couldn't. If he cracked now, he would have to admit that after five minutes of conversation, she had consumed his thoughts for far longer than these past two weeks. That he not only remembers the first time they met, but every interaction—every fucking glance in his direction—every laugh, glare, and eye roll that he received from her merciless face.

He would have to tell her that years of indifference had been for the sole purpose of saving himself from falling flat on his ass in love with her.

She interrupted his thoughts, bringing him out of his rambling panic and back to the reality of what he had done with a jolt.

"I shouldn't have kissed you." Her voice had softened, but the words still stung. "You don't have to explain anything, I…I let this go too far. Pushed it too far." She groaned and pulled a hand through her hair, mirroring his frustration.

"That's not what I was doing Evie," he reiterated. He really needed her to understand that. She was closing herself off to him, he could see the familiar curve of her slumped shoulders as she basically curled into herself. Protection from him.

Evelyn eyed him carefully for what he was sure was seven-hundred years.

"It doesn't matter." A small smile lit her tortured face, flooding him with relief and warming his body. "I'm sorry for jumping you and almost defiling table three." Her smile was a bit more wicked this time, stirring Max's desire back to life in record time. But he knew by now what she was doing. Offering an out. Joking her way out of a difficult conversation.

"I'm not," he said. Could she hear how much he meant it?

"I don't know what this is, but I have a bad feeling that things were a hell of a lot easier when we hated each other."

Max couldn't stand watching her face fall. Chocolate hair framed the soft, round skin of her face, making her look sharp as her smile faded to a sad frown.

"I never hated you," he said before he could think better of it. As it was, he would say anything to put a smile back on her face.

A genuine laugh burst out of her, and she shook her head. Her dark hair swung around her face with the motion. "You don't have to bullshit me, Chef. I'm not delicate, and one kiss doesn't change the fact that you and I have a rivalry hot enough to boil water."

Max tried another step forward. The need to hold her, comfort her, convince her that he's not the asshole that she thought he was forced its way through his blood stream. He stopped short as she moved away from him. A couple feet of distance that felt like a million miles.

"I'm sorry." He sounded a little panicked as he watched her circle the room for her things.

"No," she smiled a devious smile which threw him for a bit of a loop. "I'm sorry." Suppressing a laugh Evie pointed boldly at his crotch. "You shouldn't be seen in public with that, so it looks like you're locking up after all."

Muffling an oath, he watched in torture as she left without another glance. Her joke landing with a thud as she snagged her own tossed-out safety device and practically ran from his presence.

***

She was losing her grip on reality, sliding into a miserable abyss of bad decisions and pushy loins.

She had kissed Max.

The memory of it burned in her brain, branding her every waking moment with thoughts of him. She picked apart their time spent hate-flirting with one another, trying to piece together something that made their kiss…reasonable. There was nothing, of course. No explanation for why Max ditched his usual arrogance and replaced it with stolen glances and soft lips.

Lips, she reminded herself relentlessly, that she had kissed.

Oh, but he had kissed her back.

A wave of heat flooded her body even as her nipples hardened at the memory of that kiss. She glanced at her vibrator before checking the time. Too late.

Wishful thinking was that her pent-up sexual energy would amplify her creative mind.

Or maybe she would just melt into a horny little puddle the minute Max said *pass the spatula*.

The ding of her phone had her reluctantly peeling her eyes away from the bright blue toy. A small notification revealed a text from Maxwell 'devil horns' Easton.

Barely managing to suppress a shriek, she clicked on the notification, sucking in the words at a humiliating rate.

What if my plan of distraction backfired,
and we're both useless today?

Evelyn threw her phone away from her untrustworthy hand before typing back something ridiculous like, *I quit, meet me at table three in an hour.* Her breath shuddered out of her in a shaky laugh. He sent her something flirty, what was wrong with matching his pace?

How do you know I don't work better
when I'm sexually frustrated?

138

The shock of seeing a text from Max must have turned her brain to scrambled eggs. Which reminded her of breakfast, which was coffee. She needed coffee.

Racing to the kitchen to fulfill her task, her screen illuminated again, a small ding ringing out. She had never been more terrified of that sound.

Jokes on you. I never left the restaurant
for fear of an indecent exposure ticket.
I've been cooking all night.

> *I would be upset by your blatant cheating if I*
> *wasn't starting to worry. How long is too long?*
> *When should I call the paramedics?*

Oh, you think that's funny, do you? I 'm
not sure you remember that I already
won our bet. But if you still want to
compete, I'm okay with that.
You're going down today, Chef.

> *Hopefully not the only*
> *thing going down, eh?*

God she was out of control.

Evie grinned through her morning coffee, her shower, and her commute to the restaurant. Not wanting to attract probing questions from her roommates, she left early to avoid their curious eyes.

Truth was, she didn't have answers for herself let alone an explanation for them.

Evelyn was officially opening up to, making out, and shamelessly flirting with Maxwell 'devil horns' Easton.

The scariest part was how easy it was not to hate him.

Her grin widened a bit as she pulled up to the restaurant to see his tall figure leaning against the brick. He really knew how to commit to a story.

She waved goodbye to her driver before turning her grin on…

Oh no.

A small shiver of panic shot up Evie's spinal cord at the sight of the man casually standing before her, his blue eyes searching her face. He had a familiar scar that jutted through one chestnut eyebrow making him look constantly confused. She used to find it endearing.

His lopsided smile was timid and unsure, a look that she knew to be utterly practiced. She had seen those lips peeled back in anger enough times to know that he was anything but timid.

"What are you doing here Jimmy?" Pride swelled at the strength in her own voice.

"You haven't returned my calls," he said. His voice dripping with misery.

She didn't flinch when he spoke. Maybe it made her want to drop her bag and run away screaming, but she didn't flinch.

"I don't have anything to say to you."

"Come on Ev, you left." He moved closer to her, his steps precise. "You left me," he repeated, sounding utterly devastated.

She was not at all surprised by the feel of it, had been expecting it, actually. It started in her fingertips and actively pressed in on her until her heart swelled and her toes felt numb. Cold sympathy and guilt tried mercilessly to cut through her defenses.

It was the same feeling that drowned her anytime she denied a call from her dad after noon when she knew he would be a few beers in.

A deep sense of guilt and responsibility.

"I was sick. I told you I needed a little time to work things out."

"I left," she said firmly, ignoring her guilt. She tried to focus on the pep talks she would get from her friends. *Not your responsibility. Not your problem.* "And I think we both know that it was for the best. You have to leave Jimmy; I don't want to talk to you."

"Do you know what it's like, to come home to your apartment and find it empty?"

"Not empty, I left all of *your* shit behind," she threw back, her voice barely breaking on the last word.

He pounced as if he was waiting for it. "I came home to nothing, Ev. No note, no explanation."

"No explanation? You couldn't figure out why I left after our fight? Actually," Not wanting to hear anything more, she made her way past him and towards the safety of The Lennon. "I am not having this conversation with you, this is my place of employment, Jimmy. Go home."

Jimmy caught her firmly by the arm and spun her around to face his cold eyes.

I'm not afraid, she thought even as her legs began to shake in flagrant betrayal.

"Please take your hands off of me." Her voice had lowered to a whisper.

"You broke my heart, you know that?" He sounded tortured, but she picked out the familiar quiver of anger behind his words.

Something in her snapped, and it wasn't what she had expected. Hot anger drummed in her ears; heat climbed up her neck. Maybe she was finally learning to stand up for herself and confront her issues head on. Maybe what snapped was her will to please everyone, to fix everyone's problems but her own.

As the flames of her fury licked higher and warmed her bloodstream she thought, or maybe this is what it feels like to finally crack.

"I broke your heart, after you broke the wall right next to my face. Are you looking for sympathy, Jimmy? Or are you just here to get your punching bag back?" She pulled her arm away from his grasp with a snap before squaring her shoulders. "Either way, I hate to tell you you've wasted your time. I'm done with your abusive, toxic behavior."

She wasn't afraid God damn it.

His eyebrows rose in surprise, eyes burning with frustration. He clearly hadn't been expecting defiance from her, and with good reason. Their entire relationship had been reliable in that he could always depend on her to enable and protect him. But things had changed, hadn't they?

"You're going to hold something I did while I was wasted against me forever?" he spat, his voice losing its control.

Unwittingly, she braced for the impact of his next words. This was always the part where he told her to lighten up, stop taking her daddy issues out on him. It always seemed problematic to her that "daddy issues" were blamed on the women rather than the fathers that failed them. Unfortunately, that thought process wasn't going to help her against the verbal warfare that was about to commence.

But it didn't come. Instead, a clear strong voice echoed to her ears, breaking the early morning silence around them and hollowing out her stomach.

"I think you should step away from her."

If murderous rage had a tone, it was without a doubt Max's at that very moment.

Jimmy's head whipped around to glare at him, allowing Evie to take a step back and suck in a breath, which was hilarious because it caught in her throat the minute she laid eyes on Max.

He was closer than she originally thought, towering over them with his arms crossed at his chest. He wore a tight green shirt that made his eyes look insanely bright and the muscles in his arms aggressively rippled.

His face. That was what had her breathless. He looked about ready to meticulously—and with little-to-no remorse—murder her ex-boyfriend in the street.

"Relax bud," *Cringe.* "I'm having a conversation with my girlfriend." *Double cringe.*

"Doesn't seem like she wants to talk to you," Max replied with a smile. A smile that looked almost painful in its forced state.

Deciding that A, she didn't need him to fight her battles, and B, she didn't need *them* fighting at all, Evie planted herself in between them, facing Jimmy with more confidence than she felt.

"See? Max knows how to read a room," she said, her best attempt at being harsh. She needed Jimmy to get the message this time. "You need to leave."

He crossed his arms in childlike defiance and Evie had to hold herself back from kicking him in the shins and running into the restaurant.

She saw the moment he decided to argue. His lopsided smirk plumped one cheek, and his scarred eyebrow raised slightly. He turned the look on Max, then he opened his mouth, and her anger flashed like lightning. "I don't know what Evelyn's told you bud, but this is an overreaction and quite frankly, none of your business. If anything, I'm the one who should be mad. I was the one who was left high and dry."

Through her anger, she heard Max's step forward and barreled on before he could say anything to make Jimmy snap.

Lowering her voice she said, "You need help Jimmy. Help that I simply can't offer you." Moving a little closer, Evie locked her gaze with his, attempting to drive her point home. "I need you to leave me alone now." There was a finality to her voice that made her swell with pride. Avoiding Jimmy and the inevitable conflict between them wasn't going to last forever. It was unfortunate that the conversation was happening in front of Max, but she needed to close off this portion of her life.

And she had to admit that his presence was giving her strength.

Jimmy's eyes flashed up to Max again. He was losing control, she knew he was embarrassed to be having this argument with an audience and if she had to guess, had seen it going in a different direction.

"You have really hit rock bottom, haven't you?" he hissed. Evie blinked in surprise. Even after all this time she couldn't believe the person behind the mask. He really could turn ugly faster than she ever thought humanly possible. Squaring her shoulders again, she held up a hand when she heard Max take another step toward her and braced herself for the coming rant.

"You're sleeping with him," he stated with a curl of his lips. The statement shook her a bit. Of course, Jimmy knew who Max was, she had complained about him vehemently throughout their relationship. He was most likely trying to push her buttons not knowing that it was hitting pretty close to home.

He carried on, spitting venom with every word. "I knew you wanted a promotion Ev, but I never thought you'd stoop this low. I'm surprised you didn't go straight for Harvey! Have a lay with the old man and…gah!"

That was enough of that.

Evie looked down at her own fist in shock as Jimmy clutched his nose, blood streaming through his fingers.

Right cross, she thought, ever the student. Michael would be very proud of her form.

"I think you broke my nose!" he sputtered out, blood running into his mouth.

She barely registered Max's hands as they circled her waist and started pulling her back towards the restaurant.

"If I didn't, I'd be more than happy to give it a second try," she declared while simultaneously thinking about the pain blossoming in her hand.

Giving up on dragging her back, Max simply threw her over his shoulder and carried her, *carried her*, into the quiet of The Lennon. The hum of the refrigerators provided the only sound as he closed and locked the door behind them, cutting off Jimmy's curses.

"Ha! I told Ben those kickboxing classes would come in handy," she whooped as he silently lugged her up the stairs and towards the test kitchen. She bobbed over his back, her emotions running in all different directions like spooked ants.

"He tried to tell me that technique was useless with my puny arms," she laughed a little hysterically as her body began to shake. "But I proved that theory wrong."

Max gently shifted her back over his shoulder and set her down on an empty counter in the clean, quiet kitchen. He held her now-shaking shoulders still, searching her face in worry. His dark hair was tousled and falling over his concern-creased forehead.

The sounds of traffic drifted in through the open window to mingle with her shallow gasps as she began to cry.

"Faces are hard," she managed before burying her head in her hands, the emotion of the morning hitting her like…well like her own right cross.

Max gently separated her hands to cup her face, his big palms warming her tear-soaked cheeks. He attempted to thumb away the moisture then gave up, bringing her close and allowing her to burrow into his warm chest.

Jimmy had always known exactly what to say to Evie to make her feel like a complete asshole. He would always find some way to tie in her inability to let go of the past which made her feel childish and weak. And he had certainly never admitted to being sick before, clearly saving it for a particularly hard conversation when her guilty conscience was too relaxed.

Remorse was exactly what he had been looking for and Evie truly hated that she was giving it to him.

Max ran a hand over her loose hair, murmuring words of support and essentially turning her to a puddle. When her breaths began to even, she gave him a little squeeze before pulling away.

She needed a tissue, a coffee, and Tylenol. In that order.

His eyes were so tender with concern she almost started crying again. Instead, she flashed him a watery smile that didn't quite hit. "Good morning."

He smiled back at her, and her arm hairs tingled. Crystalline anger still coated his emerald eyes. "Could have been better for one of us. I, on the other hand, thoroughly enjoyed watching you break that asshole's nose."

She wrinkled her own nose at that, her cheeks felt tight from dried tears. "Aw well, I used to start all of my mornings like that, but I'm trying to quit."

"Uh huh, let's see that hand Mayweather." He snagged it before she could protest, receiving a wince in response.

"Faces are *hard*," she repeated. He turned her hand over, inspecting her for signs of discomfort.

He had nice hands. They were soft and strong, dwarfing hers as he rolled it over in careful inspection. She remembered those hands desperately caressing her body

146

mere hours before. Those fingers running down her sides and gripping her thighs.

The memory did nothing for her nerves, making her eager for more of the soft comfort he was providing her with.

She moved closer until her thighs pressed against his, testing out the feel of it. The feel of him.

"We should ice your hand," he murmured before stiffening. His focus captured by the gentle pressure of her legs around him.

She had to have looked completely insane. Through the puffy eyes and swollen lips, she was sure that he could read the arousal in her expression clear as day. His own flashed hot and fast before he set her hand down and took a step back causing her stomach to drop in disappointment. Why in God's name would he move his body away from her?

Maybe, she reminded herself, *because you just punched your ex-boyfriend before sobbing into his shirt.*

But what would have happened if she hadn't run into Jimmy this morning? She had a million different scenarios that came to mind, none of which involved clothes because she was thoroughly aching for the man in front of her. The events of the morning were only adding to the problem as her adrenaline began to smolder and Max's easy comfort rested over her like a blanket.

Crazy. Truly not great timing.

She was actively thinking of something nonchalant to say before he cut off her thoughts with one very simple sentence.

"I have a first aid kit at my place." There was one in the cabinet beneath her very ass but only a fool would insert that information. "And coffee."

She lit up at that, thrilled that he knew exactly what she needed.

Chapter Twelve

He knew what he was doing, right? Max unlocked the door to his apartment, allowing Evelyn in before shutting the door on the world and leaving them alone in his living room.

Nope, definitely not.

He loved his apartment. Windows and brick, just like the restaurant. The size didn't bother him, just one bedroom, a living space and a tiny kitchen off to the side. More than enough space for someone who spent more time at work than he ever did at home.

Hell, even his home looked like a mini version of work.

A bookshelf ran from ceiling to floor with cookbooks and food journals. His couch, which was the best purchase he could have ever made, was a cream-colored deep-set cushion of down feathers that he had a habit of falling asleep on after a long service.

Everything had its place in the tiny apartment, and now, he realized with a start, so did Evie.

She couldn't hide her curiosity if she tried. Her caramel eyes searched his personal space, soaking it all in before returning to him. Skin glistened where the tears had dried on her cheeks, their usual rosiness returning and relentlessly reminding him of her lust-flushed face. He took a moment to stare at her like a creep, admiration flooding his body as he took in her usual white shirt and black pants. Ridiculously bright green socks visible beneath the cuffs. He soaked it in like a sponge.

"I like this apartment."

I like you *in my apartment.*

And he was getting a grip and definitely not saying that out loud. "Let's ice that hand a bit before we wrap it."

She rolled her eyes before rubbing the back of her hand. "You think that's what I need right now?"

Her question sent his brain shuffling through a million different scenarios that all involved his hands on her.

"Coffee?" he tried instead.

"Always."

He brushed past her to the kitchen, ignoring the zip of electricity that shot up his arm when it touched her. He needed to have a serious talk with himself about not touching her if it was going to do painful things to his body.

Which was impossible since, like a complete moron, he brought her into his tiny apartment. But how could he not? Seeing her face when he pulled up to the restaurant, looking tortured and sad. He had already been willing to do anything for her even before she had burst into tears. Tears that had ripped through his core and nearly shattered his control into pieces.

And now she was here. In his personal space while his emotional control was hanging by a thread.

She had followed him into the kitchen with her perfect fucking face and her stupid taunting curves, making him momentarily forget why he had walked in there to begin with.

"Thank you, by the way." Her voice was a little shy. "I don't know how things would have gone if you hadn't shown up. And I really didn't want to work right away so this is a nice distraction." Her cheeks flushed at that, and it was a miracle his didn't as well.

Not trusting himself one bit, he focused on the coffee that was on the verge of popping open and spilling out on his clean floors. She was vulnerable, he just needed to be a good friend right now, not throw her over his couch and do everything in his power to keep that flush on her cheeks.

Christ—just stop thinking all together.

"Well, I thought that kicking your ex's ass would have been something I could lord over you for the rest of your life, but you literally beat me to the punch. Don't roll your eyes at me," he chuckled.

"Stop being cheesy then," she laughed, the sound of it finally ringing true after her confrontation with Jimmy. It reminded him of the wind chimes his mom used to hang outside of the house.

"There is something that is bothering me though." Which he should keep to himself because it's not his business, but as he continued setting up the coffee, his mouth just wouldn't stay shut. "When I walked up this morning, you almost looked sad. Like you felt bad for that prick." Hot anger rose in his belly at the thought.

It was none of his business, but he had to know. Truth was, between the anger and obvious frustration, she had looked completely crushed. He didn't know a lot about her, but he knew that he never wanted to see that look on her face again.

"Aw well, what you saw was most likely raw, unadulterated guilt, creeping in on me when my defenses are low." She gave him a small smile before continuing. "I've dealt with people like Jimmy before. Growing up, I was always the fixer in the family, the peacekeeper. When my dad would go on his drinking benders, I was right there to crack a joke and make my mom laugh or swoop my sister into a spontaneous trip to the mall." She drew her brows together in thought. "All while simultaneously telling my dad that he was happy-go-lucky and fun. I needed everyone to feel like I was on their side, even when I was ultimately enabling toxic behavior."

Her story wound its way straight to his chest, and he unconsciously rubbed the heel of his hand down his center to relieve the tension. The desire to reach out and smooth away her haunted look and bring back the spark of joy he had seen only moments ago took over.

"So, you enabled him. Your dad, and then Jimmy?" He didn't bother telling himself it wasn't his business. The hard realization that he wanted to make everything about her his business tightened his chest even more.

Her eyes widened at his understanding. "That's exactly it. I found myself conforming to him in order to prove that his behavior could be controlled. I started to tell myself that going out every night and drinking was completely normal if I could also do it without issue. I'm a fixer. And in my mind, proving that he didn't have a problem with alcohol was what I needed to do to *fix* Jimmy."

"But not everyone can be fixed, Evie."

She nodded. "Not everyone, no."

He realized he was staring at her and shook his head as if to clear it of the sad thoughts.

"I'm sorry, this really isn't making you feel better, is it?" Max asked even though he knew the answer. She was trying to forget about the past and here he was, making her relive the entire nightmare.

Thankfully, she smiled at him. A full, bright smile that had him blinking rapidly. A sad attempt at gaining a mental picture to fall asleep to that night.

"Surprisingly, just being around you is making me feel better…" She trailed off and Max stifled a laugh at the look of honest embarrassment on her face.

He couldn't stifle the grin, however, that spread across his cheeks at her words. He thought it was best to leave it at that.

Remembering the task at hand, Max moved to grab mugs from the cabinet, making Evie jump to move out of his way. Problem with that was, she didn't actually know where he was headed and ended up turning right into his chest.

The contact between them immediately had Max sucking in a breath and rapidly trying to control his hands.

She muffled an apology but didn't move. Her hands landed flat against his chest most likely feeling the rapid beat of his heart.

Max barely registered how her pulse fluttered as he held her wrists, steadying her—steadying himself. He was way too busy trying to avoid eye contact and lose it over the closeness of this fucking woman.

"You think we're fixed now?" Her voice was dripping honey, her cinnamon eyes pulling in his gaze and unraveling him way too easily. "A week ago, I would have rather put soy milk in my pour-over than tell you anything about myself." She smiled, and it took everything he had not to buckle at the knees.

"We didn't need to be fixed," he managed, voice thick as he tried to control himself. He could feel the blood pumping through his veins, could feel his body shake in anticipation. "Maybe we just needed to understand each other better."

Testing the waters, he ran a hand up her arm. A small shiver shook her body as goosebumps popped up on soft skin. He liked that. The way his touch affected her almost as much as it tortured him.

"This is completely insane; you know that right?" she laughed out in a huff.

"I have no idea what you're referring to," he lied, allowing his hands to rest on her hips and driving himself crazy. The move did nothing to stave off his desire.

She cocked her head to the side, an action that shouldn't have made his cheeks hot, and his muscles tense. A look that should never have made his stomach tighten and harden him between the thighs.

It really shouldn't have.

Whatever she was considering, he saw the moment the decision was made. She was practically vibrating with nervous energy, her stare trailing down the length of him before returning to his face with heavy hooded eyes.

"I'm talking about the fact that six years of unfiltered hatred has seemingly come undone in the past two months." Evelyn slid her hand up to his shoulder before pressing her hips into his and quite simply, killing him. "I'm talking about those *fucking* thumb caresses before the park. I'm talking, Maxwell," he was dying. Her voice was thick caramel that he desperately wanted to lick from her lips. "About how I can't think about table three without wondering when my longtime nemesis is going to finish the job he started and make me come."

Dead.

His breath caught in his throat at her words, his mind went blank, dick hard. Even if he wanted to, he would never be able to walk away now.

The coffee maker beeped, and he slammed it to warm, his eyes unable to move from her eyes, lips, literally anything Evie.

She smiled knowingly before leaning in, her lips a breath away from his.

He couldn't let her take the reins again. Not when he was ten embarrassingly short seconds away from losing control. Skimming past her lips, he brushed a kiss against smooth jaw, slowly making his way down to the curve of her neck. Her small gasp pleased him more than it should have.

"You smell like cinnamon," he murmured against the curve of her neck, feeling the goosebumps pop up on her skin. "I have obsessed over this spot," he brushed a thumb over her collarbone, sending a shiver through her body. "For years. And now that I'm here you smell like fucking cinnamon."

He should shut his traitorous mouth before it completely gave him away. But closing his mouth would mean shutting out the taste of her, and he couldn't let that happen.

He flicked his tongue over the sensitive skin just below her ear. A moan escaped her lips, bringing his laser-focused attention back to her face. Her eyes were unfocused and heavy when he dropped in to kiss her lips, softly spreading them open with his tongue and sucking in as much of her as he could take.

Her hands moved under his shirt, and he groaned in approval before doing exactly what he said he wasn't going to do and easing her back to the living room towards the couch.

The laugh that she pressed against his lips sent a jolt of lust directly below the belt.

Max caught her hands as they ran over his broad chest, every muscle flexed and tensed in anticipation of her touch. Her skin on his felt like an electric shock that very nearly killed him.

He would gladly die from that touch.

Eager for more, he lowered with her to the couch, pulling her leg over his lap as they went. Hands found their way up her shirt over soft belly to cup her breasts, twin moans of pleasure escaping their connected lips.

"Jesus, you feel so good. You..." you're perfect. He couldn't spit it out. Basic communication skills were apparently ejected from his body.

"Me? How dare you have muscles like this?" she demanded before swinging the rest of herself over and straddling his hips, moving before he could stop her and tugging his shirt up and off.

He muffled a curse as he fought down his desire, her dark hair like curtains around their faces, cutting them off from fuck all. None of it mattered.

Evelyn pulled back and drank in the sight of his bare chest with such unfiltered lust, his brain could barely process it. This was not the scowling narrow eyed glare he was used to, and when she bit her lip—yeah, he knew what image was going to keep him up at night.

Their lips came together, desperate now as he cupped her breasts, rubbing soft circles over the thin fabric of her bra until she moaned. He kissed and sucked the line of her jaw, his tongue hungry for her.

There was no way he was watching from within his own body, convinced that as Evelyn lifted her shirt over her head, revealing full breasts and the barely-there cotton beneath his hands, he watched the entire thing from outside of himself. Out of body experiences were not a common side effect of heavy petting but it should not have been shocking in the least that this woman could pull the impossible from the experience.

Max shifted Evie in his lap, involuntarily rubbing himself against her in his hunger, a rugged groan crawling from his mouth as he brought it to her breasts. Wasting no time, he reached around, unclasping his only barrier and freeing her round tits with a bounce.

"Let me just…" he trailed off, hands grasping her at the shoulder blades as he pulled her close and closed his lips over a nipple. Evie released a shuddering breath, a soft whimper that he would be hearing in his dreams for the rest of his life escaping her swollen lips.

She didn't separate herself from him, as if their bodies couldn't be close enough. Her head didn't fall back in pleasure as he flicked her sensitive peak with his tongue, instead opting to grip his hair with both hands, her lips resting against his forehead.

When he gently took her between his teeth and bit down lightly, Evelyn began to move. Rocking her hips slowly along his aching cock and sending waves of sensation through his entire body.

Pulling back, he reached for her waistband and paused as the button unclasped in record time. A little voice congratulated him knowing damn well he would never be this smooth ever again. He held her hooded gaze in question before asking, "Is this okay?" The break as he waited for her consent lasted nine years, but he wouldn't show his impatience by asking the myriad of questions circling his head. Not when they were sure to sound like he was shamelessly begging for it. *Can I take care of you? Please, let me hear that little whimper again. Do you want this?*

Do you really want me?

Evelyn's smile was slow and deadly. His erection twitched painfully against his jeans at the sight of that wicked grin before thanking every spirit, God, deity and divine being in existence when she reached for his zipper—struggling a bit before flinging his jeans open and allowing his length to spring out.

"Oh, for fuck's sake," she murmured, shamelessly staring down at him. "Of course. The eyes and hair weren't enough for you, huh? You just *had* to have disgustingly perfect abs and a big…" Caramel eyes widened as she caught herself. Flushed cheeks going a shade darker.

"Please, go on," he said just as her gaze found his satisfied smirk. Confirmation of her attraction was more than inflating his self-esteem, it was practically bursting from his chest. He ran both hands over the soft lines of her stomach before brushing his thumbs against her stiffened nipples, reveling in the gasp it elicited. "I know you love to feed my ego." She rolled her eyes, but Max did not miss her shiver as his thumbs continued their lazy caress. He leaned closer to her, lips barely brushing hers. "Is that a yes, Evie?"

The phone rang.

Nope, that wasn't happening.

She broke away from him, a triumphant look on her face.

"You gonna get that?" She had no right to sound that sexy.

"Burn it, I'll get a new one." Her laugh was cut off by her own phone's ring.

"Who needs phones anyway?" she asked bringing her lips to his neck and, fuck, licking up his pulse point. She nipped at his ear and his hips jerked. How could this goddess be appreciating anything other than her own power? The feel of her breath against the shell of his ear was nearly sending him over an embarrassing edge. Then she whispered words he hadn't even had the capacity to dream. "Yes. Please, Max."

Please? Max moaned against her shoulder before giving it a soft scrape of his teeth.

As if in answer, his phone pinged with a notification. Then another. When she pulled back again, he had never felt more dislike for an inanimate object, as he did for that unrelenting phone.

Ping ping ping. All from her phone before the wretched thing started to ring again.

They stared at each other, neither one wanting to move.

He had a sudden feeling of dread as his phone chimed again. "My dad," he said suddenly, hearing the tightness in his own voice.

Evie launched up with a gasp and stumbled towards her purse, mirroring his own desperate launch for the ringing phone.

He had a missed call and voicemail from his dad and the HR manager at the restaurant. Opening his texts, he sighed with relief at the decidedly unimportant message from Harvey. He had sent him a review of The Lennon of all things.

A nervous laugh escaped as the pressure released from his body.

He was alright. He was alright.

Max leaned against the wall and shut his eyes tight, way too close to breaking than he cared to admit. The complete mind-bending rollercoaster he had been on with Evie had distracted him from his fear, but it was not able to block him from it completely.

"Oh shit."

He opened his eyes to find Evelyn staring at her phone in complete horror. He wasn't even able to enjoy the sight of her, topless and tousled in his living room. Well, he *almost* wasn't able to. "He's alright," he said out loud, causing her expression to soften when she found him again.

"Yes, but we need to get to the restaurant. The Lennon just got reviewed by the Chronicle…they uhm." He had never seen her more uncomfortable. "They ate last night."

Realization dawned slowly, and painfully as he pulled up the article on his phone. The headline alone made him wince in discomfort. *Two Starry Eyed Chefs Come Together at The Lennon.*

"I'll grab the travel mugs," he said immediately.

"Yeah, I hope you made a strong batch," she called over her shoulder as she turned to retrieve her shirt from the floor.

Chapter Thirteen

It is an extremely visceral feeling when your body realizes you have royally fucked up. You feel light and tingly, a direct contrast to the sudden heaviness on your chest. Once you get past the panic of wondering if that was just how you are now; like you would never *not* feel like a failure, you launch yourself into an internal safe room.

She didn't say a word in the car as Max sped through the city. Why was he speeding? She wanted to tell him to stop, her preference would have been to linger in her little fantasy-world bubble before it was aggressively popped back to reality.

She had read the first two paragraphs of the article before shoving her phone in her bag and clasping it shut, convinced that the snap of the clasp would lock it away from her forever. Missed calls from Harvey, Shannon and Ben blinked at her in red with messages to go along with them.

The text notification from Shannon had given her a glimpse of what they all said.

Shannon Perry

Did you see the article? 😍 *Did you sleep with…*

Did you sleep with Max? No, but not for lack of trying. The dirty words she had said to him tapped on her forehead, relentlessly reminding her how out of control she was. Evie's body still ached for his touch even as she felt herself pulling away.

This was bad from so many different angles. From what she had read of the article, it wasn't necessarily unfavorable…it was just deeply inconvenient. Evelyn had been avoiding her own roommates for fear of having to explain to them what was happening with Max, and now some foggy version of it was plastered all over page seven.

What was happening with Max? She had no fucking clue. But apparently The Chronicle did. All she knew was that some reckless part of her desperately wanted to explore her attraction to Max and forget the rest.

Sneaking a glance in his direction, she tried not to fidget with worry. She couldn't help but wonder if the same fears that plagued her were also flooding his mind, but she knew the answer to that. He was *just* taking over a restaurant from his sick father. Evie had been a fool in not taking that more seriously.

I have been obsessing over this spot for years, her mind recalled his words while her heart rejected all of it. He didn't like her. They were recklessly using each other to forget about their fucked-up lives for a minute. It had gotten out of hand, that was it.

Oh, but she really didn't want it to end.

I'll explore that later, she thought as they pulled up to the restaurant. Now, she needed to face the music.

The silence still hanging between them, they got out of the car and began their walk of shame before Evie stumbled and slowed to a stop.

Max raised a brow, his sweet face questioning.

160

"We probably shouldn't walk in together." She said. The deep hurt that flickered before he controlled his features made her long to suck her words back into her mouth.

"Right," he said softly before turning on his heel and walking away from her.

She sighed, counted to twenty, squared her shoulders like she was about to punch someone for the second time that day, and walked in behind him.

"*…to say that the food has a quality to it now that wasn't quite there before.*" Harvey paused his reading of the article when she walked in. "Ah, Evelyn. Join us as we share in a little entertainment." His voice wasn't strained or unhappy which was a great start.

The fact that Max looked like a marble statue of muscle leaned against their dreaded pillar was decidedly *not* a great start. Harvey, save her, was seated at table three because the universe apparently had a relentless sense of humor.

She relaxed a little after realizing they were alone and inclined her head for him to continue.

"*I couldn't help but wonder if the new addition of chef Maxwell Easton, formerly of Coldwell SF and notorious Michelin guru, was the reason behind the increased passion in the ten-course meal. It wasn't until seeing him interact with Evelyn Pimm, long time sous chef turned co-CDC alongside Mr. Easton, that things became clear.*" Harvey glanced at Max before continuing.

"*The sparks flying between the two chefs were a wonder to behold. From my vantage point, I could practically see the tension between them being expertly tweezed and sprinkled onto every single dish like finishing salt.*

"*Aside from the usual heavy hitters like their house made cappelletti with beef cheek and dandelion, or the ever-decadent sea urchin crostini; a standout dish for me was the fall quail set. A colorful dish of honey glazed quail, with seasonal mushrooms and a creamy chestnut sauce.*"

Harvey was relentless. Pausing only to stab her with a knowing look or send Max an apologetic smile. His sing-song voice helped the matter zero percent, as it turned out.

"The dish was made all the better when paired with the long looks exchanged between the two chefs as the kitchen bustled around them. Their apparent passion for each other, manages to amplify the food while stomping out the stuffiness usually felt in most two-star establishments..."

Harvey read on. The reviewer briefly mentioned the wine program and fantastic pairing he experienced before circling back around to how the music complimented the chef's obvious flirtation like a movie soundtrack. He ended the article with an annoyingly delivered line of "all the restaurant industry needs is love", before handing them full praise and a lifetime of humiliation.

Harvey turned the paper around to show them a dark photograph of Max spoon-feeding her, their eyes glued on each other as the staff moved around them.

She had to admit, they looked absolutely obsessed with each other.

Silence dripped down the dining room walls and made her itchy with anxiety.

The irony of the situation was not lost on her. She had thrown herself at Max—her choice. She knew it was unprofessional and went for it anyway because clearly, she was losing all sensible thought.

She needed to make this right before losing the respect of her staff or worse, the respect of Harvey.

"It's a nice review," Max cut across her thoughts. She looked at him, wide-eyed. That review was a lot of things, she wouldn't have described it as *nice*.

"It *is* a nice review," Harvey agreed. "I'm having a hard time understanding it though." He looked at both of them, a smile in his eyes. "I was worried about putting you two together I admit, but this isn't exactly what I was worried about."

"It's nothing," she blurted out before Max could ruin her reputation further. "This is all a mistake Harvey, that reviewer was clearly just caught up in the magic of dining here." She felt Max stiffen beside her but went ahead and opened her mouth anyway. "We're strictly coworkers, there is absolutely nothing to worry about."

Her mouth went dry the minute she finished. She refused to look at Max but as it turned out, looking at Harvey wasn't great either. His eyes flicked to his son before the laugh left his face, replaced by a forced indifference that made her chest ache.

"I'm just glad you two haven't killed each other yet," he stated, before rising from his seat. "Are you finishing that dessert today?" he asked Evie, all business in an instant.

"Yes, Chef. I'm heading up right now."

"Great. Max, a package arrived for you this morning. I placed it with the rest of your ingredients for the day. Let me know when you put your tasters up." He sent his son another quick glance before turning to leave.

"Yes, Chef," they replied in unison, her voice slightly shaky, his brimming with anger.

Still unable to look at him, she stood with the intention of fleeing table three and never looking at it again. She needed to immerse herself in a recipe and try to forget that a stranger had read her longing for Max like a book.

"We're strictly coworkers?" His voice was quiet, so why did it make her jump out of her skin?

Suppressing her desire to run up the stairs, she paused at the bottom step, still stubbornly avoiding eye contact.

"What was I supposed to say Max? Did you want me to tell Harvey that I was lusting after his son in the middle of dinner service? To say that I've already crossed a line is an understatement."

Don't run, she reminded herself as she took the stairs one quick step at a time. His steps echoed behind her, catching up too easily.

"So, what? We're going to just pretend like nothing happened?"

"Yes, Maxwell." They burst into the kitchen where she finally turned to face him. She needed to end this before it got out of hand. *Too late,* the look of hurt on his face was a sucker punch to the gut. "This was a mistake." Like a slap to the face.

"I really don't think you mean that," he said, low and unsure.

"I do." She most certainly did not. "This thing between us isn't real. We need to get our priorities straight before it takes us down. And The Lennon with it."

His face went blank, his usual mask of indifference replaced the emotion filled expression in an instant. He raised his brows and leaned back on his heels in a move that said, *that was quite the outburst* before holding up his hands in mock surrender.

"Yes, Chef." His voice was all wounded pride and regret and she absolutely hated herself for it. "We should get to work then."

They worked in silence for a painfully long hour before another chef de partie walked in to work on their own dish. The young chef stumbled two steps into the kitchen, took in their quiet murderous vibes and immediately pivoted to the back of the kitchen to set up.

Evie got to work on the sauce for her dessert, heating honey over the stove and bringing her closer to Max than she cared to be. His pine tree scent mixed with the acidic smell of the honey as it caramelized.

Focus Evelyn.

Max was pissed. What she didn't know was why that was making her so sad. Him slipping back into his usual smug self was exactly what she needed. Evie had meant what she said about things being easier when they hated each other.

But she didn't hate him anymore. In fact, she had been terribly close to sleeping with him and undoubtedly enjoying every second of it.

Evie's desire to flee the kitchen was stifled by years of training and pure determination. She couldn't run from everything. But when she thought about Max's endless gaze and quiet focus, something bloomed in her chest and made her itch to run for her life.

After Jimmy, she vowed she wouldn't smother her feelings anymore. The knowledge of who she was and where her values rested was what saved her in those final months. So, she took a moment to explore them as she melted down blonde chocolate disks and added it to a food processor.

She liked Max. Liked him enough to tell him things only her closest friends knew. Why was that, when the man hadn't opened up to her at all?

I have obsessed over this spot for years. Maybe he's opening up in his own way.

Evelyn punched the start button on the food processor and slowly began pouring honeyed milk into the spinning chocolate. The sudden whirring of the machine attracted an evergreen glare that she pointedly avoided before he quickly looked back to his own work.

Two seconds of those eyes on her and her lower back tingled, her stomach danced. Her lips formed into a pout thinking about Max's anger, even as her body reacted to him simply glancing in her direction.

That was enough emotional exploration for her, and she determined that liking Maxwell was seriously foolish. Her desire to run away was still living in the basement and apparently not moving out any time soon.

Taking herself through a million pep talks, Evie managed to pull together a dessert in time for tasters with Harvey.

She tried and failed not to question Max on his own dish before Harvey arrived. It looked simple, but elegant. A pile of caviar sat on top of some sort of crisp with a dollop of snowy white sauce on the bottom. "Is that cream?" she asked, sucking in a breath when he turned his piercing eyes on her.

"Kefir," he responded. "I made it the other night, infused it with spring onions."

"Mmm," she responded intelligently. How was she supposed to work with him when he was unraveling her with a single look?

Good Lord, she couldn't shut it off for a second could she?

A loud clap brought her out of their staring contest and Harvey beamed at them, completely oblivious to her feelings of regret.

"Let's eat," he said happily, grabbing a fork and spoon on his way over. He started with Max, shaking his head at the caviar. "I'm surprised Evie let you use an ingredient this pretentious." He laughed before taking a bite and closing his eyes.

"This is Kaluga caviar, over a puffed wild rice cracker, and onion infused kefir," he explained, his business voice coming back in full force.

"Delicious. The cracker is particularly good, the caviar obviously speaks for itself. I'm thinking of pairing champagne. Something a little funky…" he trailed off in thought as Evie stole her own bite from the plate.

Shit. It was amazing, of course. How could you argue with salty caviar and tangy cream? The crispness of the cracker tied it all together to be the perfect bite, making her angry while simultaneously filling her with satisfaction.

"What do you think?" He had been watching her and she knew it was written all over her face.

She shrugged, pulling a small smile from his lips.

166

"Okay Evie, your turn." Clearly enjoying himself, Harvey dove into her dish with enthusiasm.

"You've got a burnt honey, white chocolate cream with a pumpkin seed brittle, fresh blackberries, and bee pollen." And it was pretty fucking fantastic.

She watched with sheer delight as Harvey closed his eyes and over-acted his part. He grunted his approval before taking another big bite and patting her on the back.

Max scooped himself a small taste, his brows drawn together in concentration.

"So?" she asked, realizing just how nervous she was. Seems his opinion mattered to her these days.

"Could use some cinnamon," he said roughly, before turning to clean his station.

She blinked in surprise at his back before blushing a violent red. *Now that I'm here, you smell like fucking cinnamon.*

"Okay you two," Harvey's voice cut through her fantasy. Her memory, she reminded herself. "I'm going to be in-and-out over the next week. Let's make a plan to put both of those dishes on the menu before the weekend rolls around. Also," his tone took on a seriousness as he leaned in. "I received an invitation today to the World's Fifty Best awards in LA."

Evie swallowed the scream that had threatened to escape her throat, her bright eyes snapping up to meet Harvey's. "Fifty?" she confirmed, her voice an octave higher.

The World's Best list vigorously rated restaurants around the world, compiling them onto a list of 100. They had been resting at 56 for so long, she thought they would stay there forever. Receiving an invitation to the top 50 indicated that they had moved up on the list and had her bursting with nervous happy energy.

"Fifty," he confirmed, his own excitement threatening to bubble over. "As I see it, you two are the face of the restaurant now, so I'll be sending you to receive the award."

Happy energy fell with a dull thud to the pit of her stomach.

"Wait, what? Harvey, you have to go."

Harvey cleared his throat uncomfortably. "Trust me, I would love to see us finally move up on that list, but the awards ceremony is next month and I," he paused, a small inner debate passing over his kind face. "I'm starting some treatments."

Evelyn felt a shroud of dread cover her shoulders. Her mouth filled with a million words of comfort, but her voice just would not come out. He had worked so hard—had gone through so much to get to this place.

It was wrong. Unfair.

"It's alright Dad," Max's voice came out stronger than she thought possible. "We'll represent the restaurant."

A tight fist squeezed her heart at the sad smiles exchanged between the two men. Her stupid face must have given away every emotion. Harvey gave her a small squeeze of comfort before, she was certain, getting the hell away from her tormented eyes.

When she turned to send her words of comfort to Max instead, he was already moving. Cleaning his station with a little more vigor, most likely eager to escape her company as well.

She took an indulgent look at his features while he cleaned and realized that he wore his staccato movements and unrelenting mask of indifference like a suit of armor. She had never thought of it like that before, but now she knew. She had seen him use it against her, after all.

Chapter Fourteen

Being in the water made him think of the Bible. He wasn't a religious man by any means and admittedly, hadn't read a single line from the book. He just knew that anytime he needed to cleanse his mind and clear his thinking he went straight to the water for a swim. A baptism of sorts. Wash away all of his sins and what-not.

Unfortunately for Max, his sins seemed to be resistant to chlorine. His head rose above the water allowing him to suck in a breath before dunking back under, continuing his arm strokes in determination. He loved the feel of the water as it moved around him, enclosing him in a hug of quiet musing. The ability to block out the world and be alone with his thoughts was usually a massive comfort for him—that was before Evelyn.

Now whenever he got into the water, he was consumed by images of cocoa powder hair and caramel eyes. He would painfully recount every interaction shared with her since his previous swim, breaking down every word like a lunatic. His infatuation with her was starting to irritate the shit out of him.

Tumbling through the water, he kicked off the pool wall and launched himself into another lap, determined to think about literally anything else.

Impossible.

Giving up halfway through the lane, he paddled lightly over to the pool's edge and lifted himself out of the holy water, accepting the gospel truth that his baptism didn't take.

It was Monday, a fact that he drilled into his head about a million times before heading into the gym, assuring himself that he wasn't going to bump into a sweaty Evelyn in spandex. He had been looking forward to this particular day off after stiffly working next to her all week, leaning into his usual arrogance.

The spark of annoyance and anger in her eyes used to give him a sense of accomplishment—as if he was winning the game of not falling for her. It's a funny thing, how a feeling can flip from accomplishment to failure in the blink of an eye.

Stop thinking about her, he reminded himself, which inevitably made him think about her again.

His brain begged him to meet up with his dad faster so he could focus his attention on him, and the Bloody Marys they planned to drink.

He stopped abruptly, almost slipping on the wet concrete when his name echoed through the empty pool room.

"Is that the gazelle himself?" He smothered the urge to jump back in the water and drown himself.

"Shannon," he smiled? He wasn't sure what his face was doing actually. "Out for a swim?" *Nice one.*

She beamed back at him, her blue eyes dancing with delighted amusement at his obvious discomfort. "I'm heading to the hot tub," she clarified.

Relief washed over him as he took that to be the end of it.

"I won't keep you then, enjoy…"

"I read the article." The words practically soared out of her mouth. "Such a great write up. You and Evie looked absolutely adorable in that photo." Her innocent look didn't match the tone of her voice in the slightest.

He should have shrugged, moved past her and headed out to meet his dad without a word. Instead, he laughed and tried to be as casual as possible. "Is she here?" And failed.

Her grin widened even as she shook her head. He ignored the sinking feeling in his stomach, telling himself that it was best if he didn't run into Evie in a swimsuit. Ah hell, now he was thinking of her in a swimsuit.

Yup, a quick exit was essential at that moment.

"Getting her in here is next to impossible. It's infuriating that she insists on paying for a membership just to get her ass kicked once a week."

He bristled against his will. Why did he care if Shannon doubted Evie's skills at self-defense? He didn't.

"I think that Jimmy's nose would disagree."

He shouldn't, rather.

The smile froze on Shannon's face. "What do you mean?" Her voice turned ice cold in an instant.

"Uhm, her ex?" he clarified like a complete idiot.

"Yes, I understand that." Her usual bubbliness had dissipated in a matter of seconds. "She saw him?"

She didn't tell you? He wanted to ask; the words were on the tip of his tongue. Not his business. Not. His. Problem.

"She punched him square in his stupid face. I had to clean his blood off of the sidewalk myself." The thought had his mouth splitting into a wide grin, the feeling of it foreign after spending the week in a permanent scowl.

Satisfaction flashed across her face but the smile she returned was not at all convincing.

"I'm sure she'll tell you all about it tomorrow at the park…" He trailed off. His familiarity with her schedule was making his chest hurt.

Shannon nodded and mercifully said her goodbyes before turning on her heel and striding right back into the locker room.

Max fled the gym so fast; it was a miracle he put all his clothes on correctly.

Harvey was already at their favorite seat, in their favorite restaurant, on their favorite day. Bloody Mary Monday.

Seeing him in that familiar place immediately lifted Max's spirits, allowing his brain to forget about the strange encounter with Shannon, and focus on his only mission for the day: not thinking about Evelyn.

"You started without me," he accused, taking a comfortable seat.

"You were almost late, what was I supposed to do?" The corners of Harvey's brown eyes crinkled as he muffled a smile.

Seconds after settling, his own ruby-red drink was placed in front of him, a pile of pickled veggies and celery floating on top of crushed ice.

"What's the vibe today, fellas?" Their usual server inquired.

"Keep 'em coming," Max stated without hesitation. He didn't make a habit of drinking too much as it cranked his anxiety into fifth gear, but…well, Evelyn.

Harvey arched an eyebrow in question. "Tough week?"

"Tough, stubborn, significantly more of a pain in my ass than I ever imagined possible," Max grumbled before taking a long sip of his beverage.

"I don't understand you two. You have so much in common, why don't you get along? Is this because of the towels?"

"Jesus, you too?"

"Then what is it?" Harvey chuckled before looking at Max expectantly.

He could tell his dad anything, he knew that. But he was definitely not ready for the truth about his relationship with Evie. Especially when Max had no clue what that relationship actually was.

"She's just so…" he squinted his eyes in thought. "Frustrating." That was not even close to a big enough word to describe her.

Harvey's stare made him want to chug his drink. Setting aside his own glass, he hit Max with a serious look. "You know, your mother and I hated each other when we first met."

"This is not the same," he mumbled, growing more and more uncomfortable. Was he being read that easily?

Harvey shrugged. "Maybe not, I'm just saying, not all difficult relationships—or friendships," he amended at Max's intake of breath. "Should be given up on."

Max glared at his father over the celery stick in his glass. He saw too much.

"Should I even bring up that article?"

"Can we talk about something else?" His tone must have sounded desperate enough to elicit the look of sympathy that pegged him.

"How are the new dishes being received?" Harvey tried.

Max let out a shaky breath, glad for the change of subject. "The guests have been loving them. The addition of the caviar on the menu will only elevate their experience. A couple more tweaks to the wine list and a few service changes and we'll be well on our way."

Harvey leaned back in his chair; brows drawn. "Well on our way to what?"

"Dad, I know you're happy with two stars, but…"

"I'm going to stop you right there Max. Thanks," he added to the server as she dropped another round. "The

Lennon doesn't need three stars. We've talked about this a million times. I don't want the restaurant to turn into some stuffy silent space, where the staff is overworked, and half-crazy by the end of the week."

"It doesn't have to be that way. I promise, we can keep everything mostly the same. Certain things just need to be elevated a bit, maybe buy all new stemware—"

"Max," Harvey held his hand up, softening his voice slightly. "We don't need to do this. You know that, right? Your mom loved The Lennon when it had *no* stars, getting the third one back doesn't prove anything."

He closed his eyes, trying not to think about the year the restaurant lost a star, trying not to think about the depression that hit him. Tried not to think about his mom.

"There's more to it than that."

A quiet settled between them, both thinking about the future and one of them in particular thinking how he couldn't lose the other.

"I liked the restaurant before it had stars too," Harvey replied softly.

It would take more than the Bloody Mary to wash down the lump in his throat. He opened his eyes to face his dad. His kind, humble rock of a dad.

He didn't look sick. That thought struck him every day. His gray streaked hair was full and healthy, a glow still on his cheeks. He refused to imagine a world, however small the chance, in which he couldn't look across this table at him over an overpriced drink and shoot the shit.

He couldn't handle it.

Not wanting to stress him out, he changed the subject gracefully.

"So, tell me what I should expect in LA." Well, as gracefully as he could manage.

Harvey eyed him for a full thirty seconds before deciding to play along. He launched animatedly into the itinerary for him and Evelyn, allowing Max to sit back in relief.

He needed to put his energy into work. As it was, the combination of a sick father and an inappropriate obsession with a coworker was doing nothing for his nerves. That third star was his for the taking, and he was going to get it for the Lennon. And if he was honest with himself, for his own pride.

"Oh, and remind me to talk to you about table three on Wednesday."

Max's eyes shot up in shock. "What? What about it?"

Harvey looked at him with an odd expression. "It's a little wobbly."

Max raked a hand through his hair and downed the remaining contents of his glass.

So is my self-respect.

***

The San Francisco fog is incredibly mesmerizing. It has the ability to appear out of nowhere, or slowly creep in on you. It has a mind of its own like that. Sometimes the fog burns off out of nowhere, causing you to shed some clothes and take in some sweet, sweet vitamin D. And sometimes the apocalypse ensues, and you don't see the sun for 65 days.

They had been post-apocalyptic for about a week, and Evie loved every minute of it.

She sat in her living room wrapped in an aggressive number of blankets with her head hanging out of the open window.

The air was cool and crisp, leaving tiny bubbles of moisture on her cheeks and closed eyelids.

She knew if she opened them, she would barely see the blurry lights of her neighborhood through the thick fog as it rolled casually through the city streets, licking up as much surface area as possible.

A forgotten book rested next to her on the window seat. A romance novel that she was reading in lieu of seeing a therapist. It had been her preferred method of coping longer than she could remember. Whenever life got hard, she would zip away to a fantasy world full of adoration and happy endings to escape reality. She was a libra—hiding in a daydream was her bread and butter.

This particular daydream however, had morphed into something incredibly inconvenient. She kept playing the week over in her head. Her cold words to Max, the emptiness in the pit of her stomach. The disappointed looks from guests when they realized their relationship was less "I Want to Hold Your Hand" and more "Fool on The Hill".

If the past week had been rough, she was not looking forward to being confined to a tin can sharing oxygen with the man. She would bet her rent money that he looked perfect while traveling, while she struggled not to vomit every time the plane was moving.

Which was always, in case that wasn't clear.

Ben's door burst open suddenly scaring Evie into a full launch out of her blankets and into a fighting stance. If the suddenness in which he opened the door wasn't enough, it was way too early for him to be awake.

He was holding a bottle of vodka, which was…huh?

Ben was bundled in a sweatshirt and joggers, his red hair hanging around his cheeks rather than its usual bun.

And—she looked again—he was holding a bottle of vodka.

176

Before she could ask, the front door burst open, causing her to scream before turning her fists to Shannon.

She had three grocery bags weighing down her left arm, her keys in her right hand. Her usual getup for the gym was replaced with a matching sweatsuit that looked deliciously soft, yet still elegant on her.

"Is that how you did Jimmy in?" Ben demanded, accusation dripping from his deep voice.

Evelyn lowered her fists, a flash of heat warming her cheeks.

She hadn't told them. Had been avoiding them, really. She didn't know what to say, how to explain to them what was going on in her life and how devastatingly terrifying it was. She was so afraid to actually face the facts of the past month, that she had shut everyone out to live blissfully in her own denial.

Shannon giggled, followed by Ben. She looked back and forth between her two best friends, a bubble of laughter rising in her own throat.

"You've been avoiding us," Shannon managed between her giggles as she shut the door with her foot and set the bags down on the coffee table. "So, we're bringing the park home today. Tell Mommy and Daddy all about it."

Ben took a fuchsia blanket from the pile and plopped himself down next to Shannon's feet while she meticulously started unpacking various pickles and tomato juice onto the hideously mint green coffee table. It was Evelyn's week, that meant Bloody Mary's.

"I love you guys." Did they hear the sincerity in her voice? She thought so.

"We love you too. Now tell us about how you smacked the bastard," Ben sang, getting to work on the drinks.

Once she started, the words just flew out of her. She told them about Max, about her own stupidity when she threw all common sense out the window and kissed him.

She told them about their confusing flirtation, the looks she took for desire and his (ugh) thumb caresses.

The story went on until the infamous right cross. Finishing with an admission of how she opened up to Max about her dad and Jimmy, eliciting an exchanged look between her friends.

"What?" She demanded, thirsty for a splash of insight.

"Nothing. It's just that, I'm hearing you say that Christmas," Shannon loved her nicknames. "Flirted with you, then seduced you, then listened to you, then showed understanding and caring, all while bringing you coffee in the morning." She took a long sip off her drink. "How awful for you?"

"I know right?" Evie replied.

They exchanged another meaningful look.

"Evie honey, do you think that maybe that's all a good thing?" Ben tried. "Like, maybe you're not used to the men in your life treating you like an actual human, and your wires are just a little crossed?"

"No, definitely not. Stop looking at each other like that," she snapped, pulling a hand through her hair in frustration. They weren't getting it.

She told them so.

"You're not getting it. I am not some teenage girl that thinks boys tease me when they're attracted. It's not real. He has hated me for so long, and now that he's going through something unimaginable with Harvey, I'm the closest distraction. You guys, I'm falling for a man that has no legitimate interest in me, which is not only sad, but the complete opposite of what I should…" she clapped her mouth shut, realizing too late what was flying out of it.

Wide eyes met her friend's smug faces in horror.

"You're *what*?" Ben asked.

"Not a damn thing."

"She's *falling* for Christmas," Shannon clarified with a grin.

"Nope, not doing that."

"You want to frost his Yule log!" Ben accused.

"Ha! You want him to deck your halls, *way* past January!"

She was dying a very painful death.

"I do!" Evie burst out, unable to help herself. "I don't know how it happened, but I am completely obsessed with Maxwell Easton." Her confession snowballed. "He is stubborn, and arrogant, and sweet and brutally attractive. He makes me feel mad when he's around and sad when he's not. One minute, I'm scowling at his stupid caviar dish and the next I'm longing to see him smile at me again. I am ruined," she finished dramatically, taking the vodka and pulling straight from the bottle.

"Okay darling," Shannon cooed as she took the bottle from Evie's hands and placed it a good two feet away. "Let's at least wait until noon for that. I know you're freaking out, but I think this is a good thing. And honestly, after seeing Christmas half-naked and dripping wet, I can't blame you."

She what? "I have some follow up questions."

Shannon proceeded to tell her about her run in with Max at the pool, her mouth watering against her will at the thought of him in nothing but swim trunks. She was drowning.

"I don't want to push you in any particular direction…"

"Lies!" They yelled at Shannon in unison.

"*But*," she emphasized, ignoring their outbursts. "He didn't seem like he was holding it together either. I think you should explore this Evie-Jean. Trim his tree - Gah!"

Evelyn threw a pillow at her before anymore awful Christmas analogies flew from her face.

The idea of exploring any kind of relationship with Max had her tail tucking in response. Restaurant romances weren't a rarity by any means, but this was different. This was Harvey's son. If things went wrong…she wouldn't be able to handle it if her relationship with Harvey was strained.

Her best option was to keep her head down, work her ass off, and ignore Max until he inevitably tired of her and The Lennon and walked away.

Easy right?

Chapter Fifteen

She was on a torture machine that was ten seconds away from lifting into the air and launching her into a sudden, fiery death. At least that was the image that flashed through her mental flip book every time she set foot in an airport.

A most untimely image, as it were.

Max sat next to her; his long legs scrunched against the seat in front of them in a position that screamed discomfort. She wanted to tell him to spread out a little, shift to her side and gain a little more space, but simply couldn't speak through the breathing exercises she was coaching herself through.

Evelyn sat with her hands clasped tight on her lap, her eyes shut. The plane lurched forward causing her to clasp her hands tighter, refusing to grasp the armrests like a complete amateur.

She cracked one eye open as the plane leveled out in the air, her stomach hollowing out with the movement.

A stiff motion caught her attention as Max shuffled for the hundredth time.

"You can move closer." She cursed herself when he stiffened next to her. "That is, you can stretch your legs out and invade my space, I don't mind."

He let out a sigh of relief and she tried not to gasp when his knee connected with hers.

"Thanks," he murmured. Was that amusement in his voice?

She opened one eye again and used it to glare at him. A look reminiscent of a slightly motion sick pirate.

"Are you alright Evelyn?" She tried not to pout as he slipped back into using her full name.

"I don't care much for flying."

"Yeah, I got that when you practically stabbed me for the aisle seat." How could he sound amused as they were flying to their deaths?

She opened her eyes fully, a retort primed and ready on her lips. The plane tilted, turning in midair like some kind of aluminum can curveball. Her gasp was intense, but she couldn't hear it over the beating of her own heart.

Was it hot? She was hot, it was definitely too hot.

She sucked in several long shaky breaths and squeezed her eyes closed once more.

The skin on her wrist was going cold. Was that normal? It was starting to spread through her hand, calming her fingers one at a time. Her breathing exercises must have been working.

She could hear the muffled bass of the window seat's headphones thump-thumping along with her pulse.

"Do you like sushi?" Max asked suddenly.

"Oh yes," she responded quickly, pouncing on any distraction she could. "Japanese food is second only to coffee." Deep breath.

"Favorite smell?"

"Pine trees," she answered immediately.

"Wow, I thought you were going to say coffee."

182

She should have, her anxiety was loosening her tongue. Nevertheless, her hands relaxed further. The tightness in her shoulders eased.

"What's *your* favorite smell?" she bounced back before thinking about her own answer. "And don't say cinnamon."

The grin on his face was unmistakable as he said, "It's coffee. Natural Ethiopian."

His first day working at The Lennon assaulted the backs of her closed eyelids. Max's pressed chef coat drowned in coffee. She smiled despite herself.

"What do you usually do with your days off?" He continued easily.

"Is this an interview? Are you planning on selling these answers to The Chronicle for another enthralling piece on Evelyn Pimm?"

The captain's voice sounded throughout the plane with a warning of turbulence which forced Evie out of her playfulness and back into deep hysteria. She clenched her hands into fists and held her breath.

Not helping.

"No," eyes still clenched shut, Evie jumped a little when Max whispered in her ear. "I'm just genuinely curious about the woman that I work with every day. And have kissed twice." He added, a grin thick in his voice.

Although the statement shocked some of the tension from her body, she still didn't open her eyes to look at him. Max hadn't spoken more than two sentences to her since the article blasted them back into quiet dislike. She couldn't wrap her head around why he was suddenly so upbeat and flirty.

Maybe because they were floating through the sky on a death canon.

"Why did you decide to come back to the restaurant?" she whispered. Unsure why she was asking and ruining the playfulness of the moment.

His sigh must have been a heavy one, the way the plane shuddered and rattled all of a sudden. Fingers tightened to fists once more, she barely managed to take another slow breath before he answered.

"To earn that third star back."

"Max," the catch in her throat squashed the disdain in her tone. "Why are you so obsessed with stars? You don't need them to prove you're a great chef, people can taste that in every dish."

After a full minute of silence, Evelyn reluctantly opened her eyes. With a jolt, she realized that a strong hand held hers, cool and calming. Max had been smoothing out her stiff fingers and, how dare he, was rubbing a thumb across her wrist.

She blinked before looking at the man himself who simply shrugged at her surprise, continuing his light caress.

"It's been a mission of mine since my mom died," he said. She watched a muscle in his jaw twitch, his eyes reduce down to slits. He looked as if he was highly unsure of why his mouth was moving. So was she, but wanted him to continue all the same.

He glanced at the window seat, who was scrolling through her phone so fast, it was making Evie's motion sickness worse. He must have decided she was distracted enough, before leaning in closer.

She tried not to suck in a breath and fill her nose with nutmeg and cypress.

"Dad opened the restaurant when I was sixteen. I was still a stupid kid, all I wanted to do was chase girls and smoke pot." He gave her a small smile, their hands still clasped softly. "I would wash dishes on the weekends and shoot the shit with the cooks. They used to sneak me food after the shift if I managed not to break a plate which, after my dad nearly burst a vein in his forehead, I only did once."

184

"Impressive." She could see the love in his terribly close face, it made her chest swell with something warm and uninvited.

"So was the vein. Anyway, they started me out pretty easy. Bringing me pieces of steak or some sort of grilled vegetable. The more I worked, the more adventurous things got. Oysters, pickles, aged meats, funky cheeses. I think about it now and it makes me cringe to think about how much it cost just to keep me from breaking glasses." His grin couldn't be helped now which forced Evelyn to mirror the smile. The sheer joy of it was as infectious as his story.

"I'll never forget the dish that changed my life forever. I was eighteen and had been dicking around in the dish pit for two years. I had just graduated and was on my way to college to pursue a career in tech."

Evie mocked a gagging sound and immediately regretted it as her real nausea flashed.

He gave her hand a consoling squeeze before continuing on.

"I knew there was something up when my mom was the one who brought me dinner for the night. She wasn't a chef, usually kept to the office pushing papers and making sure dad didn't spend ridiculous amounts of money on turnips." Admiration lit up his green eyes. "But when she swooped into the kitchen, I knew she held something special. Dad had tested a dish that night. Tender abalone, perfectly creamy pasta, and chestnut."

Evie's own eyes lit up with delight. "Our first staple dish."

He nodded. "I could feel the love on that plate. The abalone was so tender, there was no doubt in my mind that he went to great lengths just to obtain that result, *just* for that single element. It was like that with every bite. I felt like there was a story behind it all, and I wanted to know more. I applied to culinary school the next day."

She gave him a sympathetic smile. "Probably could have saved your money with that one."

"Maybe," he laughed. "But it fueled my obsession. After I graduated, I traveled all over the world, trailing as many chefs as I could, but I always knew I'd end up back at The Lennon. I started out as a commis like everyone else, which is where I was when we got star number two. Shortly after that, I moved up to a sous chef position, and we got our third star the following year. It was amazing, the feeling of accomplishment and pride that I felt whenever I looked at the kitchen staff—at my parents. None of it could have been achieved without each other, you know what I mean?"

She nodded, captivated by his story.

The moment shattered into a million pieces of memory when he pulled back a little, eyes leaving her face. She tried not to whine when he tugged his fingers from hers and patted her hand.

"Feeling better?"

"No," she lied. "Go on."

"There's nothing more to it, Evelyn. I care about that place, I want to see that star back where it belongs, plain and simple."

Judging by his tone, there was nothing simple about it.

"Max," she began until he cut off the speech she had been ready to badger him with.

"I was just talking you through it Evelyn. You looked like you were ready to vomit on me, I thought a distraction would keep that from happening. Which," he flicked her nose. "Seems to have worked pretty well."

This encouraged an eye roll, but she found she didn't have it in her.

"Hey, you want me to revoke your leg room privileges?"

"We only have thirty minutes to go," he responded casually.

186

She looked around in surprise to find that the sky had darkened slightly outside of the tiny windows on either side of her. They had been talking for an hour, her terror almost forgotten during his story.

Almost.

"How did you do that? It feels like five minutes have passed."

"Conversation always helped me through waves of anxiety. I have medication I can take but honestly, I prefer a good distraction."

"A distraction huh?" Her stomach flopped for an entirely different reason. Was Evelyn his distraction? Were their shared moments his equivalent of airplane chatter?

"I know what you're thinking, and you're way off," he insisted, reading her mind in a way that made her want to squirm.

"Because I'm not the kind of distraction that eases your anxiety?"

He nodded, his eyes bright.

A small ding sounded in the plane before the captain's voice calmly announced their descent into Los Angeles.

Evelyn jumped, gave in, and clutched the armrests. Giving zero fucks about what Max thought about her.

"You need me to hold your hand again?"

He was laughing at her, the smug asshole. Her attempt to think of something heated to say diminished as their tin can rattled once more, forcing her to relent.

"Yes please," she whispered.

Her hand was enveloped in his without another word and something just clicked. A sense of ease that she had never felt in her life while flying just sort of settled in her body. *Run from that*, she decided.

"I can't believe your self-satisfied face is going to be the last thing I see before I die," she said without any heat.

"A little dramatic Evelyn," he teased as her fingers slowly began relaxing.

She ignored her own brain as it told her how perfect his hand felt in hers, how the sweet brush of his thumb smoothed away her strain.

Chapter Sixteen

Friday night was an experience reserved for normal people. Restaurant workers usually had their Friday nights on a Sunday when everyone else avoided staying out too late. Occasionally, a unicorn of a day would present itself with an actual Friday night off—they'd go out with some of their normal friends with normal weekends, wait forty minutes for an overpriced drink and stand in line for the bathroom, before meandering through the crowd to yell at said normal friends in conversation.

The ordinary folks would complain about their awful boss who only provides cinnamon raisin bagels every Wednesday like a serial killer, and they'd nod in understanding. Meanwhile, the image of Chef throwing a plate at their head or forcing them to work through bronchitis flashes before their eyes.

They would end the night sleeping with one of the normal people, knowing damn well that they would never have another Friday night off to see them again.

Max found that he much preferred to just be at the restaurant and skip the rest.

He stood in front of a full-length mirror, the drab colors of his hotel room flashing back to him behind his own reflection.

There was nothing he hated more than dressing up, but he was more than willing to make an exception if it helped elevate the restaurant's reputation.

Tonight, he opted for a soft, cream-colored sweater over charcoal slacks and dark grey dress shoes. Professional without making him want to loosen his tie every five minutes.

He glanced at the door to his left.

Don't go there, he told himself for the eightieth time since arriving.

Evie's room was quiet next to his. A fact that he was actively aware of after straining his ears for two hours.

One knock, a turn of the knob, and he'd be near her again.

He shoved his hands in his pockets—left thumb still tingling from the feel of her skin on the plane.

It was a self-inflicted torture, he knew. But he just couldn't help it after seeing how sincerely frightened she had been. He would have done anything to stifle that fear, a fact that he still wasn't sure what to do with.

He ran a hand through his black hair, smoothing it back and off of his forehead.

Don't go there.

Deciding that he was dangerously close to making a mistake, he snagged his room key and headed for the elevator.

On his way to the lobby, he attempted not to stalk The Lennon on social media and spy on his staff. They were more than capable of running things while he and Evelyn were gone, there was no reason to stress.

But he couldn't help it.

What if they forget the new supplement course? What if they missed the note about Dr Shelton's shellfish allergy?

190

What if a Michelin inspector comes in?

Not worth the anxiety, he decided as he pulled out his phone and began scrolling. He barely looked up, making his way towards the hotel bar that had been booked out for their meet-and-greet.

Knowing full-well that he was about to have multiple conversations with some of the most talented chefs in the world, he scanned the room for the alcohol.

His scan stopped dead at the sight of her.

The fucking gall of this woman.

He watched as she laughed over her drink at some asshole with blonde hair. Her own hair tied in a thick braid that draped over her shoulder and sank into a silky looking emerald blouse. His eyes were drawn to the deep V of her shirt, following the long necklace that hung selfishly between her breasts.

She wore black slacks that hugged every curve and had him almost biting down on his fist to keep from drooling.

Whiskey eyes locked on him from across the room and sent an immediate shock wave to his loins.

Drink. Now.

Turning a half circle, he fled for his life.

A neat bourbon was placed in front of him and downed in a matter of minutes before being replaced with a glass of champagne. He surveyed the room, his eyes darting to the same spot repeatedly against his will.

She was chatting with Dorian Danner, which was just the type of alliterate name you would expect from a pretentious dirtbag who thought way too highly of himself.

The muscles in Max's arm twitched when he pressed a hand to Evie's back and leaned in to tell her something, before quickly easing in satisfaction when she took a full step back and turned her attention to someone else, clearly uninterested in what he had to say.

She laughed, and the wind chime sound of it cut through the crowd to jab him directly in the forehead.

"Try not to look so miserable. It's only the first night after all."

He turned to the voice, wiping his scowl away as he went. Kind eyes and laugh lines greeted him with a sympathetic smile.

Holy shit.

"Chef Klein," he held out his hand enthusiastically. "It's a pleasure to see you again."

"Celeste, please," she responded easily, pulling her fuchsia shawl tighter over small shoulders. "Buy an old lady a drink?"

"It's an open bar, but I think I can figure something out," he joked, trying not to freak out.

Celeste Klein was a culinary legend. She started running her restaurant before Max could walk and quickly gained a reputation for revolutionizing California cuisine. Credited with launching the careers of some of the best chefs out there, Celeste was talented, smart and amazingly humble. She had always reminded Max of his dad.

Her restaurant had been number three in the world for the past nine years, and with good reason.

Legend.

Only an idiot would walk away from a conversation with her, and he was no idiot. He ordered a drink for her and sat down immediately, trying his darndest not to look overeager.

"Welcome to the top fifty." Their glasses clinked together in celebration.

"It's been a crazy ride. If you had told me seven years ago that I would be back in that kitchen, I'm not sure I would have believed it," he said.

"Aw well, it didn't come as a surprise to me," she replied honestly, her laugh warm. "I remember working with you

192

years ago when I did that collaboration dinner with your father. You had a fire in you, even then."

Max wouldn't have been more surprised if she had stood on the bar and started line dancing.

"Wow, that's really kind of you to say," he managed.

"Nothing kind about it dear. I tried to steal you away from your dad, but Lennon called me with some choice words," she said. "Your mom was one of the sweetest women I've ever known, but when it came to you, she had everyone tucking their tails in genuine fright."

He laughed in delighted surprise.

"Some would say that convincing one of the best chefs in the world *not* to hire your son, was a bad choice."

"Aw but she knew, like I did, that you were an asset. She couldn't conceptualize that restaurant without you in it. You and your father? To Lennon, you two were the life force of that place—your hard work and talent built into every brick. What you and Evelyn are doing now, this amazing next phase that you're in," she patted his hand. "She would be so proud of you two."

Max blinked furiously as emotion flooded him.

He looked around for Evelyn, his heart thumping at the way Celeste looped them together in praise. He found her brown doe eyes already pinned on him, as if she knew how giddy he felt and wanted to share in the moment. She smiled at him, a simple shift of her lips that sent his nerve endings tingling.

The love he felt for her broke out of its prison, spreading through every inch of his body and filling him with sunlight.

"She's an asset too, I imagine," Celeste said softly. Knowledge and wisdom dripping off of every word.

"She is everything."

He hadn't meant to say it out loud, it just sort of…fell out before intelligent thought connected to his body and snapped his mouth shut.

Celeste chuckled softly when he cleared his throat before downing the rest of his drink in alarm.

"I think you need another one dear."

"You're not wrong."

He loved Evie. He had known for a while, his body and mind had just kicked into survival mode and suppressed the feeling, hoping it would suffocate and die. Simple.

Easy.

There was nothing *easy* about the predicament he found himself in. Loving Evie was a fucking inconvenience seeing as it was nearly impossible to work alongside her with cold indifference. And that was before he held the horrible truth of his feelings below his breastbone, constantly jabbing at his resolve and diminishing stability.

The buzz of chatter went on happily around him, everyone completely oblivious to his emotional turmoil. As if it wasn't screaming at the top of its lungs that he had fallen, face first in love with someone he had desperately tried to avoid.

A dull sting pricked his lungs from quickened breaths. He knew what happened when he started to care for people too much. The universe decided he wasn't worthy and plucked them out of his life with violent urgency. There was a reason work consumed him. A reason he didn't get too close to people or care too deeply.

Whenever he did, they were taken from him.

Max's hand shook slightly as he took the offered glass from Chef Klein. He felt sweat forming on the back of his neck and tried desperately to control his breathing. If he loved Evie, it couldn't last long. She would be removed from his life way before he had a chance to show her just how much she meant to him.

You're panicking, he told himself like he's done about a million times before. A tactic that—surprising no one—still didn't work.

Amazingly, he managed not to jump out of his skin when Evelyn rested a hand on his shoulder.

"Is this man bothering you?" she asked Celeste playfully before smiling down at him.

He was a dead man.

"He's saving me actually. I really didn't want to get stuck in conversation with Paulo about feeding my pigs acorns, yet again." She held out a hand and introduced herself to Evie with a genuine, bright smile. He could have kissed her feet for saving him from forming words and stringing together coherent sentences.

They prattled on; Max barely able to focus with her hand still resting on his shoulder.

His mind wandered back to Celeste's words, back to the collaboration dinner she mentioned. He had been a Commis at the time but insisted that he be allowed to trail during service and be a part of it all. At that point, he had worked under and learned from some seriously amazing chefs, but none as notorious as Celeste.

It had taken mass amounts of focus and energy not to screw things up at every turn, yet she still thought he was worth pursuing?

Then there was his mother. She had probably been sick at the time, he realized with a start. Yet she had fought to keep him, seeing something in him that he hadn't even realized was there. That was before the accolades, before the awards and features and stars.

Her faith in him had been unwavering and constant from beginning to end.

An end that would have torn him into a thousand vulnerable pieces if it weren't for his dad.

"You okay?" A gentle squeeze on his shoulder. "You look a little pale."

Max zipped out of his thoughts, his vision clearing and focusing on the two women he was supposed to be holding intelligent conversation with.

If he looked at Evie, would she be able to see the difference in him? As if a halo of hearts circled above his head just waiting for her to pluck one and crush it between her fingers.

He decided not to find out.

Warmth flooded the back of his neck as he grumbled out an excuse about a headache and speed-walked to the back of the room toward the bathroom. He would splash some water on his face, take a few deep breaths and get his shit together before coming back out. He would socialize with literally anybody but Evelyn, duck out early, and head to his favorite taco spot.

It was amazing how easily he could slip back into avoidance when he needed to.

***

Evelyn watched his back as he maneuvered through the crowd at a pace worthy of a stopwatch. Worry lined her forehead when she turned back to Celeste, a woman she had been thoroughly enjoying before noticing Max's ashen face.

"Maybe I should go after him…"

"I think he's just a little overwhelmed," she assured Evie. "It must be surreal to be thrust into all of this after returning to the restaurant for such a short amount of time."

She nodded, the worry not quite stifled.

"He's a good man," Celeste stated in an odd voice.

Evie's eyebrows shot up. "Yes, although a little confusing at times. You know, for someone who has a reputation for earning stars, it sure seems strange that this would be overwhelming for him."

"Well, none of those stars were for his own restaurant, were they?"

Her immediate reaction to those words was irritation. To her, The Lennon didn't belong to Max at all, and if she was being perfectly irrational, she thought she held claim to it far more than he did. She had basically replaced the very oxygen she breathed with the success of that place. It was her life force.

But that was awful, and she now knew it to be bullshit.

The story Max had told her on the plane made it very clear to her that he had a deep connection to the restaurant and the people in it. Had she really been so beautifully naive to think that he didn't care about it?

"You seem surprised by this. Didn't you expect him to come back after he lost his mom? I thought his desire to prove himself in the restaurant would have been obvious." Her words weren't harsh, but they grained on Evelyn all the same.

"Maybe I just don't understand it. I think Max is perfectly capable of proving himself without the Michelin accolades. Why does it always come back to that ridiculous star they lost?"

Celeste stared at her with an odd expression, her brows drawn together, lips slightly upturned.

She hesitated before saying, "I think it was the way they lost it that bothers him, dear. Harvey stepped away to care for Lennon, leaving Max in charge and ultimately, working himself to the bone. They were lowered to two stars a week before she passed."

Evie felt her eyes begin to burn with anger. She knew that The Lennon lost a star shortly before she started there, but never knew the full story because it simply never mattered to her. She loved the restaurant for what it was.

But this…

"They took a star from the restaurant while one of the owners was dying?" she whispered.

"Yes." Celeste's voice filled with heat. "This industry has never been a beacon of hope for mental health, has it?"

Guilt, a familiar foe, shot down her middle like hot soup. She kicked herself for misunderstanding Max so much, for constantly shooting down his methods, choosing instead to keep everything exactly the way it was when she started.

She had always treated him like some fame obsessed celebrity chef, but that was never it, was it?

"Celeste, it's been a real pleasure. Seriously, I peed a little when I saw you over here." She let out a nervous giggle when Celeste laughed out loud. "But I need to go."

Celeste nodded, a mischievous twinkle in her eye. "Go. You two should be celebrating, not listening to me ramble on."

Evelyn would have never described chatting with a legend in that way, but simply smiled at Chef Klein before scanning the room for her co-CDC.

It didn't take long to find him. He looked absolutely gorgeous leaned up against the wall listening intently to a very tall man with a love of sweeping hand gestures. She slipped in beside him, ignoring the stiffening of his shoulders. Mumbling an apology to the man's splaying hands and pulled Max to a private corner.

Then, she rounded on him.

"What's it going to take to get three stars?"

Max's brows drew together in confusion. "What? Twenty minutes with Celeste and you're ready to order truffles?" he asked, humor lighting his features.

"I'm serious. I have decided that this weirdness between us needs to end. We both care about the restaurant and want it to succeed, right? Well, that includes supporting everyone

198

within its walls. If getting that star back is important to you, then I want to help."

She stared right into his endless eyes, the reflection of her own blouse giving them an almost dream-like green glow.

He opened his mouth before shutting it again with a snap, an attempt to smother his emotions flashing over his gorgeous face.

Flip-flopping was never a simple matter as it involved putting yourself out there. Embracing vulnerability was not Evelyn's strong suit. To her, it was like blasting back to childhood screaming, *uncle!* to your awful cousin who was just going to turn around and place you in a headlock again ten minutes later.

Regret fluttered in her chest, attempting to battle the guilt that already rested in her gut comfortably. Maybe she should have taken the time to get to understand him better.

She really wished he would say something, but he just stood there, most likely trying to figure out why the fuck she was doing this.

"Max—"

"Well, isn't this a lovely reunion?" Evelyn tried not to flinch at the familiar interruption.

Dorian Danner, ignoring her altogether, burst into their conversation giving Max his full attention. "Congrats. I knew The Lennon would move up on the list after you took over," he said, holding out a hand for Max.

Evelyn's anger zipped through her veins in a frenzy.

Calm down. Don't cause a scene. You're better than that. This had been her mantra whenever Dorian forced his way into her bubble. She repeated it to herself now like her life depended on it.

Max looked down at the offered hand, his face a mask that she knew extremely well. Icy detachment radiated from him, his hand rising stiffly to accept the handshake.

"It had nothing to do with me. A lot has changed since Evelyn took your position. The dishes have more of a sense of place…more heart." Max trailed off, letting that sentence hang in the air.

Evie almost spit out her champagne at Dorian's expression.

He glanced back and forth between them; a fake smile plastered on his pale face. "I thought that Chronicle review was interesting. Are you two a *thing* now?"

Because that was *clearly* the only way Max would prefer Evelyn's menu over his? What an asshole.

"No," Max said through his own forced smile. "We just work extremely well together."

Relief washed over her at his defense, but it came with a slight pull on her heart. She certainly didn't feel the need to defend herself against Dorian, she already had to fight off enough of the industry's misogyny. But a pushy little voice in her head said, why shouldn't you be dating him? Why shouldn't you be happy?

Ssshhhh.

Her shoulders tightened when she felt Dorian's hand on her lower back. His fingers sliding over the silk of her blouse and making her want to cringe.

"That's a relief then," he whispered to her, the stubble of his chin brushing against her ear. Evelyn put all her focus on Max, watching as his eyes burned hot with anger and his hands balled into fists. His reaction gave her a bout of confidence even as she repeated her mantra in her head over and over again.

"Why don't we go somewhere quiet to catch up?" he asked, his eyes floating to her cleavage before making their way up to meet her cold gaze.

She sighed, truly unable to stop herself. Her mantra went soaring out of her head to land somewhere on the floor where she would stomp on it later.

Evelyn took Dorian's hand from her back and pivoted herself next to Max. "Quite frankly Dorian, I would rather eat these shitty lettuce cups they're serving for the rest of my life than listen to you talk about yourself for the next half hour. Would you excuse us?"

Now it was Max's turn to choke on his champagne.

Dorian's smile melted into a scowl immediately. His mouth wagged open before snapping shut again, finally at a loss for words. She should have told him off a long time ago.

Shifting to face Max again, she allowed Dorian to bow out gracefully and hopefully leave her alone for the rest of her fucking life.

"That felt good. I can't believe I just said that to him. God, he's been such a pervert from the moment I met him, but I really shouldn't have said that. Anyway, I meant what I said, let's get back to our conversation. I want—"

"Our *weirdness* has nothing to do with the restaurant." Max said, cutting through her rambling and succeeding in bringing her attention directly to his perfect face.

A wide grin spread, plumping his cheeks and warming his features.

"I just mean…" She placed a hand on his arm. Why would she do that? Cashmere clad biceps flexed in response, causing her to lose her train of thought before he tugged affectionately on her braid.

"And I don't want it to end."

He stepped closer, muscles flexing under her hand. She placed her forgotten champagne on a nearby table, afraid of dropping it and drawing everyone's gaze, knowing exactly what they would see—a horny little demon drowning in Max's eyes and grasping his bicep like a sexy flotation device.

Were flotation devices sexy? That seemed like a strange thought.

She sucked in a breath when he brought his lips down to her ear, a whisper away from touching her skin.

"Do you know what I want more than that star?"

She knew what *she* wanted. His hot breath on her neck triggered an immediate response from her body. Scolding herself as her nipples went hard, it still shocked her that such a small gesture could evoke such a sexual response.

"No."

He pulled back to look at her, incredulous. "We should change that."

A sharp, high-pitched sound filled the bar, breaking their intense stare and ruining her life.

A man that Evie didn't know, but hated all the same, tapped on the mic before launching into some boring speech about the awards ceremony tomorrow. She didn't hear a word of it, all of her attention focused on the hand resting on her lower back, the thumb sliding along the silk of her shirt.

"What do you want?" she whispered out of the corner of her mouth.

There was a long pause in which Evie felt like she would melt with anticipation. That slow caresses over the silk of her blouse had her purring like a cat and nearly whining out loud when it stopped.

"Tacos," he said simply, before taking her hand and shuffling the two of them towards the exit.

Chapter Seventeen

When faced with a threat, your body automatically shifts into survival mode, going back to its most basic instincts.

You leave the safety of your cave, immediately aware of the dangers you must face just to simply exist. You survey your surroundings, strained eyes catching on any sway of the grass—ears perked, listening for the sound of your enemies. Muscles tighten in anticipation, every sense sharpened.

Your body adjusts, pushing you forward. Pushing you to defend yourself. To fight.

Then, there are times when fighting becomes too much for your body to handle. So, you accept defeat, and allow yourself to drift into a quiet death.

Max decided that he was tired of fighting.

A knock sounded at the door adjoining his and Evelyn's rooms. He hopped on one foot, pulling black joggers over his hips before opening the door for her.

Was it cheesy to say that his heart skipped a beat? It was, yeah.

His heart skipped a beat.

She had changed into a loose T-shirt and yoga pants. Chocolate hair still hung over one shoulder in a long braid, but she had wiped the makeup from her face which was a little more familiar to him.

A laugh charged out of his belly when he read her shirt. *"Raisin cookies disguised as chocolate chip cookies are the main reason I have trust issues."*

"The audacity of raisin cookies and the people who bake them," she said before swinging into the room. "Ready?"

"Fire away."

Evie ceremoniously grabbed an overstuffed bag and upended it on to the center of the bed, spilling individually wrapped tacos out in an avalanche of carnitas and cheese.

She looked completely at ease, legs crossed, rummaging through a pile of Mexican food on a fluffy comforter. As if this was a common thing that happened to her on any given Friday night.

He demanded that his body make standard movements, take a step, grab a taco, join her on the bed.

It was that last one that his body rejected, choosing instead to lean against the generic desk and face her, carne asada in hand like a shield.

He had wanted this. To finally give-in and be alone with Evelyn. To soak up her energy outside of the kitchen, away from their responsibilities.

What was he thinking?

The knowledge that they were alone without dishes to test or lineup to attend connected to his painfully slow brain, making him sweat.

He had been using the restaurant as armor, managing to put his responsibilities in front of the feelings that had inserted themselves into his gut.

She dug into a taco and rolled her eyes in pleasure. "This may have been the best idea you've ever had," she said around a mouth full of food.

He cracked a soda and took a long sip attempting to wash his insecurities down his throat.

204

"I have been to a million of these events and it always surprises me how bad the food is. You have a collection of the best chefs around, and you serve lettuce wraps?"

She snorted. "If I'm being honest, lettuce wraps are exactly what I expected from this event. It's just as stuffy as I imagined."

Max paused with a taco halfway to his lips, remorse thick in his throat. "Jesus, I'm an asshole. This is your first time attending the awards, isn't it? I shouldn't have pulled you away like that." He should have left her alone. Left her downstairs to get blissfully tipsy and make connections. Schmooze.

She shrugged. "Should I go back downstairs and let Dorian tell me about the new aprons he's having custom made? I'd rather drink decaf."

His grin cracked like a whip, delighted by her answer.

"So, let's continue our conversation."

And his delight was gone. Dread ran through his feet, tingling his toes as it filled his body. He had a bad habit of throwing caution to the wind when it came to Evie. She had the ability to surprise him, putting herself out there in a way that made him feel like he could say anything to her. Ensuring he said something he would come to regret in response.

Do you know what I want more than that star?

He wanted her. *Had* wanted her for way too long. But she wasn't ready to hear that, and he was too chicken shit to say it.

Luckily, she gave him an out.

"How do we get three stars?"

He sat across from her and rested easily against the headboard. This was a topic he could handle.

"Mostly easy stuff. We'll need to get new stemware and make some significant changes to the wine list. Luxury ingredients will have to be added to the menu…the caviar is a nice start, but we should look into truffles. Maybe look into sourcing some wagyu beef…"

She gave him a small nod over another taco, but he saw it in her eyes. Disappointment flooded her features and made him feel like he had just kicked her puppy.

It was something he couldn't quite understand. In his mind, these changes were small, but effective. They wouldn't necessarily require a lot of adjustment, so what was the problem?

After a minute of silence, Evie squared her shoulders. The familiarity of it made him want to pull her into his arms and nuzzle, regardless of what her decision was.

"Okay," she said decidedly. "I believe we can come up with dishes that stay true to The Lennon, but still utilize these ingredients."

And it clicked.

"You're worried we're going to lose our identity."

She nodded, looking a little sad. Why did she have to look sad?

"It's not very personal don't you think? The checklist of things that you need in order to be considered the best. I'm sorry Max, but I think it's all bullshit. Think about this," she scooted forward in her enthusiasm, not even caring what it did to his insides to be so close to her. "When you tried the abalone dish, you said that it changed your life. It lit a fire in you, and you were shoveling it into your face while standing over a garbage can in the dish pit. The Lennon hadn't even been rated then."

His mouth lifted at the corners. Her description wasn't that far off.

She held his gaze, her face turning serious. "Look, Celeste told me the story about your loss—about your mom." Max felt his muscles tighten in defense. That would explain her sudden shift. "I want to help you, Max; I just don't really believe that you need that star back to prove anything."

"But you *will* help me?"

"Of course I will." There was no hesitation. Her determination to help was crushing him in a million different ways. "I'm here for you. And, uh, I'm here if you want to talk. About your mom, or Harvey."

He looked into her eyes and felt an overwhelming flood of emotion.

Shame spiraled around his head whenever he thought about that year. Panic attacks used to strike him in the parking lot of the hospital causing him to spend too little time there. The sight of his strong, radiant mother looking frail and strapped to machines would launch his pulse into a frenzy.

He would never be able to forgive himself for pushing it all away.

His mother had been dying while he had been yelling at cooks about wilted herbs and crinkled aprons.

Harvey had tried to stay positive and tell him she was strong. That she would make it through, no matter what the doctors said. Max had believed him. He thought she would come back, bouncing into The Lennon like she had been there the whole time complaining about Harvey's expensive taste.

He thought she would pull through, but Max ended up losing so much more than a fucking Michelin star.

A hand settled lightly on his knee, the warmth of it had him snapping his mouth shut, bringing him back to earth.

"I'm sorry," Aw hell, when had he started talking? "I, uhm…"

"Jesus Max don't apologize. You know you are allowed to feel this way, right? Losing a parent is hard enough but having to keep your family's business alive while also staying emotionally available for your dad, it's too much for one person to handle."

Her thumb was sliding across his skin, gently easing his tight muscles.

He didn't know why, but he was willing to bet his left arm that she would do anything he said if it meant helping him. A pain began to bloom from his chest, making him want to curl up in his taco pile and squeeze his eyes shut.

"Yeah, but it doesn't excuse the fact that I wasn't there. She should have been able to depend on me for support and I couldn't give it to her."

"You gave it to her in other ways. Look, Lennon was a smart woman. You don't think she knew what would happen when she was gone? She knew that Harvey would need the restaurant to go back to. Just like she knew that you would take care of him when he returned."

It was all too much. The understanding he was receiving from Evie made his heart ache. Is this what it would have been like if he had opened up before? He had a feeling that the answer was no. That this was something special and unique to the woman sitting across from him.

Shifting uncomfortably, Max set his forgotten taco on the nightstand and met Evie's soft eyes full on. Casual conversation about his past and his family and his *grief* was not what he needed right now.

So he shifted it all aside like he did his carne asada.

"I asked you a question earlier," he said suddenly, fully aware of his deflecting. The way he saw it, he had two choices. Open up, let her see a glimpse of his grief and fear, and completely lose it in front of her; or give in and *get lost* in her.

He didn't want to fight anymore.

"Do you know what I want more than that third star?"

***

Evelyn held a taco out to him in reply.

She knew she should bring the subject back around. Smack him and scold him for his evasiveness. In fact, she should save her own damn self and run back to her room, take a cold shower and try not to think about the man one door down.

But that was the second time he had asked that question—and she really wanted the answer.

He batted the taco away, his hand finding her knee instead and sliding gently to her thigh.

"I want you. I *have* wanted you since I first laid eyes on that red dress. Tieless and brutally unprepared for it."

She shook her head because that was obviously impossible.

"You hated me," she accused and watched his forehead crease with frustration.

She felt crazy, leaning into his words even as her mind flashed a million warning signs at her. *He's using you as a distraction, he's avoiding his grief, you're going to get hurt. You. Are. Going. To. Get. Hurt.*

She ignored all of it.

Her hand lifted of its own volition to rest gently on his strong shoulder.

"I never hated you Evelyn," he said passionately, and her breath caught in her throat. "I'm terrified of you."

His hand wound its way to the back of her head as he shifted. Pulling her slightly closer yet somehow keeping her at arm's length.

"What are you so afraid of?" She moved closer herself, their conversation circling them as they shifted. An insistent voice pressed its way into her hazy thoughts. The voice warned her, told her that boys being mean because they actually liked you was a lie you were told throughout your youth to cover up for their bad behavior.

Max's fingers brushing her collarbone conveniently wiped those warnings away in record speed.

A warm palm circled to cup her face and she was certain that her heartbeat could be heard from the next room. Could he feel her pulse while he ran his thumb over her lips? He separated them gently and she was certain that he could, the drum of her pulse vibrating through every inch of her like a snare.

"I'm afraid that there's no one else like you. Like I'll have you, and never be the same," he murmured, eyes sharp on her face. "I'm afraid it's already happened."

And just like that, all of her warning signs officially split into tinder on the ground where she set them ablaze and buried the ashes.

"Fear is so limiting," she murmured, her lips a breath away from his.

"I'm going to kiss you now." His eyes burned into hers and she knew the meaning behind his statement. Nothing was going to interrupt them this time. There was nothing in their way.

"Yes, Chef," she said with a sigh.

The feel of his soft mouth was nothing new to her and yet this was a different kind of kiss. It was tender, brimming with fluffiness and emotion. It made her legs shake.

She trailed her hands up his broad shoulders to cup the sides of his face and rose on her knees, eager to get closer. To lean into the sweetness of the kiss.

He moved, his lips landing on her chin and fluttering over her neck circling back to her mouth in a flurry of tenderness. When he nibbled softly on her lower lip, she sighed and allowed her hands to curl in his dark hair.

Her mind was void of all thoughts that weren't melting into Max, until she shifted and kicked forgotten tacos onto

210

the floor, reminding her that they were making out on a pile of food.

She felt his lips curl against hers and the pressure of it sent a shock straight to her already swollen clit.

"We should clear those off before we make a mess," he murmured.

God he was sexy. His words were confirmation that this was it, he wasn't going to stop this time—thank Christ.

She flipped over and off of him in one swift motion, causing his smile to flicker. She had no intention of going back now and would thoroughly enjoy wiping that disappointed look from his face.

Evie made quick work of tugging her shirt off, exposing her lacy bra that she silently thanked the universe for encouraging her to wear, before tugging on his hands and pulling him towards her and the adjoining door.

"We have another bed," she said, hearing the heat behind her own words. Desire flashed across his features making her stomach tingle in anticipation as they connected hard, lips pressing together frantically, tongues searching. Dim light from the vacated room cast just enough of a glow for them to navigate towards the bed before Evie's legs connected with the back of an armchair. She took the opportunity to rid Max of his shirt and, growing bold, she grabbed his careful hands and guided them directly to her tits.

A small hiss of breath released against her lips as his hands explored, gently running his thumbs along the bottoms of her breasts one hand squeezing, the other gentle. Evie was used to taking charge and going after what she wanted. In her experience it had always been met with challenge and resistance, causing her to work and work and *work* until the desired results were yielded.

That was not the case with Max.

All of her wavering attention went to that gentle hand and the delicate brush of his thumb over her hardened nipple.

Pressing her ass against the chair and arching her back, she leaned into that soft touch, a whimper escaping her lips as he quickened his pace and sent zipping currents directly to her center.

"Is that all it takes?" he asked before nipping at her lower lip, then running his tongue over it like a fucking ice cream cone. Her hands gripped strong shoulders as her body tensed with want and Evelyn was genuinely wondering if they were going to make it to the bed or just have it out in the cuck chair when the hand not unraveling her reached around to the clasp of her bra. "All I have to do is play with these perfect tits and you make the sweetest little sounds?"

Confirmation came in the form of a moan when she felt her bra unclasp and the weight lifted from her shoulders.

Her heavy breasts settled into Max's palms and fuck; she was going to come from the feel of his callused fingers against her tender skin alone. A tightness stretched her low belly, the muscles taught with anticipation as his thumbs swept over her aching tits.

She ran her fingers over his body with reckless abandon, mentally cataloguing the way his tan skin contrasted with her pale hands, the cut muscles of his stomach and the light tuft of dark hair that trailed below the band of his joggers. Max's body was disgustingly perfect, and she would be lying if she said she wasn't looking for something to indicate he wasn't a robot. The cataloguing came to a brisk end when he gripped his cock under black fabric and pumped once. Hard. As if he couldn't help but touch himself. Couldn't wait to feel friction and the glorious sensation of pressure. A strangled moan ejected itself from her body at the sight, her own hand trembling to touch herself and feel an ounce of the relief she needed.

Max's hand whipped out of his pants to grip her around the wrist, hooded eyes dashed from her eyes to her breast, lips, neck and back to her eyes before one hand gripped her breast in a desperate grasp. The other reaching around to her ass, fingers digging in and lifting until her clit was deliciously pressed against his erection.

Max's touch was molten sex on her skin. She had watched those hands delicately plate dishes a thousand times over the past couple of months, but there was nothing delicate about the way he touched her now. His movements were greedy and desperate as he wrapped strong fingers around her rib cage and lifted her onto the back of the chair. Her legs wrapped around him automatically, desperate for their connection.

Goosebumps spread along her heated skin when his lips skimmed her ear, his tongue jutting out to slide along the sensitive skin on her neck.

"You feel that?" he asked, his hips rolling into her and drawing a curse from her swollen lips. "Do you feel how much I want you? How much I need you, Evelyn?"

She did. She really fucking did. It was too much, the feel of his muscles flexing under her fingers, his skin on hers. Her heart was racing, and they still had their pants on.

Why were their pants still on?

Breaking away, she shimmied herself from the back of the chair and pushed into Max until his back connected with the wall. She took a step back, eyes locked on Max's abs, chest, soul before gripping her panties and leggings in one grip and peeling them from her legs in a move that didn't feel nearly fast enough for her.

"Evelyn." The use of her full name didn't make her want to pout this time.

She straightened to find his eyes pegged on her, one hand tangled in his hair, his chest heaving slightly with each ragged breath. She tried not to stare at the bulge in his thin joggers, his arousal pressing on the fabric.

Warmth crept over her cheeks when she realized he *certainly* wasn't fighting his stare. Bright eyes raked up and down her naked body, taking in every inch. Evie had always been comfortable in her own skin, but the way he was licking her up with his eyes made her feel vulnerable.

Like he wanted to devour her.

"You're not stopping again, are you?" She closed the space between them, her breath catching when her bare chest connected with his. "Please don't stop," she begged, remembering the reaction she pulled from him the first time she asked nicely.

His voice was gravel. "Not a chance. I've been fighting this for years but—I've lost Evie. I'm lost."

He really needed to stop saying shit like that.

He really needed to stop saying shit like that, while gazing into her eyes and making her believe every word of it.

When he brought his lips back to hers, desperation coated her tongue. She felt it in every tense grip of her ass and rough swipe of his thumb. Reveled in it as need pumped through them both.

Her hands couldn't cover enough ground. They moved over his broad chest before cutting sharply to the tie on his pants, tugging it free and pressing the rest of his clothes off in a move that she would never be able to pull off again.

He reached around to cup her ass before lifting her off the ground and stumbling over to the bed.

The move wasn't graceful, but they didn't care.

Max settled himself over her and their mouths connected in a flurry of teeth and tongues. His raking over the roof of her mouth while her hands continued to explore the smooth dips of his ab muscles. When she rubbed his lower stomach, his skin tightened before he pulled back slightly.

"Evie, if you touch me now, I'm going to embarrass myself, which is not how I have *ever* pictured this evening going."

"What did you picture then?" she asked, breathless and not even pretending to restrain herself from reaching for him again.

He lowered himself over her and kissed the skin between her breasts, pausing her hungry touches.

"What I pictured is turning out to be nothing compared to the real thing. But there are a few things…" his tongue whipped out and found her nipple, sucking lightly before pulling away. "That I have to experience. Like starting here," she whimpered as he nipped lightly on her breast.

"Then making my way down," Evie clutched the rough hotel sheets as his mouth moved down her torso to her lower belly.

He teased her nipple with one hand, the flick of it sending sensations jolting through her spine. Lips touched down below her belly button as his other hand found her center wet and swollen.

He let a shaky breath out and began stroking, circling her clit with his thumb and causing her to moan out his name. His lips trembled against her stomach as he worked, tongue flicking out as if he couldn't help himself. Sensation threatened to overtake her body as he caressed her nipple and stroked her center.

"You're soaked Evie, it's making me fucking crazy," he groaned against her hip. "I want you. I want to feel you come around me."

"You can have me," she gasped. "Truly, you have my complete permission." Stars were dancing in front of her vision while his hands did wicked things to her body. Evie savored his words, celebrating the fact that prim, pompous Maxwell talked dirty. Filthy, lust inducing words dripped from his villainous lips. She met him head on like she did— Every. Single. Time. "You know how many times I got myself off thinking about you bending me over table three?" she gritted out, gripping his hair and lifting his gaze to hers.

"Trust me when I say, my imagination has provided me with multiple ways for you to fuck me."

Max's face crumpled into a look of painful longing. The color that crept into his cheeks would assault her for the rest of her damn life. Eyes still glued to hers, he lowered his mouth until it connected with the sensitive skin of her lower abdomen. His tongue darted out, lapping at her skin as he writhed his hips, a groan vibrating through his chest.

"And I intend to try every single one of them. There's just one more thing," he said, before shifting her leg over his broad shoulder and lowering his lips between her thighs. "I need to taste you."

Evie's hips rose to meet him, her breaths heaving, stomach quivering. Sensation washed over her when he slid his tongue through her center and flicked up, grazing her desperate clit, eliciting an involuntary jerk from her hips. A tearless sob poured from her chest as he brought his lips lower, his nose raking between her folds as he slicked his tongue all the way up, pausing to give her clit the attention it was begging for. Clumsily, she pressed her fingers through his raven hair, gripping the soft locks as she pulsed beneath his skilled mouth.

Evie muffled a scream as his flicks increased in tempo and his finger slipped between folds, easing into her as he worked her with his tongue. She thought she might explode from the pleasure. Cheeks flooding with heat, lower back bowing off the bed, Max curved his finger inside of her, scraping across her most sensitive spot and working it until she felt like she might die.

A tiny voice in her head told her to quiet down, and she kindly ignored that voice, leaning into the pleasure.

She came in a rush, her orgasm washing over her like warm water as one hand clutched the bed sheets, the other grasping Max's hair in a grip that must have hurt. A delighted laugh escaped as Max gave her one last kiss and meandered back up her torso before the pulses of her pleasure had even slowed. Her limbs instantly felt limp and warm, but she wasn't even close to done with him. Little kisses rained down on her and sucked gently in all the right places as he made his way back to her mouth.

Max's eyes were stormy with desire when he gazed down at her, freezing her involuntary giggle and turning it back into ragged breaths.

"Condom," she managed without breaking their staring contest.

Muffling an oath, he tore away from her and practically jogged to his room, barely providing enough time to appreciate his excellent ass before he returned, ripping open the condom wrapper with his teeth.

She grabbed it from him. "I should help you with this." Her eyes tracked his every reaction. The way he closed his eyes, and bit down on his fist as she rolled the condom over his length, her hands greedy.

He caught her wrists before she could touch anymore, raising them above her head.

"Is this going to ruin me?" he asked, interlacing their fingers and lowering himself over her body.

"Absolutely." She was already ruined herself. Why sugarcoat things at this point? If she was going down, he was going with her.

"Fuck it," he said, taking her back to their first kiss and officially kicking her over the edge. One hand moved to clasp both of her wrists as he guided himself between her legs, cursing as his tip met her slick center. He teased her there. Spreading her arousal over himself before applying the smallest pulse to her swollen, desperate pressure point.

Writhing, hands still clutched above her, Evie lifted her hips to gain more of that contact—more of that pressure. More of Maxwell "Devil Horns" Easton. Through the haze, she realized just how fitting that nickname was. The way

Max touched her would haunt her dreams. The way he licked her, tasted her like a starving man—it was sinful.

But it was clear to her, as he continued to taunt and tease, that Max's wickedness knew no bounds. She was desperate to take him in, feel herself stretch around him.

"Maxwell," she gritted out, his name more of a whine than she cared to admit. His hand tightened around her wrists as he pulled back, a lazy grin on his face. He brushed himself against her again, watching this time as her cheeks heated and her hips jerked up to meet him. Max may have had that pleased smirk on his relentless face, but she could see her reaction getting to him. Gone was the cold, reserved man she was used to. His chest heaved as he gazed at her through hooded eyes, the green barely visible behind his blown-out pupils.

"Yes?" he inquired, his voice thick.

"You're making me crazy," she gasped as he applied a little more pressure before backing off again.

"I won't apologize for that. Making you crazy has taken on a completely new meaning to me, and I won't apologize for dragging this out for as long as possible."

Evie was about to explode.

Dragging this out for as long as possible? She couldn't take it. Her body needed another orgasm, and she was ready to apologize, praise, beg—any and all of the things that, up until this moment, would have never been done with him.

"Please," she begged. His gaze jerked back to hers. "I need you."

Watching Max's restraint crumble at her hands was like winning an Olympic gold. He groaned, growled—choked on some sort of primal sound as he finally gave her what she wanted.

More than ready, his full length slid inside of her as his hands came back to hers, clutching them above her head.

218

Twin moans of pleasure soared out of their throats as he filled her, pausing to allow Evie to adjust to the fit.

His eyes fluttered closed; his hands tightened around hers.

Slowly, so slowly, he pulled out almost entirely before easing even deeper inside of her. Feeling herself stretch around him was a painfully luscious experience.

His breath hitched when she circled her legs around his torso, and they started moving, their rhythm catching like they knew exactly what to do with each other.

Their bodies moved, mouths searched and explored, fingers tightened.

She was certain she could stay tangled up in this man forever.

"You feel so good Evelyn. So fucking good."

Good was an understatement.

She raised her hips, eager for more of him. He thrust deeper, connecting to her most sensitive spot and shocking her body with pleasure.

"I need you to come for me again Evie," he groaned, sounding absolutely tortured.

"Don't stop," she gasped, completely falling apart at the seams. Her mind lost in her lust.

His rhythm quickened, working her clit at a pace that had her plunging to release before she even registered how close she was. Her legs tightened even as they began to tremble with satisfied exhaustion and, realizing he had released her hands, she gripped the back of his neck, bringing his lips to hers and kissing in a tangle of lips and tongue and breath.

As if the feel of her pulsing around him was too much, Max practically growled as his movements became more frantic, his pace frenzied. His release rocked into her, sending shock waves bursting through every single nerve ending she had. When he collapsed his full weight against her, their hands frantically clasped together once more, tethering them as they rode out the pulses of their pleasure.

They were ruined.

Chapter Eighteen

I bought a cinnamon candle.

Thanks for the update.

I thought it would smell like you,
but it smells like cookies and
now I have a sweet tooth.

Great, bake me some cookies.

Raisin cookies?

How dare you? Terrible people
put raisins in cookies. Should
I be questioning your character?

Come over tonight and I'll
bake you anything you want.

Chocolate.

Give Harvey my love.

Max grinned like an idiot down at his phone. In fact, he hadn't been able to wipe the smile off of his face since Friday. He was actually finding it difficult to think of anything other than the past weekend.

I finally got to wake up next to Evelyn. A simple thought, but one that he had a million times a day.

They had left the adjoining door of their hotel rooms open for the rest of the weekend, but still gave each other as much space as they needed. Which wasn't much as it turned out.

"What are you grinning at?" Harvey asked.

If there was anything that could remove his goofy, elated feeling, it was seeing his dad hooked to an IV.

Putting his phone away, he focused on the man sitting across from him. Always so strong, so brave. He wasn't even breaking a sweat and there was a long sharp pointy object in his arm.

Max was not a fan of hospitals, and most definitely not a fan of needles. His eyes snapped away from the IV the minute they landed there, opting instead for Harvey's eyes.

He took a deep breath before his anxiety could kick into high gear.

It's just a needle. These are professional doctors; they know what they're doing.

Not working.

"I am going to bake some cookies when I get home."

"Don't put raisins in them, Evie will never speak to you again otherwise." He winked at Max, picking apart his words easier than he plucked herbs.

Everyone knew at this point. The awards ceremony made sure of that.

They had been waiting patiently for their name to run across the giant screen, certain that it should have already happened. He remembered Evie's nervous face, the line that formed between her brows while she worried.

She had to talk him off the ledge a couple of times after they called numbers 50-45 with no Lennon in sight. He had been certain that they made a mistake, that they weren't on the list and were never meant to be there.

When the restaurant finally flashed on the screen, relief flooded through him in a wave before warming his body with excited pride.

Number forty-three in the world.

They had both jumped out of their seats. Him in a basic suit and her in dark green velvet because she loved to torture him.

It was a good minute before he realized they had embraced, and another thirty seconds before his brain told him they were kissing. Cameras flashed; hundreds of people cheered.

And everyone knew. *What* they knew was a different story.

He was still trying to figure that out himself. There was no way he was going to tell Evelyn he loved her. The thought made him jittery, and he had already said too much over the weekend.

But now there was photographic evidence of Max grinning at Evie's face nestled between his palms with such obvious adoration, it made his eyes burn.

So…there's that.

"Should I be worried?" Harvey asked, bringing him out of his thoughts.

"No," he answered automatically, not wanting his sick dad to worry about anything more than he already was. "Wait, worry about what?"

"You and Evie. I will admit that, when the Chronicle wrote that piece, I was kind of excited by the idea of my two favorite people, well…getting closer."

He let out a nervous laugh and shifted in his seat, drawing Max's eye to the tube in his arm as it shook.

He suppressed a shudder before answering. "You shouldn't worry, I've seen the way Evelyn handles unruly men," somehow, he managed to smile at the memory. "And we are going to remain completely professional."

"It's not her I'm worried about," Harvey said softly, voice dripping with understanding.

Awful man.

He knew that Max was a goner, and things were getting away from him now. How did he convince Harvey that everything was okay and not to worry if he couldn't even convince himself?

Fears he had worked tirelessly to block began creeping into his nightmares the minute he decided to return to the restaurant. He didn't have a defense mechanism for them anymore. Would he ever be able to turn cold and dismissive on Evelyn again?

Truth was, when he asked her if he was going to be ruined, the answer already swam in his gut.

"Does it hurt?" he asked suddenly, changing the subject. They were not going to talk about the intricacies of his love life while his dad was receiving chemotherapy.

Harvey heaved a sigh before resigning. "No. I will have a rough couple days ahead of me, but that's why I've got you to run the restaurant and bring me some of those cookies you mentioned. I'm on the same page as far as raisins go, by-the-way."

He smiled at his dad, and maybe it didn't meet his eyes, but that was the best he could do.

He knew Max so well. When to push, when to challenge, when to back off.

Max hated seeing Harvey strapped to machines. Hated knowing that he would be sick for the rest of the week and there was nothing he could do. It felt eerily like history repeating itself as his uselessness zipped into sharp focus. Max knew his only contribution was to cradle their legacy in his hands and keep it safe.

He would not drop the ball again.

Max remembered his time in this exact hospital when his mom was sick. He had completely shut down—terrified of what it would feel like to lose her. The finality of death was something that he had always struggled with. His anxiety would rear up, forcing him to either panic, or put safeguards in place to protect himself from the pain.

The panic attacks he had endured that year and for years afterward had left him completely exhausted. Originally, his fear of death and losing his mother had been the triggers. Then it turned into the fragility of life and losing loved ones.

He closed himself off from friends and family. Evelyn.

Maybe it was cowardice, but diving into work and immersing himself in a demanding activity saved him from slipping into madness. His walls were strong now.

Right?

After sitting with his dad for two hours in the hospital, Max canceled on Evelyn. He needed to get his mind right before heading back to the restaurant tomorrow. Needed to calm himself after spending way too much time in a hospital room.

"Are you alright?" Even through the phone her voice kicked him in the chin, dazing his thoughts and making him want to tell her all of his secrets.

"I'm fine, just a little more tired than I thought," he replied, his voice indeed sounding tired. "I think I just need a good night's sleep."

She paused, and the silence grated on his nerves, knowing that he would break if she pushed. He was one nervous tick away from falling to his knees, begging her to ignore him and spend the night cradled in his arms.

"Okay." One word and he knew he'd fucked up. "I'll see you tomorrow."

"Yeah sure." *Yeah sure?* He was sliding back into his usual mask against his will. "I'll bake those cookies tomorrow," he said knowing damn well how distant it sounded.

She responded with her own *yeah sure* and they hung up.

Max ran a frustrated hand through his hair before kicking a pillow across his living room. Unable to stand the clutter, he immediately picked it up and placed it on the couch again.

Too many unwelcome thoughts flew through his brain.

He was worried about his dad, of course. Worried that Harvey would be miserable all week, worried that he wouldn't be able to support him enough. He stressed over the restaurant, and whether he could run it successfully.

But he worried about Evelyn too. Why had he gotten so close to her—let her in? He could lose her at any moment, and then what? The cycle would start all over again.

Shaky hands filled a water glass as he thought about Evie. He didn't regret a damn thing, but things were different now. She didn't feel as strongly for him. She wanted to support and comfort him because she knew that he was miserable.

Evelyn the fixer.

His hands shaking a little more now, he grabbed the anti-anxiety medication that he reserved for panic attacks before popping one in his mouth and downing his glass of water.

He knew himself enough to know that he was about to launch into a bout of toxic thoughts that would keep him awake all night. Best to nip it in the bud before it latched on and took over.

Max raked his blankets from the bed and lugged them to the living room, setting himself up on the couch. He had a process for soothing his anxious mind, which worked eighty percent of the time.

Turning the tv on low, he picked out an old eighty's movie with Tom Hanks. One he had seen about a million times. He muttered a couple of lines as they were delivered on screen, but otherwise let the movie drone on as his meds kicked in. Over the years, he figured out that there was always comfort in the familiar.

His last thought was of big brown eyes and green velvet before he drifted off into a deep sleep.

Chapter Nineteen

She was grumpy.

Evelyn pushed a strand of hair out of her face as she looked over the week's menu and planned out some new additions.

Eggplants were out of season; she would have to move on to another vegetable before the end of the week and was actively searching through her recipe books for all of the mushroom dishes she had collected over the years.

She could call some of her sources and most likely get her hands on some chanterelles by the end of the week, and although that would be amazing, there was a porcini dish that she was dying to try…

She made a note to herself to call her porcini source and get a timeline for the next feasible harvest.

A small creak sounded in the building, causing her to nearly jump from her chair. It had taken all of her energy not to sit by the window and watch for Max's car all morning, and now she was anticipating his arrival at every shift in the floor.

Evie had slept a total of five minutes last night. Her head filled with Max's voice from the other end of the phone.

Gone was the bright, happy, desire filled tone. RIP.

He had spent the afternoon in a tough situation with Harvey, which she reminded herself of every time she focused on her hurt feelings.

Was she freaking out a little by the fact that they were back to reality? Yes, absolutely.

She barely understood their relationship before, how was she supposed to know what was going to happen now that they had shared a bed?

It was more than that, she knew. But she was determined to avoid thinking about that until she absolutely had to.

"Knock knock."

That voice. It was painfully familiar. The voice of a man who was all business and no emotion.

"Brought you a coffee," Max stated easily as he stiffly entered her office.

"That's because you're a smart man with great survival instincts. I'm exhausted." Ugh, she hadn't meant to admit that. He was going to know that she hadn't slept a wink because she was a psycho who had grown attached to him in a mere three days.

He stayed quiet and unreadable. If he knew of her inner turmoil, he said nothing of it.

She rose from her chair to accept the cup as he set it awkwardly on her cluttered desk. Clearly, she wasn't going to greet him with a hug, with a touch. Nothing of their weekend had traveled back with them.

She avoided his gaze as she sat back down, hurt spreading through her abdomen like heartburn. She had it bad if such a small thing could cause this much pain.

"I wanted to discuss those changes that we briefly covered."

Briefly covered? Did he mean before he seduced her and changed every fucking thing?

Was *that* what he was referring to?

The man was infuriatingly confusing. It was a miracle she didn't have whiplash.

She nodded, unable to speak. Unable to open her mouth and allow him to hear her undoubtedly emotion filled voice.

She wouldn't be the vulnerable one. Not this time.

He rambled on about ordering as her sadness faded into a dull heat. She would yell at herself later. Kick her own ass for allowing herself to think that he had actually meant anything he said to her. How could she have believed he had wanted her? Max had barely given her a second glance before he came back to The Lennon, how could she be so stupid?

He had played her. Using false emotion and intimacy to soften her into helping him change the restaurant.

And she had fallen for it.

"Hey," he nudged her foot underneath the desk. "Do you still want to do this?"

Did it matter? The hard truth was that she would do anything for him because she was a pathetic lovesick asshole.

"I said I wanted to help, so I'll help." She met his indifference with her own and it felt incredibly bad. She didn't feel protected at all.

He stared at her with narrowed eyes. His lips separated, then shut again before he could say anything more.

They were back to reality; the hotel room had been a fantasy land and she couldn't be sadder about that realization.

***

Lineup was one knowing smirk away from turning her permanently tomato red.

Sitting next to a stiff, shell of the man that she had spent the weekend tangled up in was a new form of torture for her. Combine that with the fact that Karla had done nothing but glare at her since she arrived, and Evie was a hop-skip away from running herself through the dishwasher, claiming worker's comp, and never returning to this fresh Hell ever again.

In fact, she was furiously trying to figure out how to avoid Max for the rest of the night when she got a call from Harvey.

"Hey, you should be resting…"

"Oh boo." She could see his big hands wave away her concern as if he was standing in the kitchen with her. "Is Max close by? Put me on speaker."

Evie stiffened, her eyes connecting with Max's back as he set up his station.

"Is everything okay?"

Max turned around at that. Clearly, he had been eavesdropping a bit.

"Yes yes, I just have a menu update for you two."

She reluctantly beckoned Max to her side and tapped her phone to allow Harvey's voice to sail to their ears.

"Dad, you should be resting." Max cut in, furious.

"I have a quick menu update and then I promise, I'm going to drown in my own boredom for the next five days." Evelyn's lips twitched despite herself. Max still looked pissed.

"I'm sure you two are working on the seasonal changes and I wanted to see how you'd feel about moving to quince for that dessert Evie?"

Evelyn's shoulders tightened immediately as Harvey continued like nothing was happening.

"I knew that dessert was going to be a hit, and I was not disappointed. I'm thinking that it needs to be a staple at the restaurant. Wouldn't you agree Max?" His voice was playful, and happy, and all of the emotions that Evelyn should have been feeling at that very moment.

She looked up at Max, a threatening smile playing at her lips.

Max barely looked at her. That is, his eyes were pointed at her, but he was practically staring through her. His lips in a tight line.

He was pissed. Because, she had done it. She had finally created a staple dish for The Lennon. One that might very well be the last they ever add to the menu.

How fucking inconvenient.

"I completely agree," Max stated, evergreen eyes boring into hers.

They stared at each other, her heart pounding in her ears as she waited for him to really look at her. Grin at her, hell she would even take an eyebrow raise over this closed off version of him.

He gave her a lopsided smile that looked more like a grimace before silently turning back to his station to set up.

Evelyn stood there like an idiot, holding her phone even after Harvey congratulated her and hung up. She forced her limbs to move, one foot in front of the other as she half celebrated the fact that she, Evelyn Pimm, put a staple dish on the menu. Her hands were shaking slightly as she opened the walk-in and bolted inside, immediately letting out a shaky breath that hung in front of her in a puff of fog.

Tears filled her eyes as she struggled with warring emotions that pulled her in two different directions, threatening to rip her in half.

She desperately willed her tears to recede before running hot down her cheeks and embarrassing her in front of the entire staff. She was a leader, co-CDC, and now she had her own staple dish on the menu. And yet…

I completely agree. Delivered with such meticulous detachment, it might as well have been a slap across the face.

She should not feel so miserable.

"This is ridiculous," she said to herself, breath puffing out in a thick fog. She needed to simply talk to Max. Evelyn had to believe that their shared weekend had meant more to him than just a distraction. That her fears were unfounded, and he couldn't just be taking advantage of her.

Squaring her shoulders, Evie left the cold comfort of the walk-in to find the kitchen bustling with nervous energy. She caught sight of Max prepping at the cold station but before her confusion could blossom, one of the line cooks filled her in.

"Phil seems to have come down with some sort of bug, Chef. Max jumped on his station for the night."

Crap.

Her plans to corner him into talking flew out the window as she charged towards the pass to finish setting up. The Ballroom Blitz was already wailing through the dining room, giving her the kick in the ass that she needed to ignore everything else and get to work.

But her insecurities became unbearable in a kitchen she usually thrived in. If Max wasn't trying to avoid her, he was unconsciously doing a fantastic job of it. She called out demands from the pass, her own business voice in full swing as she tried not to hold his gaze anytime she caught him looking.

Evie avoided the memories. Waking up next to him, his big hands holding hers as they gave in to each other. Shutting her eyes tight on the memory, she balled her hands into fists and tried to think of anything but him. Literally anything to stop her from thinking of Max's soft touches and even softer words.

When service ended, Max hit the ground running. Cleaning his station in what felt like two seconds and bolting up to his office with barely a word. Now she was waiting for everyone to leave so she could silently fall apart and long for the days when she hated Maxwell "devil horns" Easton.

Evie grew more and more heated with every passing minute. She piled her workload onto table three and began shuffling through recipes with so much determination, she barely registered when Max plopped a plate in front of her.

Her stomach did a pathetic little flip when their eyes met.

"Have you been baking this whole time?"

"I promised you cookies without raisins." He smiled at her. His first genuine smile since they returned from the fantasy weekend.

And she broke.

"I suppose you stayed back to discuss the pending changes. Should I be taking notes?"

He hesitated at her tone, brows drawing together.

"You're mad."

"Yes Maxwell, I'm mad. Who the hell was working today and what happened to the man I spent the weekend with?" She held up a hand before he could answer. "It doesn't matter. I am a woman of my word so; I will still help you with your third star." Her voice broke on the last word making her feel even more angry.

Funny, Max had been the one who claimed to be ruined.

"Wait, hang on a second—"

"Why did you say those things to me?" It burst out of her before she could think about it. She charged out of her seat, anger spinning in her stomach like a cyclone. "Were you trying to soften me up so you could make all of these ridiculous changes to my restaurant?"

"Evelyn, you were the one who told me you wanted to help. I assumed it was because—well it doesn't matter why, I guess. You've clearly changed your mind."

234

"Right, like you *just* figured out that ridiculously priced stemware and gold leaf aren't my cup of tea. Is that why you turned to ice the minute we were back? You finally got me on board and didn't need to keep up the ruse anymore?"

He rose from the incorrigible table three, fire lighting his beautiful face.

"Wow, is that the type of person you think I am Evelyn? I said those things to you, because I was tired of holding them in."

"And then I suppose you got it out of your system, huh?" She was brimming with sadness. His calm tone forced harsh words off her traitorous tongue. "It seems there's nothing you want more than that third star after all."

His eyes snapped to hers and she immediately wanted to take it all back. The hurt that splashed across his face could never be unseen.

"Are you mad because I still want to go for three stars, or because you came across another person that you can't fix?"

Now it was her turn. She shut her eyes tight as her pesky inner voice yelled at her to run for her life. A real "I told you you'd get hurt" kind of moment. She wanted to continue to yell at him, but she just couldn't. Evie saw the truth of what he said so clearly, it hurt. And a hot tear snuck out of her closed lids, running slowly down her cheek as she fought against her own idiocy.

He had known how easily she could be manipulated; she had made sure of that hadn't she? By letting him in more than anyone else she had given him a secret weapon to getting the restaurant back.

Just get the fixer to fix everything.

But who was going to fix her? Put the pieces of her life back together now that she realized that, yet another person had tricked her into complacency?

"Evie," he said, miserable. He sounded like he was in pain. "I didn't mean that. I know I've been a bit distant…"

Her eyes snapped open when she heard him take a step towards her. She knew damn well that she would fall apart at his touch.

"You're right. I can't fix this," she said quickly.

Evie slung her bag over one shoulder, rapidly blinking her tears into submission as she wheeled around to run from the pain of it all.

"This restaurant is your white whale Max, and I thought I could do this, but I can't. I can't drown with you, okay?" she said, her voice breaking as she turned.

And ran.

Skirting tables and chairs on her way out of the restaurant, Evie did what her instincts had told her to do from the beginning and ran from Maxwell in a blurry-eyed race to escape.

"Evie…" it was barely more than a whisper. He had probably realized how much of a mistake he had made by getting involved with her and lost his ability to speak.

Whatever it was, she wasn't waiting around to find out and collapsed against the door, out into the cool damp night. The scent of chocolate cookies was replaced by foggy city smells, breaking her down into sobs like a lunatic.

How was she going to work the rest of the week? The thought sent a new panic through her as she walked hurriedly towards nothing. How was she going to face him now?

Harvey. She wrapped weak arms around herself, hugging away the foreboding. Harvey would never look at her the same after this. Her and Max would have to slip back into their rivalry, but it would have a new kind of heat to it. A very real, raw heat. Harvey would land right in the middle of it like he always did.

Evelyn finally stopped walking and pulled out her phone to request a car. There was only one reasonable thing for her to do, upset and unsure of her life at this hour.

236

Chapter Twenty

Her trip was short and awkward. The driver kept shooting glances back at her tear-streaked face as he drove, clearly uncomfortable with a crying woman in his car.

She had given Ben a quick warning before heading his way, a text that he most likely wouldn't read until well after his busy shift. When she walked in and he immediately snapped his eyes to her in worry, she laughed at her silliness. He would never ignore a text from her.

"Here, now." He pointed to a stool in front of his polished bar, and she sat without hesitation. "You're glowing. You look like a fucking fairy princess. Let's run away together, buy a house in Italy and eat nothing but carbs for the rest of our lives." A drink was set in front of her in what could only be described as a chalice. A tiny umbrella poked out of the mountain of crushed ice on top. "What did he do?"

Evelyn sucked down half the drink before launching into the story. The day's disappointments slapped her across the face as she recounted them. Her realization that LA was a lie, the knife edge of Max's indifference, her own hurt feelings.

Slap, slap, slap.

Halfway through her story, a man sitting next to her shook his head and asked her, "Why do men think they can tug on our emotions like this?"

To which she enthusiastically nodded her head and thanked him. Ben listened quietly as he worked. His bar-backs assisting with keeping her friend mostly in front of Evie.

She finished the last of her drink with a flourish. "And then I ran out of there before I cried in front of him and embarrassed myself further."

Ben paused for longer than necessary. His blue eyes pierced her with a speculative gaze. His hair was down, and the red waves framed his face making him look extremely intimidating.

"I'm confused," he finally said while rubbing his beard.

"What is there to be confused about? I opened myself up to a man who was using me to—"

Her rant petered out as she realized she didn't know the exact answer.

"Why would he have to use you to make changes to HIS restaurant?" Evelyn sat back in her chair, shocked.

"Because Harvey trusts me. I am co-CDC damnit." The man next to her gave an enthusiastic *hell yes you are!* before clinking his glass to Evie's.

The bar was nearly empty as they approached last call, so Ben leaned over the polished wood and pegged her with a knowing look.

"Evie-Jean, I know this isn't what you want to hear, but I think you misread the situation, no—don't do that," he scolded as her eyes filled with tears again. "That man is head over ass in love with you. I'm not saying it's okay for him to close himself off, I'm just saying that maybe he had a reason."

Evelyn's stomach hollowed out at the mention of love. Max couldn't love her, not without an ulterior motive.

"He said I couldn't fix him. He took something personal, something I told him in confidence and used it against me. I'm not trying to fix him, he's fucking perfect."

"Then maybe you're trying to fix something else, darling."

She leaned back in her seat and shook her head. "I don't want tough love from you, asshole," she murmured.

"I know love. And normally, I would already have a pyre built to burn the witch. But—look, it's no secret that past relationships have been conditional for you. I just think you are throwing up walls around yourself because you're scared, not because there's any real threat."

Evie let the thought sink in. If she truly focused on it, she could be honest with herself and say that Max going cold wasn't a surprise. It wasn't, because she had expected it. She had written their story before they had a chance to live it.

The expectations left behind by her dad and Jimmy were embedded in her. Evie could always be depended upon to comfort and care for people, no matter how much they hurt her. She would always provide a smile, words of encouragement and praise—she was reliable. She had been so determined not to be taken advantage of again, that she didn't even give Max a chance to do the opposite.

Great waves of realization crashed over her as Ben set another drink down on the mahogany bar.

"The call is coming from inside the house," she whispered.

"Yeah," Ben's eyes softened to melted ice cubes. "Maybe don't lock yourself in, eh?"

Amazingly, she smiled.

The beautiful thing about hard truths is they do in fact, set you free. If Max wasn't using her for his own personal gain, she had been too guarded to see it. Her freedom from her own negativity and toxic thoughts was soaring through her like a bird in flight.

"So, what are you going to do now?" This from the bar patron as he gathered his jacket to leave.

And her bird of freedom flew straight into a window, feathers spiraling through the air.

She looked at Ben hopefully, then slumped over when he shrugged back.

Hypothetical: say you mistakenly accuse a man, who smells like hot cocoa and snowfall, of using you for his own personal goals. Let's say, he is in a very sensitive situation in his career, which you also told him was his white whale, basically exclaiming that his goals were ridiculous. Then, as if that wasn't enough, you tell him that you're not going down with the ship—bailing on him after telling him you would be there.

How do you fix it?

Evie rose slowly from her bar stool, an idea formulating.

"You going to go shimmy down his chimney?" Ben asked, a gleam in his eyes.

She chugged the rest of her drink, which proved to be difficult but her commitment to drama was stronger.

"Ben," she said as she set her empty glass on the bar with a snap. "Call me Ishmael!" Turning on her heel, Evie skirted around bar stools and tables towards the exit.

Slurred words of confused encouragement drifted to her from the bar as she left.

***

The knock on Max's door sounded hollow, representing her exact feelings at that moment.

Her skittish foot padded the tile floor with a tap tap tap that was only adding to her stress but still, the nervous tick continued on through every silent minute.

He wasn't home.

Where the hell was he at eight in the morning on a Thursday? She shifted the bag of tacos in her arms, the crinkle of paper echoed through the empty hallway as she pulled out her phone. Evie had hastily scribbled "*I'm sorry* on each taco while dodging glares from her Lyft driver on the way over.

Maxwell 'devil horns' Easton

Can we talk?

Her hasty text had been sent at almost two in the morning, so it made sense why there wasn't a quick reply.

But she should have received one by now, right?

Deciding he was at work; she ordered a car and took the longest drive of her life to The Lennon. The perfect strawberry sign swung in a light breeze as she pulled up, but no welcoming lights were on.

A quick circle of the restaurant told her what she already knew—he wasn't there.

Before she could order another car to shuttle her to the gym and really solidify her inner stalker, she set the bag on his usual seat across from her desk and got to work.

Her plan formulated last night after her chat with Ben. She needed to make up for fully bailing on Max, show him that it wasn't who she was.

Diving into a project always helped her calm down. She went to every single test kitchen for that very reason—to immerse herself in a recipe. It was a mysterious, curse inducing thing. You never knew if what you were doing was going to work or taste like hot garbage.

She approached this task in the very same way. Trying to avoid a dumpster-fire situation, she gritted her teeth and began writing her lists. Tedious things.

Evelyn worked tirelessly, every creak in the floor had her freezing in her movements. Listening intently for any sign of her co-CDC.

She had been so focused on the task at hand that she hadn't realized the time until hearing a commis' excited voice drift upstairs.

With a yelp, she bolted down only to find that Max hadn't arrived yet.

She gave the arriving commis some extra tasks for the new menu before launching back upstairs to finish her project.

A text dinged in her pocket; a sad, heart-rending sound that had her desperately punching in her password and drinking in the message.

Think I may have caught Phil's flu.
Can you cover me today?

She read over the text twelve times before answering. Each rendition of Max's imagined voice became more and more monotoned and emotionless. Her brain ran through a thousand different responses before she landed on one thumbs-up emoji that made her miserable the minute she sent it.

Her body felt shaky and nervous as she printed her work and busied herself organizing the pages. An annoying voice at the back of her head asked if she was wasting her time. She had already had it out with Max, what if the safe move was to cut her losses and run?

It made her sad to think about. Her feelings for him had rushed through her body and took up residence. They certainly weren't going anywhere. Maybe that was it. Maybe she'd be stuck pining over her ex-enemy for the rest of her miserable days.

Maybe.

Another chime sounded from her phone and the rate at which she drank in the notification was truly pathetic. The disappointment felt when she realized it wasn't from Max wasn't any better.

A simple reminder glared up at her from the unrelenting cell. *Wish Dad a happy b-day.*

Crap.

Through all of her nervous scrambling, she had forgotten about her dad's birthday.

After a few rings, his lilting voice greeted her from the speaker.

"Happy Birthday!"

"Thanks honey. Another year around the sun," he said, laughing over the sound of his television in the background.

She sighed with relief. It took one line for her to hear that he hadn't had too much to drink just yet. He went on in his carefree sort of way, completely oblivious of her assessment. "How are things with you? Emily showed me that fun award that your restaurant just won. Looked awesome!"

Evelyn softened a bit at his words. She knew that, although he hadn't been particularly present for most of her childhood, he cared about her. He cared about her in his own way.

"Yeah, it *was* awesome. Is Em taking you out to dinner tonight?" She knew the answer, and let her dad babble on about the restaurant and how nice it was to be taken out. She felt a small tug at her conscience and tried to fight back the guilt. She would send money to her sister to contribute to the birthday she had forgotten about.

A familiar pop sounded from the speaker as her dad opened a beer.

"Is that the dear sound of an ice cold PBR being cracked?" she asked, seamlessly gliding into a state of acceptance. She knew she was enabling, but at this point in her life, it was so much easier than being angry.

"Well, it's my birthday, so I went with the champagne of beers," he joked back.

Addiction was a strange maze to navigate, and Evie knew she was most likely doing everything wrong. The thing about it is, eventually you hit a wall. There comes a point where you stop trying to fix the people in your life who frankly don't want to be fixed and start focusing on the things that you can repair. The things that you *can* control.

Evie could control the way she approached her relationship with her dad, and maybe it wasn't right, but she was really trying. That had to be enough.

"I love you dad. Enjoy your birthday, and be safe, okay?"

"I love you too, honey. It's good to hear your voice. Call me more often, would ya?"

And Evie decided she would.

Chapter Twenty-One

Running on a full two minutes of sleep can be tricky. Add a busy day and emotional chaos to the mix—let's just say that Max was a little loopy.

He called in all last week. Maybe it was cowardly, and maybe calling in gave him more anxiety than he's felt in months, but he simply couldn't do it. He couldn't face Evelyn until he had worked some things out for himself.

His anger toward Evelyn had almost immediately cooled when he finally saw her again after a week away, lips pouty and cheeks flushed.

Almost.

He was still pissed, even when it took mass amounts of his energy not to smooth her worry lines away with his lips. Even when he wanted to pull her into a hug, apologize and smother her neck with his face.

"How are you feeling?" she asked timidly.

"Better," he lied. His voice came out clipped and irritated.

Stop that. He scolded himself before spitting out what he really wanted to say.

"Will you come over tonight? I'd like to..."

"Yes," Evelyn cut in, her eyes filling with brightness.

Max stifled a grin before nodding and getting the hell away from her.

They danced around each other all day. The only difference between this and last Wednesday's service was the unspoken knowledge that they had both fucked up.

His scattered thoughts bounced to the visit with his dad a few days ago. He had looked well. Well enough for Max not to feel guilty about the bomb he dropped on his lap. Harvey had been confused, then proud, then delighted. He supported Max one hundred percent of course, which gave him a little thrill, nonetheless.

The smile that tugged at his lips was smothered when he caught Evie looking at him. If she asked him what he was smiling about, he would tell her, and ruin his period of solitary hysteria.

Dinner service lasted for days. Months. Every minute was a torturous fight to avoid Evelyn and stay calm.

When he finally made it to his apartment, he poured himself a glass of wine and took deep breaths while waiting for her arrival. Every nerve in his body sparked like he had short circuited. The anticipation of having Evelyn in his apartment again, having her nearby.

It was driving him crazy.

A quick knock at the door nearly startled him into knocking over his glass of barely touched Bordeaux.

Calm, and I can't stress this enough, the fuck down.

He took an indulgent thirty seconds to smooth down his dark hair and straighten the loose, light blue T-shirt over his jeans before opening the door and immediately forgetting what he was going to say.

All of it flew out of his brain at torpedo-like speeds when he saw her, hair up in a messy bun, soft, red velvet hugging every single curve. Light pink immediately tinged her plump cheeks when she saw him, making her look shy and so fucking sweet, his mouth craved salt to balance it out.

246

His eyes landed on plump, pouty lips that were lined in the same red as the dress and he suddenly forgot his own name. In an attempt to organize his thoughts again, he raked a hand over his face—it did absolutely nothing.

"It's a nice dress." The only words that would flap off his thick tongue.

"It was. The damn thing is about two sizes too small now," she said as her eyes surveyed his face. "May I come in?"

Why, when he was perfectly content to gawk at her in his doorway? When she scooted past him, he took a moment to gather himself before turning to face her again.

"I'm sorry Max. I—"

He held up his hand because apparently, his body turned to curt hand gestures at the loss of his speech.

She eyed him suspiciously, clearly growing concerned.

Out with it.

"I'm mad." Perfect, fucking wordsmith.

"Yes." She replied slowly, like she was talking to a child. "And you have every right to be."

"Can you put a jacket on? I can't think." He snagged one of his coats off a rack by his front door and shoved it over her shoulders, trying desperately not to think about how her skin felt when his fingers skimmed over her.

She pulled it tight across herself in frustration.

"Better?"

Nope.

"Yes." *Out with it*, he demanded of himself. "I'm mad. Not only at you, although to be clear, you're not totally out of the woods." His lips twitched when she rolled her eyes at him, a move that he could easily watch for the rest of his life.

"But I'm mad at myself for shutting you out. After spending the day at the hospital, I just couldn't stop myself from thinking of The Lennon and losing my mom and…I was doing a really shit job of grappling with my anxieties."

She released his jacket a bit, revealing the red velvet beneath and reminding him to get on with it. "Then, Dad called to tell you about your dessert, and things suddenly became so clear to me." She cocked her head at him in question. *Out with it Easton*, he told himself sternly.

"I'm leaving The Lennon."

Watching her face flash with emotion would have fascinated him like usual if it wasn't breaking him into a million pieces. Sadness, guilt, anger, regret. How could one person feel all of that without hyperventilating?

"Max…"

"I had a conference call with Celeste Klein. Several actually," he let that hang in the air for a few seconds, still unable to process the information himself. "And she's agreed to invest," he paused, fear suddenly washing over him. "In my restaurant. I'm leaving to open my own place."

He barreled on at her stunned silence.

"You were right. The Lennon doesn't need to change, and I don't want to see you, or my dad washed clean of it. The success of that restaurant is owed to you two and, regardless of that third star, it's my favorite place in the entire world."

A smile spread across her face, even as her eyes filled with tears.

"When your dish was approved to be a staple, everything just clicked. You were always meant to run that restaurant, Evie. You bring genuine light to that place. I figured it was time for me to take my excessive tweezer-work somewhere else."

He held his breath as she shifted from foot-to-foot, wanting desperately to know what she was thinking.

"You're going to need this then," she said simply.

Max looked at the folder she held out to him in surprise. He hadn't noticed it before now, too enamored with…well with her.

"What's this?" He flipped open the folder to find a painfully organized checklist. The title made him grin down at the paper like a goon.

Max And Evie Take On Moby Dick

He scanned it, understanding sinking in before he flipped the page to find a list of purveyors and companies. Page upon page of organized lists and timelines flashed back at him. The whole thing was a serial planner's wet dream.

"I know you have already done this a million times, but I'm a visual kind of gal. I thought it would be helpful to make a checklist of things to do, timelines etc. the Michelin guide just came out, so I figured we have a couple of months before these things need to happen. You can have it, if you want…"

The shyness in her words shattered him. Disbelief shrouded his features as he stepped forward, a good two feet still between them.

"Why did you want to do this for me?"

She hesitated for the longest three seconds of his life.

"Because I adore you," she blurted in a rush. "I wore this ridiculously tight dress to try and smother my dense words from last week and remind you that you liked me once too." She kept going, the words spilling out as if she didn't know what they were doing to him. "I realized that I would buy a million stuffy chef coats and sit through countless meetings with snobby wine reps if it meant seeing your face light up." She took a step toward him, the distance between them like a rubber band about to snap.

"I wanted to do this for you because I needed to keep your pine needle scent and thumb caresses close to me for as long as possible, but I'm too late. I'm so happy for you Max. Opening your own restaurant will be challenging but I know you'll be amazing. You always have been."

Color rose in her cheeks again when she finished her admission. Her gaze fell to her feet, she pulled the coat tighter. A move that told him she put herself out there and now it was his turn.

He set the folder gently on the couch and lifted her chin, closing the distance between them and almost losing his mind with affection.

"I'm leaving the restaurant Evie," he said softly. "But there is no way I'm letting you go." She blinked, lips separating in surprise. "I love you," he said without another second of hesitation.

Evelyn's eyes widened to big whiskey-filled pools, and he held the moment in his hands like a gift. He soaked in her rush of confused uncertainty before her cheeks inevitably blossomed with color and were plumped as she beamed up at him.

"Even with my terrible taste in socks?" she whispered, raw emotion weighing down the joke.

He trailed his fingers down and around her waist, finally getting his hands on the red velvet he had been pining over for years.

"Socks, coffee addiction, blatant disregard of proper towel usage," he allowed his thumbs to caress her lower back indulgently. "I love all of you."

She sighed before sliding her hands up his front and clasping them behind his neck. Cheek resting against his chest as she relaxed against him. He couldn't help but notice how perfectly she fit there. Like she had always meant to be in his arms.

He finally managed to relax after what felt like years. Probably was years, as he had been wanting to hold this woman in his arms for a while. She adored him, and he loved her, and everything just sort of clunked into place.

"I was thinking of naming the restaurant *Eighty Dollar Spoon*," he said slyly. "Thoughts?"

She laughed against his chest, "What, was *Imploding Ego* already taken?"

Epilogue

Three Years Later

Evie hurried out of the gym, waving goodbye to Shannon with a promise to bring snacks to the park. She was heading to her favorite place, to meet her favorite people, on her favorite day. Bloody Mary Tuesday.

Her kickboxing session had gone extremely well which encouraged her to sneak a donut from the corner store on her way to the restaurant. The stickiness of the maple frosting stuck to her fingers, and she licked them unconsciously before rounding the corner and running into a familiar figure.

"Easy there Mayweather, I'm not looking for any trouble." Max smiled down at her, his green eyes shining with humor. It was still amazing to her that a single look could turn her into a puddle.

"You certainly look like trouble to me." She circled his waist, trying not to touch him with her tacky fingers.

Not missing a beat, his features turned suspicious in an instant. He bent his head down, slowly licking her lips with a low hum. Christ, this man was going to be the death of her.

"Evelyn, did you have a little snack before breakfast?"

"We're going to be late," she said, face stern for about two seconds.

They grinned at each other like a couple of idiots before their lips met in a dizzying soft kiss. For some reason, she was reminded of a time when the thought of kissing Max would have been the most ridiculous idea in the world. Those days were most certainly over.

She prattled on about how they were to oversee snacks for the park while they skirted around chairs, heading for the usual table.

Harvey was already seated like always, a red drink with what could have been confused with an entire garden salad tumbling out of its top.

"You started without us," Evie accused.

"You were almost late," he replied, the corners of his eyes crinkling.

The server placed two matching drinks in front of them without asking—she knew the drill—and they raised their Bloody Mary's in toast, glasses and greenery connecting in the center of the table.

"What are we drinking to?" Max asked shyly.

"Oh, I don't know. Nothing comes to mind," she teased. "We could drink to the inhumane amount of pancakes I'm about to consume?"

Max flashed a grin in her direction.

His restaurant buildout had lasted a meager year and a half longer than anticipated, but the time had finally come. After he hit the ground running with permits, recipe testing and ordering, Max had hired an amazing staff, and had just opened reservations for the following month. The first week had been booked out within twenty-four hours, the second week wasn't far behind.

Pride filled her eyes, and she knew that she would see it mirrored in Harvey's.

She thought of the planner she had given him, and how it was nearly all checked off. Evelyn was absolutely certain he only used it to make her happy, which worked pretty damn well.

He had ended up naming the restaurant Prudence, an ode to their favorite Beatles song. The love she felt for him burst through her every time he mentioned it. The man was a ridiculous romantic.

"How about we toast to our health?" Harvey suggested casually, drawing their attention to him.

He hadn't lost his hair but *had* lost a lot of weight. Dark circles bruised his under eyes, but his color was back. In fact, she thought he looked better than he had in months. Harvey had finished his last round of treatment and had been awaiting results from his oncologist.

"Dad?" Max asked weakly, his hand began to shake a bit making the celery tremble. She placed her free hand on his knee when it began to bounce in agitation.

"Cancer free," he said with a wicked grin. A whoop escaped her lips before he could finish. Max let out a shaky breath, eyes immediately brimming with tears. "I got the call yesterday. We did it kids."

"YOU did it," Evie emphasized as relief filled her body in a rush. Cancer free, she had never felt such pure elation.

"Jesus Dad. Okay," he nodded. A giant smile stretching his cheeks, pesky little tears sneaking out of his evergreen eyes. "To our health. And fuck cancer," he added as they clinked their glasses together.

"Fuck cancer!" They exclaimed, ignoring the surprised looks from surrounding diners.

"Oh, speaking of," Harvey said after taking his celebratory sip. "Shannon invited me to the park today to go over some things, so I'll be tagging along."

Max glared at his father's mock innocence.

"Are you serious? You're teaming up with them *again* this year?" he asked in disbelief.

Understanding struck Evie as her own outrage burst out of her mouth.

"I thought we were going as the Sanderson Sisters this year!" she exclaimed.

"I know, I know. But Shannon and Ben pitched an idea to me that I simply can't turn down. I've secured the trophy for three years now, and I intend to make it four." He took a nonchalant sip from his drink. "It's nothing personal."

Evie locked wide eyes with Max. Her traitorous roommates...

"If you recall, Evie and I secured that trophy for you year one. So technically, you're only two years strong, old man," Max stated with a wicked grin. All signs of tears were gone as his joy pushed through to merge with his competitive streak.

"Ah, but I'm not sick this year, young one," Harvey said with the biggest smile she had ever seen.

"Fine," Evie said, her own competitiveness brimming. "We'll take Frances then."

She could see Max nodding affirmation out of the corner of her eye, and knew he was shuffling through the many ways they could win with Frankie on their team.

Harvey's features formed into an overly sorrowful frown; brows scrunched together in mock sympathy. "Sadly, it was the news of Frankie's talent this year that drove me to this tough decision."

Evie gasped before pointing her fork at him. "How dare you hold out on us! Spill the tea."

"Britney," Harvey said with a sigh. "And I don't mean to step on your head while you're drowning," he went on. Eating an olive as if he truly didn't mean that at all. "But it's Toxic."

"Christ," Max managed before taking a long pull from his drink. "The nude bodysuit."

"The blue flight attendant getup," Evie added sounding crushed. "Wait, what are you three going to do then?"

"Like I'm going to tell the competition. The Show is in one month. We've reached critical planning mode here," Harvey said with a laugh.

Max brushed her hair back and leaned in, interrupting her own laugh and causing her breath to catch.

"Don't utter another word," he whispered, her stomach hollowing out at the feel if his lips against her ear. "We'll plan something that will bring the house down."

And she fully believed him.

Evelyn sucked down another gulp of her drink before leaning into Max. He automatically put his arm around her and kissed her temple as if it was the most natural thing to do. She soaked up every detail of the moment like a sponge. Harvey's cherry-stained cheeks, her own happiness and relief, the taste of spicy tomato juice on her tongue.

Max's thumb floating lazily along her skin, making her arms break out in delighted little goosebumps.

Perfect.

Acknowledgements

Wow, this is so insane it makes my palms sweaty. This book would not have been possible without the inspiration and support of my family. Mom and Katie, thank you for being the best family a girl could ask for. You always encourage me to go for the things that I want, and this book is one of those things. Thank you to my husband, David, for hanging in there through my manic writing sessions. You provided me with the tinder, spark, and fuel for this story, all I did was fan the flames.

Thank you to my fellow shadow baddie, Darcy. I will forever read alongside you and will never *not* find a reason to bring up Daddy Az. Thank you to Liana, Kelsey, and Ali, for all of your input along the way. You live within these pages, and your unwavering support had me breathless on more than one occasion.

Thank you Audrey and Beth, for your friendship and love and encouragement and just about a hundred other amazing things.

There are no words to express how grateful I am to anyone who gave my book a chance. Thank you, reader. You are as appreciated as that first sip of coffee from Evie's mug each morning.

About The Author

E. J. Hopps is a restaurant obsessed, perpetually dehydrated romance writer hailing from the Northern California coast. When she's not spinning her daydreams into written word, you can find her pouring sake at the restaurant she runs alongside her husband, or cozied up with a good book and her dog, Dozer.

With her heart firmly rooted in both the world of fine dining and the promise of happily ever afters, Hopps seeks to captivate readers with steamy restaurant romances, inviting them to savor the magic of her world with every turn of the page.